SHE T
GOES (

By
Sue Holmes

Cover design by Trisha Lewis

Edits & Layout & Publishing via Van Velzer Press
First Edition, 2020/2021

ISBN: 9 7 8 - 1 - 9 5 4 2 5 3 - 0 2 - 5

Printed in the United States of America

VanVelzerPress.com

THE
BEGINNING

Chapter 1
Michelle (New York)
Scene 1

A click on the remote control caused the huge garage door to shudder to life with a groan. Her body was warm within the cabin of her Mercedes, yet her heart turned cold at the sight of the empty space where he normally parked his car. She inhaled sharply from the instant pain of realization; he wasn't there. Another expectation shattered.

Having pulled inside and in no rush to face the dark and empty house, Michelle waited for the lone lament of Katie Melua on the radio to finish.

She was exhausted from a grueling work schedule; she had accepted a temporary assignment in another city which was tough enough on its own. The constant juggling of the needs of an ailing relationship just added to the load she constantly carried on her shoulders. Slumping forward while scary mind words ran amok, screeching the stammering and disjointed status of their relationship, Michelle sighed. *So much for distance making the heart grow fonder, more like, outta sight, outta mind.* Eight weeks had passed since they last spent time together and the eerie presence of his absence engulfed her core.

Silently, Michelle let herself into the house. The hall light cast a stark light across the open-plan living area. Tonight, it felt hostile and unwelcoming. In days gone by she would have passed from room to room, taking a quiet pleasure in switching on each and every lamp in the house and watching the beautiful home she had painstakingly created come to life.

As exacting as she was in her career as a banker, she was equally emphatic about lighting. With an aversion to overhead lighting, Michelle much preferred the warmth of lamps, each one had been purchased with infinite care and precision during business trips to many places the world over. She bought them as memories, part of her life tapestry; *he* had been silent at the arrival of each and every one.

Still wearing her cashmere coat, she took a seat at the dining room table; the room was chilly and dark. A noise at the kitchen door alerted her to the imminent entry of her housekeeper. *Dear Rosita, always so happy to see me,* especially these days when time at home was limited. This was supposed to be one of those two weekend visits tacked onto a work week in her home city and he had been mysteriously unavailable, travelling on business, quashing any hopes she harbored that distance would improve and strengthen their relationship.

Holding the tears back, Michelle watched in silence as Rosita busied herself making tea. "So, you're here and he's there," said Rosita as she placed a beautiful tea set on a silver tray in front of Michelle.

"Yes Rosita," she said with a wry smile, "joke's on me—except this time, I'm not laughing anymore, I guess the punch line falls flat now."

An awkward silence fell between the two women. Rosita asked politely if there was anything else needed. When Michelle shook her head, Rosita took this as her cue to depart the sadness of this house and return to some reality shows in the warmth of her condo. As she left, she reminded Michelle she would be taking her mother to the hospital for a series of tests, so she wouldn't be in to work the following day.

Alone again, draping her coat over the back of a chair, Michelle walked to the den, carefully setting the tray down on a glass coffee table. She kicked a floor switch with the pointed toe of her stiletto shoe; instantly the room was bathed in a soft warm light. She rifled through the contents of her handbag, in the process placing reading glasses, cigarettes and a smartphone on the table.

Balancing red reading glasses on her nose to study the remote control, soon the plasma screen and stereo system flashed to life at a push of a button. Lighting a cigarette and pouring tea, Michelle studied her cell phone, complaining to herself about the size of the lettering which seemed to get smaller with every passing week.

She skimmed through email messages while sipping tea, the highlights in her long hair shimmering golden in the warm lamplight. The last message was bitter and sweet; a message from Ruby confirming the travel details for a birthday reunion in Greece in a few months' time.

Michelle couldn't believe she would be turning fifty later this year, the big Five Oh. She always lied about her age so none of her co-workers were aware of the "oh" birthday that was looming upon her—but how could one pull off a lie to four school buddies who were all born in the same year and were determined to have this huge reunion in Greece?

Her thoughts turned to these four friends, each of them living in different parts of the country. She had remained in constant contact with her best friend Ruby and with the assistance of Facebook had re-established contact with Tilina, Alex, and Charley. Thanks to the tools of modern-day communication, cell phones, internet, Skype, Zoom; they managed to stay in touch but it had been years since they had all been in the same place together.

This grand birthday bash was Tilina's idea; wanting them to link up for a reunion and make the reunion work as birthday celebrations for all of their milestone 50th birthdays. Michelle was dreading the rapid approach of this birthday ushering her into old age; she had been relieved to have it turned into a general celebration.

One intoxicated evening, while lamenting the "woes of the oh" birthdays, the thought of coupling a birthday celebration with the insatiable desire for a reunion conceived this brainchild of a grand birthday reunion bash. It all made perfect sense to lighten the solitary load and make the reunion work as a massive x5 birthday celebration for all of their 50th birthdays.

Michelle was looking forward to the sanctuary and companionship of her friends for this momentous occasion, so had gladly said to count her in on the trip.

Ruby, the best organizer of the lot, took charge of the travel research and planning, communicating the details of each likely prospect via email to all concerned. Michelle, unlike the rest of the crew, hadn't gotten too involved with the planning, making it clear that so long as the weather was hot, the place was far from the maddening tourist crowd, and the beach was good, she was happy.

Skimming through the email she noted Ruby booked a five-bedroom villa in some small seaside town with an unpronounceable name in a region of Greece with a name which, quite frankly, looked Greek to her. She wondered how airline connections to this hidden place in the world would look, but decided she would leave that to the joint skills of Ruby and her work assistant. Michelle knew her own energy and diplomatic skills would be needed in the negotiation with the man she thought she was in a relationship with. She grimaced as she visualized the future discussion with him; three weeks' vacation in a luxurious villa without him. She could already hear the accusation in his voice, a long weekend away with him was an impossibility in her schedule and yet three long weeks with her friends was a can do? And that was just the mild possibility of his reaction to this trip. With a sigh, Michelle thought about this man and their situation which the years, and each small choice from both of them, had brought their relationship to . . .

He had proudly told all who cared to listen that he was a businessman. Always consumed with the intricacies of complex deals and swathed in a self-fashioned cloak of intellectualism, he cut a very dashing picture to the world. In truth, it was the fruit of *her* labor that kept the cupboards well stocked with his favorite imported foodstuffs. It was *her* house in which he proudly entertained his friends during many of her absences. It was *her* performance bonuses that paid for the extravagant comfort he had become so accustomed to living in, *her* corporate incentives that ensured his place at her side at amazing celebratory events after many a successful sales campaign. In short, his entire lifestyle was compliments of Michelle—she could never remember a time that he produced his credit card at the checkout line, even when the shopping basket was full of his personal items plucked from the shelves.

With the latest work assignment, she seemed to have more "alone" time on her hands than usual and found herself noticing more and more things about the relationship that were not adding up to a simple one plus one makes two. Becoming unsettled with the demanding, needy nature she seemed to be acquiring of late, she had sought guidance from a psychologist. Michelle approached the initial counseling sessions draped in a heavy cape of shame and guilt, utterly convinced the fault lay with self and patiently awaited the inevitable chastisement that was bound to follow. Eye opening, mind altering, discussions took place as different viewpoints and aspects were reflected to her as a patient. In this process, Michelle started to understand the true nature of the man she had been sharing her life with for so many years. Subliminally questioning her presence in the relationship but simultaneously understanding an overwhelming terror of being alone. While there was no question in her mind as to how she wanted this relationship to develop, she noticed the commitment phobia he exhibited when they first met was still apparent ten years later. She had just pushed it to the back of her mind as the years flew by. It was something that niggled at her as of late. The past twelve months of therapy gave her the confidence to become more daring about voicing her wants and needs to him, a new trait he was not taking kindly to.

His demeanor was deceptive, a cunning manipulator cleverly masked by a quiet and apparently friendly manner. In private, he was a passive/aggressive personality type. His cold and dark silent moods could crumble even the strongest character, his hypomanic tendencies were only obvious to those who could see past the expert disguise he managed to master after many years of practice. He instinctively sought the company of dynamically open people, knowing they would provide an endless source of energy for him to feed from. Like all accomplished parasites, he derived his life existence from the various people who were unknowingly willing to play host to him since his survival depended upon a diverse range of relationships that would sustain his every need; certainly he was too needy for just one person to cater to his emotional demands for constant attention.

Michelle had provided the perfect main host, she was a strong and able woman who rose to the many challenges in her life; quitting had never been a part of her vocabulary. An only child of academically brilliant parents, she learned at a very young age to be satisfied with the mere acknowledgement of being a daughter to her parents. Her earliest experience with relationships was of one-sided input; it simply never occurred to her a relationship should, or could, be anything different.

Her thoughts were startled by the ringing of her cell phone. Checking the display before answering, Michelle's body shivered, knowing a confrontation was coming. Breathing deeply, she softened her voice to answer, she was not in the mood for another fight, there were too many of those lately.

"Hello," she said gently.

"It's me," he said breezily.

Idiot, she thought, *of course I know it's you.* "How're you doing? How'd the meeting go?" She listened as he bemoaned his misery, the meeting was a waste of time, the people were unprepared, the drive had been terrible, he had just sat through the most boring of boring dinners.

Silence echoed on the line. "Hello?" he said, unsure as to whether the connection dropped while he was talking.

"I'm here," she said softly, "I'm listening," but she was aware the normal sympathetic response from her side was absent, it left the moment she walked into that empty house, realizing all her efforts to spend a long weekend with him were in vain. Her voice sounded hollow in her ears as she spoke. "So, I guess you could've been here this weekend after all." There was no accusation; it was merely a statement of what she felt was the truth, delivered quietly.

Immediately he became defensive. With a long suffering sigh and in a tone of irritation he snapped, "I'm busy working on a huge deal, I don't have time for your hysteria or neediness, I could do with some support, but that seems to be in very short supply these days."

"I understand entirely what you mean. In fact, so well do I understand your grievances, when I end this call, I'm going to start packing, and I am not going to sleep until everything that can be remotely construed as belonging to you is taped up in a box and delivered to your office. By the time you return to this city, the locks on my doors will be changed. Goodbye." With that, she clicked the end button.

Suddenly she was a woman with a mission! The incessant sound of a clock ticked in her head as she paced to an outdoor storeroom where she knew a number of flattened cardboard boxes were kept. Taking a roll of packing tape, she wrestled the boxes into their new life as a square again. True to the words she uttered not so long ago, she began to pack. Methodically she moved through each room, rifling through every drawer, nook and closet shelf; placing anything identified as "his" into a box.

Cold threads of dawn cast an eerie light on the stack of packing boxes now gathered within the entrance hall. Michelle had worked diligently through the night knowing her window of opportunity was small, his physical distance after their phone breakup allowed her to make a clear-cut decision to rid herself of the parasite that had drained her lifeblood for so many years. The mental clock continued ticking, reminding her this work was not complete; she couldn't allow herself the luxury of sleep, not just yet. Instead, she headed for the kitchen and busied herself with the coffee machine. As it spluttered to life; she bounded up the stairs to take a shower.

Warm needles of spray stabbed at aching muscles. In spite of the lack of sleep, she felt surprisingly awake, her mind was racing over the details of things she needed to do as the business world sprang to life. The tasks that had to be finished that day would take a lion's share of the day, so she took the day off work. Determined to embrace this newly appointed role as a single woman in charge of her life and her destiny, she spent extra time on her makeup and dried her long blonde hair into a casual down style. Selecting a new pair of skinny jeans and a pink cashmere sweater from her wardrobe, she threw on her favorite pair of UGG boots and was ready to face the world—well, after a cup of strong coffee she would be anyway.

Tapping away at the keyboard of her laptop, Michelle accessed her closest friend in the world (next to Ruby of course): Monsieur Google, the professor of all modern day knowledge. Who needs to squint at a telephone book when you have a wireless access laptop and dear, faithful, Monsieur Google at your fingertips . . . and you could make the font whatever size you needed and fool yourself that eyeglasses were only necessary in certain lighting.

"Mini Movers and Storage, *aaha*," typing a number into the telephone, she smiled sweetly to herself.

"Yes, good morning to you too, I would like to arrange the urgent pickup and storage of some items of furniture and several boxes from my house to your storage this morning." Providing the requested details from the storage clerk, she listened intently to the person on the line then answered, "Well actually everything is ready to go, so if your driver is passing this way right now, he can pull in and collect everything, there is even a hot cup of coffee for him to take along." Finishing with a chuckle Michelle said, "Great, I'll keep an ear out for the buzzer when he arrives. Thank you and enjoy your day."

"Well that was easy," she remarked to herself, "now it's time for the locksmith." Fingers clicking the keyboard of the laptop once again, she skimmed through the various options Monsieur Google provided. "*Mmh,* emergency locksmith, yes, I'll go with that, this is an emergency. I gotta get these locks changed before that son of a bitch gets back to town and tries to loveball me into changing my mind."

Her fingers punched in the telephone number and within minutes she arranged the services of the emergency locksmith … still the clock ticked in her head.

Spinning on the heels of her UGG boots, she rifled through her stationary drawer and located a box of orange dot stickers. Once again, she worked methodically from room to room, this time applying orange dots to the few pieces of large furniture that belonged to him and that were today shipping out of her life for good—courtesy of Mini Movers and Storage.

As she poured herself another cup of coffee, the gate buzzer sounded. A quick glance at the gate camera confirmed the locksmith's truck idling there. Pushing the button on the internal intercom system, the gates of freedom opened.

The locksmith passed through unobtrusively. However, the moving truck was another story. Mini Movers Storage Company announced its arrival in a belching roar of exhaust fumes and barely squeezed through the gate. Michelle could feel the curious stares of neighbors from behind their curtains when the enormous box truck blasted to a halt at her front door. While the load was relatively small, the heavy piano took much effort to move. At one stage, she thought it might be destined to remain there but so determined was she to rid her home of every trace of this man, she called in the assistance of Andrew, a friendly pump attendant at the local gas station, to assist in the piano relocation process. Andrew was only too happy to help the rather stunning woman he associated with a Mercedes and generous tips.

The sun was beginning to set when the truck finally pulled away. Michelle stood with the inventory of its contents and a large brass key which the driver assured her would open the lock on the storage unit. The last self-assigned task of the day was to head to the florist where she ordered the biggest funeral wreath they had in their catalogue, specifically choosing Saint Joseph's Lilies which would most certainly trigger his flower pollen allergy. Taking a large envelope and marker, she placed the papers and key inside to be delivered with the funeral wreath and scrawled his office address details.

Later that evening the security buzzer sounded; the gate camera identified a forlorn Rosita who had stopped by to drop off some dry cleaning, standing at the gate, wondering why on earth the gate wouldn't open. Michelle pushed the button for what she hoped would be the last time that day and allowed Rosita access to the property.

Tidying her hair and putting on a matter of fact face, she awaited Rosita's arrival at the front door. Tempted to explain the new locks and security code as a glitch in the security system, Michelle realized now was as good a time as any to start letting people know that "he, himself" was no longer part of her world. Rosita nodded in understanding, wondering what had taken her employer so long to finally come to her senses and throw that useless twit out of her life.

Sensing no need for further explanation or discussion, both women took their leave to get on with their respective evenings.

Scene 2

Moving from room to room in her beautiful home, Michelle engaged in her favorite evening ritual: the illumination. Step by step, she savored the peaceful serenity of her abode, thankful that some years back she had escaped the claustrophobic clamor of Manhattan high rise living and escaped to the suburbs. Growing up in Texas conditioned her craving for space and terra firma beneath her feet. Yes, the daily commute could be tough, but time spent on the weekends in the spacious silence and pleasure of her garden made up for it.

Michelle sighed as the jets of the modern tub beckoned her tired aching muscles. She walked purposefully to the liquor cabinet; she opened the glass doors of the steel fridge and selected a bottle of Veuve Clique champagne. Champagne in the tub had always been one of her many favorite indulgences. After filling a silver ice bucket and selecting a beautiful blue crystal champagne flute, she busied herself preparing the bathroom for her intended relaxation.

The bathroom was ready for her cleansing ceremony. Stripping off her clothes; Michelle stood in front of the mirror and surveyed the woman she was now. She was indeed a beautiful woman. Time had been kind to her, a combination of great genes, unwavering beauty disciplines, and the gym together resulted in her looking a good ten years younger than she actually was. For the second time that day, she stepped under the shower, selecting a strong massage option and quickly washed the dust and sweat from head to toe. Breathing deeply, she let the warm water wash over her, hoping the ache in her heart would disappear with the lather down the drain.

Stepping out of the shower, she wrapped a soft white towel around her wet hair and eased slowly into the large tub. Michelle sunk under the water and lay quietly listening to the music of Katie Melua once again. Katie's beautiful lone voice seemed to be a constant companion these days. As she languished in the sad melody of *Just Like Heaven* Michelle began to sing along to the lyrics, with visions of their "us" playing in her mind which started the tears flowing in an attempt to wash the pain from her heart.

"Enough feeling sorry for you," she told the woman in the mirror as she toweled herself dry and moisturized her body. Pulling on one of her favorite sweat suits, she slipped her feet into a pair of oversized slippers. It was going to be an evening on the couch and hopefully she would manage to fall asleep early and get a good night's sleep. Of late, sleep was a rare commodity, perhaps it was the combination of a demanding job or the anxiety of this crumbling relationship. Whatever it was, she was becoming very familiar with the 3am gremlin hours. In the cold dark hours, she would often lie rigid in bed, wrestling with every imaginable fear she possessed, watching in terror as they mutated into realities ... little green men racing over her bed, their monster-like faces vomiting one abuse after another at her.

She stood gazing blankly into the bowels of the refrigerator, willing some morsel to tempt her slumbering appetite awake. She realized she hadn't eaten since a business lunch the day before but after the events of the past twenty-four hours, a bottle of Merlot or two (not a good idea on an empty stomach) and a packet of pretzels seemed the most appealing items on the menu this evening.

Sauntering into the living room, she placed her snack on the glass coffee table. Holding one of the bottles at an arm's length distance, she squinted at the label trying to decipher what her random wine selection was. *No matter, whatever it is, tonight it will do, I just need something to numb the pain in my heart.* Michelle was determined tonight she would sleep, even if she had to knock herself out with both bottles and deal with the headache in the morning. At least she would be able to treat *that* with some aspirin.

A feeling of panic started to swirl up from her toes. With a sense of urgency, she reached for her handbag and pulled out two small plastic containers of prescription pills. They were tranquilizers and sleeping pills her general practitioner prescribed some time back "just in case" she needed calming or sleep assistance. Michelle generally avoided taking any medication, but tonight was different. Tonight, she wanted calm to envelope her soul even if it was chemically induced. Pouring the wine perhaps a little too generously into her glass and squinting at the dosage instructions on the bottle, she swallowed a few tablets and then lit up a cigarette.

She was startled by the ringing of her cell phone. Michelle didn't recognize the number calling, and assuming it to be business-related, she answered in a formal manner, and was visibly surprised to hear it was *him* on the line.

Suspecting she would not have answered if she knew it was him, he was calling on an internal hotel phone. The tone of his voice was ice-cold indicating he had been smoldering on his anger since their conversation the previous evening.

The combination of champagne, wine and medication provided an unusually defiant calm. This evening the energy of suppressed anger and rebellion made her feel invincible. Reveling in the secret knowledge that today she had torn him from her lifeblood and knowing the death of this relationship would follow as a consequence, she felt confident in her ability to step aside from the passive manipulation that had become a key feature of their relationship.

Thinking back on it, she was amazed at the skillful manner in which their two personalities attracted each other: she a woman with an overwhelming hunger to be needed and he, a man who needed someone to take responsibility for him. The extraordinary fit of the two personality types, the parasite and the host, had perfected the movements of an intricate dance sequence they were happy to perform for many years. They danced their complicated dance, each step complimenting the next move of the other, happy in their respective roles, until she started to make changes in the way demands of her own were presented. Soon Michelle was no longer willing to dance the sequence that had become her role. In a desperate attempt to gain the upper hand in the relationship once again, over the past month he unleashed his fury at her, delivering devastating but skillful blows of verbal and emotional abuse aimed at mutilating her self-esteem. He watched her initially crumble under this assault but from somewhere in her, a sense of survival emerged and his strength turned to weakness. This evening for the first time he realized his lifeline had slipped from his grasp and he was angry, very angry.

The telephone connection cracked with tension, he attacked with verbal venom, aiming to injure. "I believe there was a moving truck at our house today, you bitch," he spat the words at her. "You've done me in, I bet you've cleaned me out, your insatiable desire for material possessions, corporate power, and position, that's all you want: money and control over every person that crosses your path."

Stunned by the ferociousness of his attack, she was silently thankful for the distance between them for she knew she would never have been able to handle this wrath in person. Pressing the phone to her ear, she listened intently to his abuse. Even now affording him more respect and attention than he deserved. With shaking hands, she reached for the bottle of pills on the table and swallowed several more of them, emptying her wine glass in the process. She needed to remain calm and the pills and wine were certainly doing the trick tonight, so much so she was losing track of how many she had taken.

"Is that all you have to say?" she sighed.

"Listen to me you scheming bitch," he yelled attempting to elicit a more emotionally turbulent response. He was surprised that thus far she was able to remain calm so he aimed his final blow at her heart, delivering his words with the precision of a surgeon's scalpel.

"I never loved you," he sneered. Relishing in her gasp, he continued, "I never loved you, not in the way a man should love a woman. You've never been my special someone."

A nasty chuckle emanated from his mouth. "You made life so easy for me, that's why I stuck with you all these years." A grime of sarcasm coated his wrathful voice. "Convenience?" He exploded, "I don't even like you."

In a blinding moment, she realized their truth; they had never been a relationship. A desperate power struggle, yes, but never a relationship. His final words were her epiphany. Removing the phone from her ear, she pushed the power off button the second the final words left her mouth: "Good-bye," she whispered, then she watched the device power down. Katie Melua's sad lyrics continued to play as she poured yet another glass of wine and swallowed just a few more tablets.

She stared vacantly into nothingness, allowing the full impact of his betrayal to cast a gray light of dawning upon her inner being. She shook her head as she considered the many lost opportunities with other men because of her blinding love for him. She thought of the wedding they would never celebrate; every word he had ever uttered to her, every declaration of love and promise turned now instantly to stone. How could she ever believe any of those memories after what he just told her?

The ultimate betrayal was the children she had yearned for but never had because he never wanted to become a father. Fooling herself that their relationship was sufficient to replace and therefore satisfy the deep need for her to bear a child, she had terminated an unplanned pregnancy early in their relationship. Sadly, she contemplated her approaching fiftieth birthday knowing she would never feel the warmth of a child of her own.

How long she sat in the darkness of that night swilling glass after glass of wine after the handfuls of medication she would never know.

Michelle's only recollection was an overwhelming tiredness, a comforting blanket of darkness embracing her as she lay on the couch and closed her eyes.

Chapter 2
Ruby - Anchorage, Alaska
Scene 1

Good morning to you, Ruby Campbell speaking, please connect me with Michelle Lansdowne," commanded Ruby in a most important business-like voice. It had been weeks since she'd last heard from Michelle. This in itself was not unusual, Michelle's work often involved long absences away from home in far flung places, but Ruby awoke early that morning with a strange feeling of unease. Her first thoughts dwelled upon Michelle. Calls to Michelle's cell were automatically diverted to her recorded voicemail message which had remained steadfastly repeating the same thing over and over again. Hence Ruby's call to Mitch's office.

A professional voice answered without wavering, "Ms. Campbell, thank you for calling. Ms. Lansdowne is currently out of the office, do you wish to speak to her personal assistant?"

"Yes, please connect me," Ruby responded. At least the prim but efficient Emily would be able to give her some idea of Michelle's whereabouts. Piped music played a soothing tune while Ruby waited.

"Thank you for calling, this is Emily Jones speaking, how may I help you?"

"Emily…how are you?" Ruby allowed an exaggerated warmth to exude from her voice, these assistants were often a little too protective of their managers and Emily fell headfirst into this category. "It's Ruby Campbell speaking, I'm on the hunt for that elusive woman called Michelle."

"Hi Ruby, I'm well, thanks for asking. Michelle's currently out of the office."

"When do you expect her back? Tough question I know, all the travelling she's done of late, I can't seem to get through on her cell so was hoping you could give me a number I can contact her on or pass on a message when she calls in."

"She's on vacation, I'm not expecting her to call for the next week. If I hear from her I'll tell her you've called, I'm sure she will call you right away."

Sensing Ms. Efficient Emily had effectively ended their conversation, Ruby said her goodbyes with a gnawing sense that this vague exchange didn't bode well. Several hours passed. Ruby dialed Michelle's cell number only to be greeted once again by voicemail. "Mitch, it's Ruby, I'm looking for you, can't get you on the cell, office Emily says you're on vacation. What's going on, you there? Mitch…call me…please."

Ruby pushed away from the desktop computer in the open office living space of her home. She glanced momentarily out of the window and saw the flickering headlights of Will's car weaving its way up the steep driveway of their sprawling hilltop home. The elevated position of their abode provided splendid, unhindered views of Anchorage City, the surrounding mountains, and the sea inlet from nearly every window within this lavish dwelling. Ruby had fallen in love with the house the moment her eyes looked outwards from that living room window. Ten years had passed and she still stared in amazement from the windows. Every day Mother Nature painted a beautiful picture for her to marvel at. She loved the winter views the most, the peaceful serenity of the deep white snow that covered their surroundings for weeks on end were mesmerizing.

The rumbling of the garage doors signaled Will's imminent arrival. Ruby made her way to the kitchen where she busied herself making a cup of tea she had very little intention of drinking, a puzzled frown on her face as she stood idly waiting for the kettle to boil. *Vacation, Mitch? Vacation? She never said anything about this, especially before our big vacation. Marathon training, yes…work, work, work, yes… definitely no mention of a vacation.*

Will came into the kitchen in search of dinner and found his wife gazing into the steam of the kettle. "You okay Ruby? You're mumbling to yourself."

She spun around noting his puzzled look. "I woke up with a bad feeling this morning and the first person I thought of was Michelle. I've been trying to get hold of her all day, her cell's on voicemail and her assistant tells me she's on vacation…Michelle on vacation? Last time we spoke, she was working like a demon trying to get a project completed so it would be running smoothly by the time we go to Greece and now she is on vacation? Nope, I don't think so. Mitch would have told me if she was going away. I'm not buying this fairy dust sprinkle, something's going on and believe me it is not good!"

Will shook his head, after thirty-two years of marriage to Ruby, he had learned to trust her bad feelings. She was a lioness when it came to protecting those she loved and there were times when he suspected her bond with Michelle was infinitely stronger and deeper than the one she shared with him. He adored Michelle, yes, the financial savvy of the woman unnerved him; beyond that there was an underlying vulnerability and humility that endeared her to him. It somehow contradicted the air of independence that oozed from her. Will figured it humanized her in his eyes. She called him Houston, had done so for ages. He smiled as he reminisced on the reason. Many years back, Mitch spent the Christmas Season with them. Her incessant struggle with the ruthless Alaskan winter temperatures prompted him to brew up a large pot of German Glühwein, a heated wine laced with numerous spices, traditionally served in open air German Christmas markets to keep people warm while they shopped and socialized. Sipping this delicacy became a daily must for Mitch. One morning she greeted him in the kitchen with a forlorn look, "Houston, we have a problem," she mimicked with a smile pointing to the empty pot on the kitchen sink. "We're out of rocket fuel!"

Will ensured that the rocket fuel pot was replenished on a daily basis any time she was visiting and consequently, the name Houston became her nickname for him.

"Well, we'll have to track her down somehow. Have you called that twit boyfriend of hers or what about that Spanish housekeeper she has? You know, the help always knows what's going on in everybody's house."

"Great idea, I think I saved her number in my cell on my last visit, hopefully she still uses it. What was her name?" Ruby started to scroll down her contact lists. "Rose, Rosa, *aah* Rosita—here it is," Ruby said with a flourish and pushed the call button.

"Rosita? It's Ruby, Michelle's friend, remember me? I came to visit last year."

"Miss Ruby, I remember you well," the heavy accent carried a warm welcome as the woman spoke softly.

"Rosita, sorry to trouble you, I'm looking for Michelle, she's not answering her phone. I need to talk with her, do you know where she is?" The phone echoed with silence. "Rosita, you there? Rosita, can you hear me?" Ruby pressed her ear closer to the phone, she thought she heard muffled sobbing on the line and then a mumbled conversation in Spanish with another person and then a scrambling and fumbling as the other person appeared to take the phone from Rosita. At this stage, Ruby could now hear Rosita wailing in the background, she swore she could hear something about Mother Mary causing fingers of fear to clutch at Ruby's heart.

"Hello," a male voice spoke tentatively, "this is Roberto, I'm Rosita's son. I'm sorry Miss Ruby, something bad happened to Miss Michelle that's why she is not at the house or the work, I'm sorry…"

"Oh my God, what's happened? Is she alright? Dear Lord please don't tell me she's dead!?" Ruby listened in horror as Roberto related an almost unbelievable story.

A week previously, Rosita arrived in the early morning to clean and found Michelle unconscious on the couch. There were medicines and empty wine bottles on the coffee table, so she called 911. The ambulance came and took Michelle to the hospital. The boyfriend had been to the house a few times since, he said Michelle was alright but would stay at the hospital for a while. He took a suitcase of personal items for Michelle and that was all they knew. They were worried about Michelle because there had been trouble with the boyfriend and he hadn't been living at the house before this incident, but they didn't know who to call and weren't family so they had no knowledge of what was going on; all they knew was what he told them: Michelle was alive, no visitors or phone calls were allowed, and she would come home soon.

Ruby got off the phone and headed straight for the liquor cabinet in the living room with Will trailing quickly behind. She splashed a tot of whiskey into two crystal tumblers, set them down on the large wooden coffee table, and plunked herself onto the black leather sofa next to Will. She stared into the warmth of the fireplace while her mind skimmed through the details of the call with Roberto.

In tears, she related the story to Will who sat shaking his head in disbelief. Michelle, suicide? Never, not the Michelle they knew. Ruby took a healthy slug of neat whiskey, her face scarlet with fury and emotion. Snatching her phone, she dialed the boyfriend. Attack had always been Ruby's best form of defense. Restraining her fury and fear on a tight rein she took a deep breath as she heard his voice. "Bradley, this is Ruby speaking," pausing deliberately to gauge his reaction, she gave him a space to speak before she lashed into him.

"*Aah* Ruby, I've been meaning to call you." He sounded nervous.

"Bradley, I've been speaking with Rosita, she tells me Michelle's in the hospital? Is it true, what happened, why didn't you call me?"

Ruby had always intimidated him, there was something about her feline eyes and mannerisms that made him feel uncomfortably transparent and small. He heard her breath coming down the phone in short, sharp intervals and sensed the heat of anger rising as she spoke. A skilled chess player, he decided to disarm her by adopting a cool and friendly matter-of-fact stance. "Well Ruby, I've been waiting for things to settle down before I called you. Frankly, I've dreaded this moment and yes, have probably put it off for too long. I'm not sure how to tell you, but seeing as we're in the moment and there's no gentle way to put this, I'll be brief and to the point. Michelle overdosed on prescription medicine and alcohol, a potentially lethal combination as you know. Fortunately, the housekeeper found her in time and called the ambulance. The medical staff performed a gastric lavage procedure on her and other follow-up treatments. I'm pleased to say she's nearly recovered."

"Bradley, are you trying to tell me Michelle overdosed...as in tried to commit suicide? Michelle...suicide...are you nuts? She'd never do that. If you told me she'd been knocked down by a car while training for one of her stupid marathons, or got kidnapped in one of those godforsaken places she works in, I'd believe you, but suicide? No honey, I don't buy that story, not one little word of it."

"Well Ruby, that's what happened. Michelle's not been herself lately. She started seeing a therapist and you know what those people are like; they talk all sorts of shit into your head. It put a lot of pressure on our relationship. She started to become very needy, clingy, and demanding all sorts of commitments and actions from me, which Ruby, quite honestly, I just don't have space for that kinda pressure in my life. The next thing I know, she's taken on some work assignment that means she's spending weeks at a time away from home and then, one evening she comes home, has a shit fit because just for a change, I'm the one traveling on business. There and then, she decided to throw the towel in on us, just like that. Ten years, *poof,* finished! She packs my stuff, dumps it into a storage depot and sends me the key in a funeral wreath! She changes the locks on our home, refuses to take my calls and the next thing I know, I get a call from the hospital."

Unconvinced, Ruby had listened in silence to the man's ramblings. "So, where's she now? What hospital? Why isn't she answering her cell?"

"Right now, you wouldn't want to contact her. She's not the sweet, dear Michelle you know. She's a mess; hysterical crying, ranting, raving. She's gone bonkers I tell you. She left me out on the street, no home to go to. I can't face my friends I'm so embarrassed. I've got nothing, she's taken it all and after what she did to my piano, well quite honestly she can rot in that hospital for all I care."

"Piano? You're talking about the Steinway piano you put a deposit on and she eventually bought for you because you couldn't afford the payments?"

Ignoring Ruby's snide comment he continued, "You know Ruby, you've gotta be careful moving precious instruments of great value like that. She bundled that piano into a truck and it was shoved into the storage container, not sure it will ever be the same again."

The irony of the piano discussion struck a painful chord deep within Ruby. After more than ten years of sharing his life with Michelle, this man spoke with more passion and pain about an untuned piano than he did about her beautiful friend. Mentally summing things up in an instant, Ruby made her approach cautiously, she knew Michelle was in trouble and needed her. Ruby had to find Michelle and she was speaking to the only person who could point her in the right direction. "I'm devastated by this news; I never knew there were problems between you and her. Sounds like I need to have a good chat with Mitch, which hospital is she in?"

"She's in a private psychiatric clinic," he sighed.

"You're fucking kidding me!"

"Her therapist insisted she be discharged into a mental institution. Michelle wasn't keen but I persuaded her, it's the best thing for her Ruby."

"What's the name of the clinic? Give me the phone number so I can speak with her."

"Ruby, due to the nature of Michelle's condition, the clinic has her on a controlled visiting and phone call policy. She has no access to her cell phone, you can't contact her. She's starting on a counseling program. Michelle's gone crazy, she's not eating. You know she's always been borderline anorexic. I'm not sure when the booze or the drug habit started, best thing is to leave her alone and let her battle this out for herself. She's finally got her comeuppance in life; maybe this episode will humble that arrogant bitch once and for all."

Barely able to contain the flaring anger that outburst caused, Ruby spoke in a very quiet, controlled manner. "Bradley, you've got two choices…either you give me the name of that fucking clinic or I'll get on an airplane tonight and when I land I will make you give me the name of that clinic. I might not know where you live anymore, but I certainly know where you work. Trust me, I will hound you until I get that information; my efforts will be nothing short of spectacular until you tell me where Michelle is."

The coward emerged from Bradley.

Thoughts of facing Ruby's legendary wrath and fury was something he didn't want to experience; her tone was tighter than he had ever heard from her, she wasn't playing.

Coldly he spat the name of the clinic at her and disconnected the call.

Scene 2

Reciting the precious name to commit it to memory, Ruby grabbed her iPad and Google-searched the clinic. Will thoughtfully placed another whiskey in her hand as she scanned the website of what appeared to be a very exclusive private psychiatric clinic situated in a beautiful country setting. The bios of the clinic's therapeutic team indicated this was a full-on psychotherapy center, which also specialized in the treatment of drug and alcohol addiction and eating disorders. Ruby's heart went cold when she read about the Electro Convulsive Therapy unit. In her wildest imagination or worst nightmare, she simply could not imagine her beloved friend Michelle would ever be admitted to such a facility; Mitch was always so together, so under control. It was just beyond her comprehension. Downing this whiskey, she sat back in her chair and thought deeply about the situation.

The story was not sitting well in her mind. Admittedly she hadn't spoken with Michelle in two weeks, but the last time they did chat, Mitch was Mitch…cheerful, funny, busy. She mentioned she was training for a marathon, that she was working crazy hours with this new assignment and spending very little time at home as a result of the business travel. Yes, Ruby was aware Michelle had been seeing a therapist, but there was no mention of any trouble with Bradley. The booze, the drugs…where was this coming from all of a sudden? Mitch was so fitness orientated, she seldom took more than a single drink and apart from the odd cold, she never seemed to get sick. The pieces were not fitting together, something wasn't right and Ruby was determined to get to the bottom of it. If all of this was true, she would have to be very careful in her approach to contacting Michelle.

An idea crept into her mind and she sat up boldly. Scanning the bios of the medical professionals, she selected the name of a German-trained female psychiatrist; the bio stated that Dr. Helga Schwartz was the mother of two children. Gambling on the fact that it was now late in the evening in New York, she worked on the assumption that Dr. Schwartz was reading bedtime stories to the little darlings and definitely not on duty at the clinic.

Testing this theory, Ruby called the clinic and, feigning a heavy German accent, inquired if Dr. Schwartz was still on duty and was advised she was not. Proceeding full steam ahead with this plan, she then asked to be put through to the General Psychiatric Unit, where she spoke with what sounded to be a very young nurse. Continuing in her German accent, she fumbled and tumbled in broken English as she tried to communicate with the nurse. "I'm Mrs. Becker, Dr. Schwartz, she calls me three days passed, but I'm on vacation, she leaves message for me to call urgently about Michelle Lansdowne. I must talk now, very important."

The nurse listened carefully, Ms. Lansdowne was categorized a high-risk suicide patient, her extreme reclusiveness and constant sadness justified the concerns; the man who appeared to be her partner was now only noticeable by his absence. This call from nowhere was indeed a relief, at least there was someone who seemed to care about this patient. "Mrs. Becker, Good Evening."

"I'm very worried, Dr. Schwartz, she says, Michelle is trying suicide, I can't believe this terrible news." Ruby's loud sobs penetrated the line, "she's my relative, I need to speak with her, please, can I speak with her?" After a blubbering gasp of breath, the wailing continued, "Oh *mein Gott, mein Herz ist gebrochen*... I'm broken with sadness."

In spite of the language difficulties, the young nurse was extremely sympathetic. "Mrs. Becker—" she started but got no further as Ruby was fully committed to her plan now.

"I try cell phone for Michelle, no answer, please let me *spre... spre, spechen mitt* her, *bitte, bitte,* please." Ruby was now wailing in between the German and English with real anguish in her voice.

Under the mistaken assumption that Dr. Schwartz had contacted Mrs. Becker, the nurse interrupted the bawling Ruby, "I will bring Michelle to the phone," she said very slowly, "you must wait a few minutes, I will fetch her."

"*Danke, danke,* thank you, I wait."

A third whisky appeared at Ruby's side as she waited; a fumbling noise indicated that someone was picking up the phone.

"Just a moment Mrs. Becker, I'm going to transfer you to Michelle on another phone," said the kindly nurse.

A few moments passed before Ruby heard a faint voice say, "Hello?"

"Michelle, Mitch—is that you?"

"Ruby," she whispered. "Oh my God Ruby, is that really you?"

Her eyes brimming with tears, Ruby replied, "Yes baby it's me." There were a thousand questions in her head but in true Ruby style and three whiskies in her bloodstream all she could say was, "What the fuck is going on Mitch? Where the fuck are you?"

"Ruby," she whispered again. "I'm not exactly sure precisely where on Google map I am, but I'm in a clinic of sorts and oh Ruby, it's awful. There are drug addicts and alcoholics and very, very skinny weird and crazy people wandering around. I'm so scared Ruby, there are no locks on the doors so anyone can come in my room."

"Oh my God," uttered Ruby.

"They took all my stuff Ruby, went through my toiletries bag, took my scissors, my tweezers, my razor, my cell, they think I'm going to kill myself. There's this room that looks like a bank vault, it's painted white with a little window in this big door and they lock people up in there."

"Mitch, I just spoke to Bradley, he told me you took an overdose, he told me you tried to kill yourself. Mitch that is why you're there?"

"Ruby, you have to listen to me, it's not like that. Please believe me; I didn't try to kill myself. I know I sound crazy but it's not what it seems. Listen to me Ruby; I made a stupid mistake. I've been working out really hard, training for a marathon. I pulled something in my groin so I went to the doctor and got pain killers and anti-inflammatory pills. I've not been sleeping well. Jetlag on these business trips is a big culprit so I got some sleeping pills at the same time. You know, it's been really tough going lately, working crazy hours, traveling, bucket loads of stress at work."

Ruby took a huge swig of the latest whiskey as she listened intently. "Mitch, tell me what happened."

"I finally snapped and kicked Bradley out of my life. Anyway, I had a weekend at home and decided to take some time off just to chill out a bit, you know get the boat back on keel. I dosed up for the groin and stupidly decided to crack open a bottle of wine. Then Bradley called and we had a huge fight on the phone, so I proceeded to get shitfaced on my own, opened another bottle of wine and just to make things even more interesting, I swallowed a bunch of tranquilizers and sleeping tablets so I could have a good night's sleep. Well the pills worked like a bomb, I woke up in the hospital with pipes in my nose, pipes in my stomach and I had slept through the best part of it, the ambulance ride, complete with siren I believe!"

Ruby thought that it was so typical of Michelle to crack some ridiculous joke in the direst of moments, a trait that could drive Ruby mad with frustration. But the faint hint of her wicked sense of humor convinced Ruby that Michelle was far from suicidal. She listened as Michelle confessed she hadn't been in a good space the past few days, she was suffering from extreme fatigue and felt exhausted and emotionally drained from the whole experience. In retrospect she realized she was bulldozed into the clinic by Bradley. Naïve in her belief that he was acting in her best interests, she allowed him to act on her behalf when discussing her treatment with the medical staff. With her resolve weakened by the strong sedatives administered, Bradley exacted his revenge for the breakup. In a fit of uncontained fury and spite he told her he had washed his hands of her and it was up to her to fend for herself in this mental institution. The malicious intent of the man had triggered her survival instincts, realizing that the fog of medication was impairing her thought processes; so two days ago she deliberately stopped taking the prescribed medication.

Needing more information on her condition, she gained access to her file one evening when the nurses were busy with a delusive drug rehab patient and discovered firsthand Bradley's untrue but damning account of her mental state of mind. He had indicated in the report that her decision to end their relationship meant that there was not a sound support structure available to her if she were released from the clinic and that he was convinced she would attempt to harm herself again. Michelle's refusal to join the informal group therapy sessions offered at the beginning of her incarceration and the fact she was not eating had been duly noted in her file.

"Michelle," Ruby said sternly, "you need to get out of that place now!"

"I know Ruby, I don't belong here, I've an appointment scheduled with the psychiatrist tomorrow morning and I'm going to demand to be released."

"From what you've told me Mitch, we'll need to have you released into the care of someone responsible, someone who will take care of you until you're over this."

Michelle sighed in agreement. If she had someone who could act as a responsible caretaker the doctor wouldn't be able to refuse her discharge, but Ruby was so far away with her own life to take care of. Michelle had other friends and acquaintances, but there was no one she could ever expose her current vulnerability to, she also knew that under no circumstance could she allow her employer to ever become aware of the situation. She had to pull herself together, put this episode behind her and get on with her life.

"Mitch, I've got an idea, give me a half hour to figure it out and I'll call you back. Make sure you act calm and happy after our talk so the nurse will put my next call through to you."

Scene 3

Ruby's brother Nigel recently completed a three-year contract on a construction project in the Middle East; it had been a very lucrative financial opportunity. For the entire duration of the project he had lived in a "dry" expatriate compound where all his living expenses were provided as part of his package. Nigel took the generous vacation allowances in cash and stashed this with his tax-free earnings into an offshore bank account. Nigel devoted his down time to the study of East Asian religions. In the absence of a reliable Western hairdresser, he grew his copper-colored hair out long, fashioned it into a ponytail and happily immersed himself in his interpretations of Buddhism. It was here he first learned of, and become quite enchanted with, the practice of traditional Japanese Reiki.

At the end of his contract, he decided to take a sabbatical, or as his sister termed it, a gap year, bought a round the world ticket and started his journey in search of Reiki Masters who would teach him more about this ancient Japanese philosophy.

Nigel dutifully kept his sister informed of his whereabouts and progress and Ruby was quite accustomed to the infrequent calls from unpronounceable and pretty much unknown places in the world, so she had been quite surprised when he called a few days prior from New York of all places. There was a famous Reiki Master based there; Nigel decided to become a Reiki student, happily substituting the Ashram in India for a YMCA hostel on the west side of New York.

A quick glance on Skype told Ruby Nigel (aka Yamada) was online. His face flashed onto the monitor as he accepted her call. "My favorite sister," his warm voice filled the room.

"Your only sister Nigel," laughed Ruby.

"You only say that when you want something Ruby, what's up?"

"I need a babysitter in New York."

His curiosity piqued, he leaned further in toward the camera taking up her whole screen. "Tell me more …"

Ruby quickly updated him on Michelle's plight; they had all grown up together and he had always had a soft spot for Michelle. Nigel was a very easy-going guy, always ready to lend a hand. "Sounds like she's in a tough spot, give me the address and I'll be there a half hour before you say. It'll be good to catch up with Mitch. It's not a hassle, I'm sure her spot will be a bit more comfortable than the Y so it's a sweet deal both ways!"

Blowing him a kiss, Ruby said her goodbyes, poured herself another whiskey and called the clinic to pass on the news.

Scene 4

Michelle was packing the last of her meager possessions into the suitcase that Bradley crammed the odd mix of clothing he had dropped off at the clinic for her. Anxious to rid herself of the wild woman appearance of the past days, she took great care over her makeup and hair that morning. She hardly recognized the pale, gaunt face staring back at her from the mirror; her jeans hung precariously from her frame, but the fire in her eyes returned as she promised herself she was moving on.

A nurse came to the door to announce a man at the reception area who gave his name as Nigel Campbell who wished to see her. He understood that since his name was not on the list of visitors, his visit had to be approved by the psychiatrist before he would be allowed inside. The nurse informed Michelle with a quizzical look that Mr. Campbell was quite prepared to wait. Unable to conceal her curiosity, the nurse asked Michelle if Mr. Campbell was perhaps a spiritual man, to which Michelle replied, "He is both my spiritual angel and brother." Smiling to herself for the first time in days, Michelle thought, *screw your visitor's list, I'm outta here girl and I ain't never coming back!*

Michelle sat nervously, dwarfed by an enormous leather chair in a book-lined office. Although she had been consulting with a therapist for a while, this felt different; more serious implications and definitely terrifying. This was the first time in her life that she had ever seen or spoken to a psychiatrist. She had only ever seen such people in movies and wondered curiously where the couch was. She noticed a large box of Kleenex tissues on the desk and idly wondered how many boxes this doctor's patients used in a day.

Dr. Wilson was a large man who filled the room the instant he entered. Her first impression of him was 'hair' which appeared to grow profusely from both his head and face. A pair of heavy glasses sat squarely on his nose as he eased behind his desk and studied her file carefully. He asked what seemed to be very routine background questions which she answered very politely.

Sensing resistance, he leaned forward to look her squarely in the eyes and said, "I have the toxicology reports here and you need to understand, Michelle, that if the housekeeper had not found you when she did and taken swift action, you would not be here today."

"I understand sir, it was an accident and I am very grateful to everyone for saving my life."

"I want to discuss and get your agreement on your treatment plan today and strongly recommend you stay in the clinic and follow a six-week program which will focus on dealing with the various issues that have been detailed here."

"Doctor, with the greatest respect, your valuable skills will be better spent with people who truly need it. I'm a well-qualified, highly paid professional business woman, I need to get back to my office and get on with my life. I don't belong here, I don't fit the profile of a patient in a psychiatric clinic. My incident was a one-time accident of my not paying attention to the timing of the medicine I took in relation to when I had some evening wine."

"Ms. Lansdowne," he said leaning back, "would it surprise you if I told you that eighty percent of the patients in this clinic have the same business profile as you?"

She was taken aback at this information and changed tack, "Doctor, I'm a single woman, I agree with you that the treatment would be hugely beneficial and it's something I intend to do, please understand if my employer were to find out about this, I would lose my job." Taking a deep breath, Michelle continued, "I would like to return to the clinic for treatment each Friday and during vacation time."

He looked at her skeptically. "Michelle, your file states categorically that you have no support systems whatsoever at home. After a failed suicide attempt—albeit an accident—you need to prepare yourself for the emotional rollercoaster that you WILL experience across the next few months." Lowering his voice and adopting a gentle tone he continued, "A support system is vital for you, which is why I reiterate my recommendation that you stay in the clinic for further treatment."

Michelle blinked back the tears as she leveled her gaze at him. "Doctor, I have been betrayed by a person whom I loved with all of my heart for nearly ten years and it hurts deeply, BUT I am a special person and there are many people who love and care for me. One of them is actually outside right now and he has come to take me home and help me settle back into a routine. You can release me into his care and know that my support system is impenetrable."

Picking up his pen, he reached for a prescription pad and scribbled page upon page of medication and instructions which he handed to her along with the official clinic discharge paper that Nigel would have to sign.

An hour later, Michelle made her way to the reception area with her suitcase and stopped dead in her tracks when she saw Nigel.

Copper ponytail complimenting a bright Indian pajama-type top; his ensemble fit the description of spiritual healer that the nurse alluded to earlier that morning. She fell into his warm, chubby embrace and felt safe for the first time in days.

Having dispensed with the discharge formalities, they stood at the entrance of the clinic waiting for a cab. The medication had been placed firmly in Nigel's possession; after this episode, she vowed that no medication of any shape, form, or color would pass her lips.

Michelle planned to battle her gremlins single handedly.

Nigel had already decided on a spiritual treatment which would include his new found knowledge of Reiki.

Chapter 3
Charley - Houston, Texas
Scene 1

The fading light of the day filtered through skylights, the pride of her art studio, bouncing warm shafts of light off numerous mirrors adorning the walls to reflect differing viewpoints of the life-sized piece of clay that stood inert on a fixed sculpture stand in the center of the room.

The highly acclaimed, much sought after, yet very reclusive sculptress, Charlotte Stein, pondered this latest piece of work, a commission by a wealthy client. His wife was expecting their first child and he wanted this special event immortalized in bronze form. Charlotte moved slowly around the lifeless column of clay, satisfied with the beginnings of the sculpture from which the form of a woman's torso and legs were starting to emerge. The wedges of clay, which were destined to become arms, rested expectantly to the side of the work.

A distant rumble from Charlotte's stomach alerted her to the time. She had been in the studio since midnight, working with a savage discipline and superior power of concentration; this creative drive banished most human activities such as sleeping, bathing etc. from her consciousness. She was now looking forward to dinner, a daily ritual shared with her mother, Marjorie, who occupied the main house.

Charlotte had lived with her wealthy parents at the family's gracious country home in Houston, Texas, for most of her life. Academically challenged by dyslexia but blessed with artistic promise and talent from an early age, Charlotte ventured abroad to study Fine Art and Sculpture at an art college in London. An ill-fated attempt at marriage to a fellow student in her early twenties crumbled, sending her fleeing back to the protection of her mother.

Charlotte's return filled the void in the newly widowed Marjorie Stein's life. Realizing that Charlotte's business skills didn't match her artistic ability, Marjorie assisted her daughter by guiding her talent and developing the body of work into a successful business enterprise. Marjorie was a former public relations and marketing specialist, she used every ounce of her skills to create and manage the 'Charlotte Stein' brand which soon become synonymous with world class pottery, sculptures, and ceramics.

Charlotte's father had left both mother and daughter well provided for in his will, the lack of financial constraints and the strong bond between mother and daughter worked well and the years passed by in quiet companionship with neither woman showing any need or desire to change their status quo. They were both attractive women; there was certainly no shortage of potential male suitors, yet the wholeness of each of their worlds was such that neither noticed, nor even considered, the pursuit of anything that would remotely risk any disruption in their lives. Especially a potentially huge disruption like a love affair.

Charlotte's reclusive personality was tempered by regular interaction with her mother who become the face and the driving force of the business and as a manager ensured Charlotte's appearance at various events. Across the past couple of months Marjorie noticed her health and stamina were not quite what they used to be. Ordinarily, she scoffed at her advancing years, fiercely maintaining independence, firm in the belief that an inactive lifestyle was a definite precursor to mindless rambling and dribbling in an old age home. She kept her mind active and in touch with the changing times through involvement in her daughter's business; she still drove herself everywhere she wanted to go and took brisk walks with the dogs on a daily basis. She indulged in a glass or two of red wine every evening, having read of the health benefits of this very pleasant task on many internet sites; Marjorie was deeply committed to this enjoyable practice. Of course, she skipped over the smoking parts, certainly the odd cigarette to accompany a wonderful Merlot was not part of

WebMD's advice but one had to have a vice, even as a mature woman.

At the age of 75, knowledge that the years were passing rapidly came to Marjorie at night when she would roll in her king-sized bed like a marble in an empty bucket, struggling to fall and remain asleep for any length of time. The hour before dawn regularly brought an anxiety she had never known before; she wasn't afraid of dying but was worried about how Charlotte would cope one day when she was not around to manage the financial aspects of the business. Marjorie had always been a practical woman and took heed of what she believed were life's silent warnings. Therefore, she had spent hours in consultation with Gilbert Mylechrest, the attorney who had looked after the family's affairs for many years. She trusted him implicitly and between them they came up with a financial solution to protect both Charlotte's business and inheritance. In short, should Marjorie wish to relinquish the reins of the business, or if she passed away, Charlotte's business affairs and personal well-being would be professionally looked after by Gilbert's well-respected law firm which had been in existence for decades.

Marjorie understood the complexity of Charlotte's artistic character. Her daughter's very being was a series of contradictions: small and waiflike; she possessed both physical and mental strengths that were astonishing to watch. In an artistic frenzy she had the tendency to work for days on end without sleep, single handedly tackling a bulk of clay that weighed almost a ton. With the determination of a pit-bull terrier she would wrestle with the tools of her trade until from somewhere, creative brilliance triumphed and a sculpture of such exquisite form and detail would emerge that the final versions were purchased as soon as they were offered to the world. In moments of rest she slept for days on end or withdrew into a private world of childish fantasy watching endless animated children's tales, taking particular delight in fairy tales. Frustratingly naïve about modern issues at times, she possessed the wisdom of a wizened soul that had been roaming the world for centuries. Contrary to the well-meaning sympathies of friends and remedial experts regarding her daughter's disabling dyslexia, Marjorie viewed this to be Charlotte's salvation since it had protected her from the academic world that would and could never make sense to her beautiful, unique mind.

Marjorie caught sight of her daughter as she ambled across the well-manicured lawn towards French glass doors leading into the living room of the main house. Dressed in jeans and a t-shirt, Charlotte's ruffled blonde hair was still damp from a refreshing shower and the smile on her face indicated a satisfying day in the studio.

"Hey Mom," she sauntered into the house. Lady, their chocolate-colored Labrador, trailing in her wake. "I could take on a man size steak. What's for dinner?" Pouring a glass of wine for each of them, she cleared the coffee table so she could collapse on the couch and put her feet up. Mother and daughter chatted about their day, waiting to be summoned to the table by the housekeeper, Lela. "I received an email from Ruby today; she's been waffling on about this trip to Greece for ages and it looks like she's pulled it off—all the girls have pretty much indicated they're in."

Marjorie smiled as she thought about Charlotte's four childhood friends; Ruby, Michelle, Tilina and Alexandra. Many years had passed since they'd been regular visitors to the house, each one of them had moved away in pursuit of their adult lives. Apart from the odd snippet of information here and there from Charlotte, she wasn't very up to date with where they were all at. She had often likened them to Belgian Truffles, the finest of fine chocolates that she simply adored. She could never select an overall ultimate favorite for as perfect as they were in their own unique individuality, their combination seemed to stimulate every human sense one could imagine.

Pouring another glass of wine, she smiled at her daughter and said, "Tell me more, tell me the where, what, and of course the when of this grand travel adventure."

Marjorie reveled in the unusually high spirits and animated conversation of her daughter that evening. Charlotte's introverted personality and androgynous appearance often caused people to treat her with indifference, not knowing what to make of her or how to categorize her in their minds. Marjorie was reassured to see her daughter's obvious pleasure at once again being drawn into the close-knit bond of these four remarkable women. With the wisdom of maturity, Marjorie knew instinctively that across the years each one of them would have faced their own unique and challenging journeys. Marriage, divorce, children, careers, husbands: all these life experiences could battle-stain even the strongest and bravest warrior. How wonderful it was that these women would collectively find each other again and unknowingly create a resting point on their life journey where they could pause, re-connect, reflect, and draw strength from the nurturing and safe environment they had always provided for each other. That they were reconnecting just now when her worries about Charlotte's life after her passing were surfacing; well it was perfect timing. It was Marjorie's fantasy that they would all be there for each other. Yes, there had been numerous heated childhood squabbles where one would fall out with the other, but Marjorie had observed firsthand how remarkable the bond of female friendships operated. *It's just simply the way it is,* she mused to herself.

"Ok, so five stunning women are due to take up temporary residence in the playground of the Greek gods, I predict a chaos that will make the Greek Debt Crisis pale in comparison…has anyone warned the Greek Head of State?" she said with a laugh.

Charlotte assured her with an almost comical seriousness that this trip was definitely not planned as a manhunt. They were mature women. Tilina had been divorced for a few years and was very anti-men at the moment. Michelle had a lifetime commitment to her career. Ruby and Alex had been happily married for years and that she, as in one 'Charlotte Stein' well, she was certainly not the most social of creatures. In her usual self-deprecating way, she mused that the girls had probably invited her to ward off any unwelome male attention in the first place. Suddenly Charlotte's upbeat mood crashed, other than a man-repellent, she confessed she couldn't think of another reason the girls would even have invited her along.

Marjorie was shocked at her daughter's lack of confidence and belief in herself. "Dear, why be so hard on yourself? You're a beautiful, kind, sweet human being, you're intelligent and talented, your friends invited you because they love and appreciate who you are."

Blinking back tears Charlotte's voice softened to a plea, "I'm not sure if I really want to go Mom, why don't you come with me? We haven't taken a trip together for so long and I really hate being away from you. Dealing with strangers is difficult, I'm not sure I would know what to do with myself outside of my art world. The years have passed and I'm sure we've all changed, what if we don't like each other? What if they don't like me anymore?"

Marjorie moved to the couch where Charlotte sat and scooped her daughter up into her arms. "I'm concerned about you Charlotte; you shut yourself away from the world and distance yourself from life's endless opportunities. It's time to understand your fears are only as real as you want them to be." Looking deeply into her daughter's blue eyes she said gently, "Why not look at this as an artistic adventure, travel with your eyes wide open, look for new ideas, new colors and bring them home to your studio." Her eyes misted with emotion. "I'm an old woman now and I won't be on this earth forever, life's taught me many things, trust me when I say you should clasp the loving hands of friendship that have been extended to you and believe that your friends will hold your hand because of the warmth and strength it provides them as well."

Marjorie looked up as their housekeeper struggled through the dining room door, a tray laden with the evening meal was gratefully placed on the table before a disaster happened. Later, as they sat at the dinner table, Charlotte's blue eyes twinkled as she raised her glass in a toast, "A toast and a promise to travel with my eyes and my heart wide open…to Greece!"

Scene 2

Charlotte returned to the studio in high spirits after dinner, the wine relaxed her allowing work on the sculpture to progress easily. Definitive body parts were clearly visible from the former sausage-like shape. She formed the arms which were now roughly attached in an approximate position on the torso. She had slightly exaggerated the length and graceful form of the arms and legs in order to create a central focal point with the heavy breasts and extended belly. The absence of an armature inside the clay meant that any part could still be easily moved but she was now at the stage where the clay had to dry a little in order to become firmer. In the light of morning she would study the piece from all angles and decide what to do next. The positioning of the various parts looked right to her and the overall structure felt balanced, she didn't envision any major changes and believed that the next task would be to focus on the fine details like the hands and the face.

Preparing to turn in for the night, she stood idly in the kitchen waiting for the microwave to warm some milk for her nightcap. She heard barking that sounded very much like Lady. Glancing out of the window she noticed that the lights were on in the main house. A little puzzled, she decided to go across to see what was going on. As she drew closer to the house she broke into a run. Through the glass doors Charlotte could see Lady was clearly agitated. As she burst through the door she saw her mother lying lifelessly on the floor.

Marjorie was dressed in her nightclothes and her body felt warm to the touch but she wasn't breathing. Dialing 911, Charlotte started CPR in an attempt to revive her. The paramedics took over as soon as they arrived.

Charlotte watched in horror.

Eventually they stopped and one of the paramedics stood before her talking. He put a hand on her shoulder and repeated those hollow words: "You have our sincere sympathy." His words disappeared into a long dark tunnel of disbelief. She looked beyond him, watching a sheet being placed over her mother's still form.

She asked for some private time with her mother and the medical personnel withdrew to accommodate this quiet request.

She sat on the floor cradling her mother's head in her lap, rocking from side to side in vain, entertaining a brief fantasy that Marjorie would open her eyes and smile. At some point Charlotte stopped and stared at her mother's peaceful form, realizing her life would never be the same again.

She repeated the promise that she had made earlier that evening, "Mom, I promise I'll travel to Greece with my eyes and my heart wide open…just like you wanted me to."

Scene 3

Sleep escaped Charlotte as she wandered aimlessly around the main house later that morning. She moved from room to room, not quite sure what to do with herself while somewhere in the distance, she was aware of the home telephone ringing constantly and the quiet tone of Lela's voice dutifully dealing with the callers.

Fay Kantor, the family doctor, arrived at the house later that afternoon; Lela prepared a tray of tea and summoned Charlotte to the dining room to meet with her. Besides being their family doctor, Fay had been a close friend of Marjorie's for many years and it was on this basis she offered both her friendship and her support to Charlotte during this very difficult time. Fay's gray hair and gentle demeanor indicated she had dealt with many situations like this during her long career as a family medical practitioner. Her presence was soothing as she spoke with Charlotte and officially advised that her mother had died from cardiac death more commonly known as a sudden and severe cardiac arrest. She quietly assured the grieving daughter that death would have been quick and painless.

With a desperate look in her eyes, Charlotte asked Fay if there was anything she could have done to have changed the outcome. The doctor looked at her sadly and shook her head. "Rest assured the paramedics and you did everything you could to resuscitate her."

Accepting the tea offered, Fay waited to answer any more questions Charlotte might have. In a soft voice she outlined the medical and legal procedures that would need to be followed prior to a funeral before turning her focus to Charlotte's personal well-being throughout this process. Doctor Kantor was aware of the very close bond between mother and daughter and understood the emotional shock and numbness Charlotte was currently feeling. She emphasized the need to take care of health and rest during this time and prescribed a very mild sedative that would help Charlotte to cope and sleep better for a few days. Fay recommended the names of a few funeral homes that would assist with the final preparations and suggested she meet with Reverend Crawford at the church to discuss the type of funeral service she had in mind. Their conversation drifted across many subjects that afternoon and Charlotte felt comforted by Fay's sincerity and very down to earth manner. Charlotte needed to be with a person who would allow her to speak if she felt like it or respect her silence; Fay seemed to sense this and guided her mind through the planning process.

After dining with Lela that evening, an overwhelming tiredness permeated Charlotte's body. Subconsciously seeking the comfort and presence of her mother, she gravitated towards Marjorie's bedroom. A glass of water stood on the bedside pedestal; eyeglasses lay open across the book she had been reading. The sheets were drawn back almost as if they were waiting for her. Charlotte sank into the hollow that her mother's body had left the night before and drew the covers up. Imagining the warm arms of her mother around her, she lay quietly, taking in the familiarity of her mother's room. She felt a small piece of sanctuary in the room she had always associated with comfort and safety.

Drifting into a deep sleep, she dreamt that her mother came to her. It was a beautiful sunny day and they were sitting on the front patio admiring the garden and discussing her mother's funeral service. In vivid detail her mother described what she wanted. "Bright colors, bright colors Charlotte, please no black—celebrate my life which has been abundant and colorful." With a wistful sigh Marjorie's ghost continued, "Open the house, let the light stream in from every window and fill the rooms with flowers, vases of beautifully scented, happy flowers. No stiff, somber wreaths." With a flick of her hair she added with a smile, "Dress me in casual chic, I will, after all, be making the acquaintance of the Almighty Creator after the ceremony. Play heavenly music, speak of your love and memories of me. No coffin, no burial, scatter my ashes in Greece, I've always wanted to go there and this way I will grant you your last wish, for me to travel with you." A serious look crossed her mother's face as she appeared to think deeply. "Oh and ask Reverend Crawford to prepare a beautiful sermon based on love, serve champagne and canapés in the rose garden afterwards and make sure you sing Amazing Grace at sunset."

With a sigh of relief, Charlotte drew closer to her mother. "I was so scared Mom, I thought you were gone forever and that I'd never see you again."

"Charlotte," she smiled, "while you may not see my physical presence like before, remember that the spirit and the soul are eternal. You're not alone my beautiful daughter, whenever you need me, just sit quietly and know that in the deep recess of your mind, you will find me."

Charlotte awoke the next morning with a deep sense of inner calm; she set about preparing her mother's memorial service, exactly as she believed her mother wanted it to be.

Marjorie's family and friends came together the next day to celebrate her life, sipping chilled champagne and nibbling on delightful canapés. They shared special memories and anecdotes about her life. At sunset, a soloist accompanied by a bagpiper, performed the haunting song Amazing Grace. Charlotte released seventy-five beautifully colored butterflies, each one symbolic of a year in Marjorie's life.

Fluttering en masse, they carried the last notes of that beautiful song into the heavens.

Chapter 4
Alex - Seattle
Scene 1

Alex stepped out of the shower and was immediately taken aback as she caught sight of a woman's shapely naked form in the mirror. In a split second she came back to reality, realizing it was seven o'clock on a Sunday morning and she was alone in the gym's changing room. The image she admired was in fact, hers. She stared in absolute amazement as she surveyed the mirror, hardly recognizing the happy and vibrant person staring back with confidence. As she toweled dry, a smile crossed her beautiful face as she cast her mind back to what, in hindsight, seemed like two very short years ago.

Feeling absolutely overwhelmed and worn down by her life then, Alex took refuge from a fierce thunderstorm in a dimly lit booth of a downtown coffee shop. Lost in the dark depths of despondency and despair, she brutally assessed every aspect of her life while thunder rolled above the café. Solemnly she vowed over her fifth Mocha Java that she was committed to changing her life and she embarked on her Project Phoenix Program.

Alex engaged the services of a life coach to guide her. Initially meeting weekly, their time was spent sometimes over lunch, a walk in the park, or a coffee. Their discussions led Alex to the secret place within where hidden, mothballed, or shelved, her dreams had been hastily stashed in the mistaken belief that her worth lay in the unconditional nurturing of her loved ones.

* * *

Alex was what her mother always termed an 'oh fuck' baby. Conceived by high school sweetheart parents at the after party of the prom, she was the sole reason these two incompatible people were joined in holy wedlock. To this day, her harridan mother never let her forget this. Every wrong turn, every minor missed opportunity in her mother's life, was attributed to the ill-fated pregnancy that ruined her mother's life. Throughout Alex's childhood, she wished that her mother had put her up for adoption, or god forbid, had an abortion, she was convinced that either option would have spared her from the mental anguish Alex suffered at the hands of this angry and resentful woman. In her quiet sweet way, she wondered what would have become of her five siblings if she had not been there to protect them, when, as rhythmically as the season, the hurricanes of blame engulfed the family home and things really got out of hand.

Alex learned self-preservation at a young age. She was a quiet, withdrawn child who buried herself in studies, longing for the day she could escape the mental hell that home life was for all the children. Alex found a mentor in her high school math teacher. Under his guidance she discovered a passion and penchant for mathematics. She was a gifted student so he encouraged her to consider a career in computer science or engineering. Emphasizing the need for a formal qualification in this field, he assisted this prize student with university applications. Making her escape from the family home and funded by loans, some small grants, and several part-time jobs to supplement her living expenses, Alex embarked on her university career. She completed a Bachelor of Technology in Electrical Engineering and finalized her studies with a Master's Degree in Engineering and Computer Science. When she left the university, she held tangible proof that she was a highly qualified engineer capable of developing complex IT systems.

Alex met Kevin while working on an IT project for a civil engineering company. Their attraction was instant and with the help of a failed contraceptive device, Alex followed in her mother's footsteps, walking down the aisle pregnant. But Alex silently vowed at the altar that she would never become like her mother. Melanie was born, closely followed by a little sister, Abigail. Alex embraced the role of mother, sidelining, well perhaps just slowing, her career by choosing to work from home on selected software projects that came her way. Kevin earned well so there was no financial pressure on her to provide for their family.

She lavished love and devotion on her two daughters and husband. They enjoyed a successful, quiet and peaceful life in suburbia. As Kevin progressed in his career, his work seemed to take him away from home for prolonged periods of time. Alex was an undemanding wife and assumed the majority of the responsibility for raising their two daughters.

Once the girls started school and became more independent, she returned to full-time employment. A pleasant family status quo prevailed within weeks; giving the entire family a cheery weekly routine. She was happy with the way life turned out, especially after the hellfire marriage of her parents who finally divorced some years back. Alex was deeply grateful for a peaceful home. She would have liked to spend more time with her husband, perhaps having a more passionate relationship with him, but he was just not that type of man. He was quiet and dependable, a caring husband and father which, judging by her conversations with other mothers her age, was a rarity.

The years passed by all too quickly and before she knew it, young Abigail headed off to college in San Francisco. Kevin and she settled into the rest of their lives—well that was what everyone thought; everyone except Alex, who learned at a very young age the art of strategy and patience and how to wait until the time was right…and the right time was approaching rapidly though she didn't know a change was in the air…until that sudden storm.

* * *

As this new life vision materialized, the necessary actions for change became instinctively obvious. Alex became conscious that her lifelong tendency to remain in the background was reflected in a mousey, and at times, dowdy appearance. The new order and balance Alex introduced into her life included a rigorous physical training routine. Naturally tall and slender, she soon reveled in the distinctly foreign sensation of a stronger and more defined body, she had been working on her new look for the past twelve months to lock in this new, strong shape. In a moment of invincibility, she decided to have breast enhancement surgery. Modest 32 AA cup bras were replaced with daringly sexy 36 D works of art. She gasped at the thrill of her own cleavage, enjoying the spectator value of the appreciative glances received from arbitrary men she came into contact with.

Experimenting with color and different hairstyles, she finally settled on a deep chocolate brown color which accentuated the medium length with dramatically layered cuts. The warm tones of this hair color enhanced her dazzling green eyes. Alex applied makeup to highlight this newly attractive face.

Stepping back into the present moment, Alex stashed the makeup and skin care products into a polka dotted red and white toiletry bag perched on the marble topped vanity unit and headed towards the main area of the locker room. Donning her favorite low rise, Diesel jeans, a white fitted long-sleeved button up shirt and high-heel ankle boots, she was ready to take on the world. Facing the woman in the mirror, she stood back and remarked, "Might be Sunday morning but girl, you got a busy day of work ahead." As Alex closed the clasp of her watch, she observed the discreet Phoenix bird tattoo on the underside of her wrist—this symbol was her constant companion and personal reminder of her new found self.

The remarkable change in Alex's outward and inward demeanor was attributed to the high tech nature and success of her business. Only Alex knew the decisions and changes she had made in her life were caused after a terrible secret was unearthed followed by some self-discovery in the midst of a raging rain storm some two years previous.

Scene 2

Leaving the gym, Alex noticed that the world at large was still asleep. Cruising along the freeway she let the roof down on her brand-new sports car: a cherry red Audi TT, a recent gift to her, from her, in celebration of the closure of a large software contract which would keep her team busy for the next year. Her qualifications and programming skills as a software engineer had always ensured a reasonable annual income, but her decision two years ago to create her own startup business launched her career into another stratosphere completely.

Alex established Magenta Integrated Tech, a web-based technology company. In this traditionally male dominated profession, the move attracted a lot of attention in the industry. Alex's extensive history in IT, her professional background, and groundbreaking patents attracted additional whizz kid computer geek specialists who wanted to work with her, much preferring her management style to a stuffy old-fashioned type of office setting.

Magenta was born in the distance of a preferred background role where Alex had observed the obvious gap between the technical and creative genius of the IT world and the stuffy end users of the final products. The polar opposites of the people that clustered around the various boardroom tables provided a source of endless amusement to her. During intense discussions, Alex would often steal a moment to sit back in her chair and observe suited executives trying to interact with the sneaker clad, black gothic, t-shirt brigade. She was determined to bridge this gap with Magenta and create predominantly client focused, high tech innovative solutions for an exclusively corporate clientele.

Scouring hundreds of resumes of former Wall Street employees who had unwittingly become casualties of the financial crisis following the COVID-19 pandemic, she drew from this sadly endless source a handful of well qualified individuals who met her predetermined sales skill criteria. Following her instincts, she gravitated towards high energy, passionate people who had hands-on knowledge of the business challenges, intricacies, and jargon of the financial institutions that they had once worked for. Rationalizing that this strategy would provide the platform from which to source the need for IT solutions, which Magenta's technical and creative team would in turn provide. Painstakingly she created a sales hit team letting an aggressive remuneration model, based on team performance, drive the desired sales targets.

Team Magenta's philosophy was the core of their success and the company went from strength to strength. Within a short span of time, the collective brain power and skill set combinations secured several lucrative contracts with major financial institutions and large corporations.

On reflection of this success, Alex realized her core knowledge and years of experience had always been there; she had merely stepped forward into the limelight and started to strategically direct where she wanted to be after that fateful dark afternoon.

Alex brought the car to a standstill in the undercover parking lot for the office block. While waiting for the roof to close, she rummaged through her purse for her access card and office keys. The parking lot was still empty and she looked forward to a productive morning of uninterrupted working time.

The busy clip of her heels alerted the complex security guard, who greeted her enthusiastically. "Good morning Miss Alex." A big smile revealed a perfect set of teeth in his small brown face. Raj adored Alex and in spite of her being the big boss at Magenta, she was never too busy for a few cheerful words.

"Good morning Raj," Alex said while setting a brown paper bag on the reception desk. "Fresh pecan nut and raisin muffins and a cuppa Joe for Sunday breakfast, the muffins are fresh out of the oven so they should be good." She smiled. "I'll be outta here at 12:45pm, kick the door if you don't see me by then!" Raj nodded and reached for a muffin.

She sipped at her coffee while waiting for her computer to power up. Activating the voicemail on the speaker phone she listened to various messages from the engineers who had been working over the weekend. There was also a message from Ruby confirming they were all set to go and that in a few weeks' time they would be feasting on Lamb Kleftiko and sipping Ouzo cocktails.

Dear sweet, bossy, managing, and directing Ruby, thought Alex, *that woman hasn't changed a bit since school days.*

Alex looked forward to the reunion and wondered how it would be to finally set eyes on each other again after all this time. Yes, they'd spent many hours in their "wine down" cyber space meetings but she couldn't help but wonder how the reunion in Greece would work out. One thing was for sure, if it hadn't been for Ruby's organizational skills (and the fact she was a housewife with spare time on her hands) the dream of a grand birthday reunion would never have materialized.

Alex turned her attention to the last voicemail message, listening to it several times, writing down the exact, carefully worded dialogue of the caller.

Her eyes rounded as she spoke the words out aloud, "Oh, my goodness, I think someone wants to buy Magenta!"

Scene 3

Clutching a folder full of papers, Alex tore out of the office at 12:45pm. She had scheduled her monthly "catch up" lunch with Arnie, the Chief Financial Officer of Magenta at 1pm. She looked forward to this time; it was their habit that, over a few glasses of wine, they would discuss all aspects of the business. She valued Arnie's calm insight and drew on his many years of corporate expertise.

Arnold Willis was a former client; they met eighteen years ago on a project. In those days, Arnie was unhappily married and had an eye for young attractive women. Realizing that any pursuit of Alex was futile (due to her unmistakable devotion to her husband) he was happy to fulfill the role of mentor and friend to this beautiful and intelligent young woman. In hindsight, he was thankful for the friendship they had cultivated over the years. Arnie was coaxed out of retirement by a desperate Alex, who within three months of establishing Magenta, realized the company needed the help of a good financial person that she could trust. Arnie fit that bill perfectly.

The old school gentleman stood up as she approached the table, an embrace and kiss on the cheek dispensed the need for any other formalities. Exquisitely dressed as usual, he cast an appreciative glance over Alex. In spite of having remarried some years ago and declaring to the world he was "happy as pie" he still had a deep appreciation for beautiful women.

"Looking good Alex, you sure you haven't got a boyfriend on the sly?" he joked.

She smiled at him, flattered at the compliment. Ignoring the usual flirting those words brought to mind, she suddenly realized it had been a few days since she and her husband had last talked. Kevin was on site at a project which usually meant that it was very difficult to contact him, nevertheless she made a mental note to call him later.

They turned their attention to the menu, knowing that if they didn't order immediately, they would forget about food and wine because they tended to lose themselves in a forest of discussion points with the alarming ease of two good friends. Alex pulled out the financial statements Arnie sent that morning for review. In an attempt to coach her on the intricacies of company finances, he made it a rule that she provided a summary of her thoughts on where the business stood at that precise point in time for each monthly meeting.

After listening to her, he smiled in agreement. "We're in good shape girl, the business is cash flush, showing a healthy trend and all operating expenses covered by day three of the business month. We're lean and mean, sales increasing, we're in for another good month."

"So, my vacation is approved?" She chuckled as he nodded in agreement,

"Indeed, in fact, your vacation's way overdue!"

As Alex turned to pour more wine, she handed him the piece of paper on which she had transcribed the message from that morning, watching his eyes widen as he read. She passed him some additional papers containing some information obtained on the credentials of the caller she got from Google that morning.

"Seems like we're not the only ones who've figured Magenta's a gem," he said rubbing his face thoughtfully. "I can't say I'm surprised, the marketplace is small, word gets around. How do you feel about this Alex?"

"Blindsided—in one respect defensive, in another, flattered... confused—I don't know Arnie. I need some time to think about all the implications. I've always believed if you don't know what to do, do nothing. Sooner or later, the answer comes to you."

Alex smiled wistfully at Arnie. "You know right now my focus lies elsewhere; the timing is either so wrong or so right, I'm just not sure. Perhaps my time away in Greece will help me to put things into perspective."

He looked at her in a fatherly way and said, "I've been on planet Earth for a few more years than you. I've learnt life deals certain cards at the most inopportune times. Go to Greece, do what you have to do, and leave this with me."

For the rest of their lunch they discussed a strategy to tackle this new issue; agreeing that as the CFO of Magenta, he would handle the preliminary discussions with the would-be suitor during her absence. An experienced hand at these types of transactions, he would feel out what the exact nature of the proposal would be and then prepare her upon her return from Greece for any further communications or meetings. "Who knows," he ended with a chuckle, "you might fall in love with a Greek god and decide never to return to the USA!"

Alex laughed with him, "Yeah dream on Arnie."

"So where exactly are you going to in Greece?" he inquired. "I went there many years ago, loved the laid-back nature of the Greeks—very un-American you know, I bet it'll have changed somewhat since they unified Europe."

Alex explained their final destination was somewhere in the Pelion region, between trying to co-ordinate and juggle air travel from the various locations that they each lived in, it had been a difficult trip to arrange.

Finally, they agreed they would meet in London where a privately chartered aircraft would fly them to Volos in Greece. From there they would pick up a rental car and drive the short stretch to their villa.

Alex assured Arnie she would leave a full itinerary with him. "But that's weeks away, in the meantime I've got a lot of work to get through. I've scheduled my final meeting with the lawyers to finalize my financial planning around what we discussed, so in more ways than one, I'll be good to go!"

Chapter 5
Tilina - Los Angeles
Scene 1

Tilina's German Shepherd, Peggy, whimpered at the sight of the suitcase destined for Greece on the bed. Peggy's doggie sense intuitively warning that the sight of this item was not a good omen for daily fun and games. It usually meant that Fred and she were dispatched to the kennels where they would be confined to a cage to await Tilina's return. Endless days of slop doggy dinners, without a hint of the bacon tidbits Peggy adored, would follow and she would be reduced to howling at the moon until her human mother would magically appear and take her home.

Their animal lives of privilege had started when they were acquired to fill a gap created by the divorce—now five years later and in the absence of a successor, with no likely prospect either, there was no doubt of their priority rank in their owner's affections. Not that they had much to complain about, Tilina was pretty much a homebody these days. In fact her divorcée status suited them. Tilina treated the dogs even better than her children who visited during college breaks and holidays. Those were normally great occasions, Tilina seemed a lot happier when her children were around, the walks and meals certainly became even more interesting as Tilina went to great lengths to ensure that her sons were well taken care of during their stay.

Tilina had made sure that her divorce was acrimonious, determined to score every cent she could wring out of Glen. She approached her legal strategy in a manner in which Napoleon would have been proud. After two years of legal chess, she left the divorce court a wealthy woman. Filled with a great excitement and anticipation, she waited for her newly claimed life. What she hadn't expected was the harsh and stark reality of life as a divorcée. Their mutual friends still smiled and engaged in polite small talk when she happened upon them in the grocery store, but the social invitations received as a couple dwindled to a point that the highlight of her social life was ordering take out and watching a movie at home with Peggy and Fred on the couch snuggled against her sides.

The only males that ventured into the near proximity of her bedroom were her sons. The final undoing of her plans for a smooth transition into singlehood was the speed at which her ex-husband had moved on.

* * *

Tilina remembered well the day she first set eyes on the other woman. It had been a "chance" meeting Tilina engineered once she learned about 'Dad's girlfriend' from her youngest son. That put her on alert and led her to start eavesdropping on a conversation between her eldest son and his father. She discovered that the lady in question would be visiting that weekend and was looking forward to meeting the boys for the first time.

Tilina's brain went into overdrive as she plotted her "oh I was just in the neighborhood and thought I would drop by" visit. She took hours with her makeup and hair, and deliberately dressed for the game of sexual innuendo that she intended to stage—nothing like a "he is not quite over his ex" performance to shake the foundations of a new relationship which could only be in a work-in-progress stage. Dressed to the nines and battle ready to take on the fiercest opponent, she parked her car at a discreet distance from the former family home and waited for her adversary to arrive.

Glen's car was in the driveway, lights glowed in welcome from the curtained windows; she could imagine the dinner preparations taking place in "her" kitchen. Her ex-husband prided himself on newly acquired chef skills and, she had to admit, he was an absolutely charming host when the occasion arose. The boys would be enjoying a root beer with their old man, shooting some balls at the pool table; there would be some country music playing and…suddenly Tilina felt a wave of sadness crash over her. This was her life, her husband, her children, her home and in a moment of temporary insanity, she had decided it wasn't good enough for her. Sitting in the darkness of the stationary vehicle, Tilina realized she wanted her old life back and would stop at nothing to reclaim what was rightfully hers.

She had wanted more excitement, more personal fulfillment, more independence…she craved space to connect with herself, she wanted her own money. The more he begged and pleaded for her to reconsider and give marriage counseling a try, the more stubborn she became. She was tired of the habitual reconciliatory discussions over a bottle or three of wine that always ended up with things returning to just how they had always been. The last "discussion" they had went nuclear just as they popped open bottle number two; every unsettled argument, disappointment, and perceived rejection she felt during their twenty-two year marriage was hurled at him in a relentless barrage of bitter, resentful anger and ultimately signaled the total annihilation of their marital union. The following day, she packed everything of value that they possessed and moved out—in vino veritas be damned—she wanted a D I V O R C E.

Tilina enjoyed the initial adrenalin rush of the divorce. In the beginning their friends rallied around her in what she thought was support; she reveled in the attention. Fueled by anger, Tilina engaged in gossip which spread through their social circle in an endless round of he said, she said, they said. Empowered by a seemingly sympathetic audience of friends, she delivered blow after blow about Glen and his continued reconciliatory attempts; listing with disgusted joy the reasons Glen should never be given another chance.

Then suddenly everything changed.

He stopped phoning, emailing, and visiting. The unthinkable happened…this person who was so valueless and unworthy of her, met someone else…which was why she was sitting like a stalker outside of what was once their house.

The beam of a car's headlights focused her attention. A car drew up at the curbside. Confidently, Tilina stepped out of her vehicle and walked towards the house, timing her simultaneous arrival at the front door with that of the woman who just arrived in the car, skillfully giving the impression, that she too, was an invited dinner guest.

Her estranged husband looked gob smacked when he opened the door and stared uncomfortably at the two women, recognizing the spite in his ex-wife's eyes. He mentally saw the promise of happily ever after with his new lady friend evaporate in front of his eyes...or so he and Tilina thought.

Instead, this exquisite creature instantly disarmed her opponent with the graceful charm that had attracted him in the first place.

With a beautiful smile she engaged in small talk with Tilina, skillfully maneuvering through the minefield of questions aimed at her finding ways to compliment Tilina on her high and gorgeous cheek bones, her stunning straight black hair, her bravery in moving from Texas to LA.

Tilina had intended to laud it over the intruder, scare her off, but was completely stonewalled by the classic beauty and poise of this highly intelligent woman. After a half hour or so, this delightful woman had talked Tilina to the front door.

Standing on the sidewalk beside her car that evening, Tilina realized that Glen had been her backbone. Throughout their married life he epitomized the perfect husband and she had been too damn self-centered and downright spoiled to realize it.

Suddenly, the divorce seemed very wrong and she set about trying to win her husband back from the clutches of this loose woman.

Scene 2

It was at that point when Tilina lost the plot of the story she had been writing for the next chapter of her life; somewhere in her bitterness, a twisted madness emerged. The coat of blame for the demise of her marriage was instantly placed squarely on the shoulders of the other woman who was now in an "adulterous" relationship with her husband. In Tilina's manic mind, she become the victim, the much-aggrieved wife, and Tilina wore this status like a medal.

An aggressive and self-righteous stance had always been her favored method of confrontation, so Tilina sent threatening emails and text messages to the perfect one. To her chagrin, never once did that woman stoop so low as to respond personally. Instead, swift legal action was taken in the form of a restraining order which was delivered by an official of the court. Tilina kicked her own ass for that piece of stupidity, obviously the woman was an attorney and a good one at that, so this line of attack was quickly abandoned.

Undeterred, Tilina moved in on her ex-husband; after all, had he not been the one that had come around to her house and begged and pleaded for her to return to the marital home where they could sort out their differences? She believed that once he realized she was ready to 'come home' he would ditch the new woman. She sent emails, long chatty ones, birthday greetings, Christmas updates and *oh my goodness perish the thought*, a long begging email which finally brought the very much longed for/dreamt/fantasized about reply from him in the form of a phone call.

"Tilina, I hope this is a convenient time for you." Her heart raced when she heard Glen's voice on the phone.

"Yes of course." *Fool,* she thought, any time of the day or night is convenient for me to speak with you. She had been waiting for this call, she paused noticing there was a slight hesitancy before he spoke again.

"I need to see you; we need to talk."

"Sure," she said as lightly and brightly as she could. "Where and when were you thinking?"

"Maybe we could have dinner together this week, Restorante Berinato is still very good."

She smiled. "Thursday at 7pm is good for me, I'll see you there."

She was beside herself with excitement after the call; Restorante Berinato was an Italian restaurant that they used to frequent. It was off the beaten track, very private and very romantic. Careful questioning of her son confirmed that the wonder woman was on an international business trip. Things were certainly looking good for their planned reconciliation. Tilina was determined that by the time that bitch returned Tilina would have taken her rightful place back in the marital bed.

In the days that preceded their date, Tilina hit the spa with a vengeance. Her entire body was exfoliated, wrapped, oiled, waxed, manicured, and pedicured in preparation for the wild, raunchy, make-up sex she planned to have with her husband.

She couldn't wait to get her hands on him. Apart from intermittent sessions with DIY toys; sex was a delicacy that had disappeared off her menu for far too long. Tilina shopped for new outfits and went a little wild in the lingerie department; Glen's sexual appetite was insatiable and she knew what he liked. She intended to give him a little of what he didn't know he liked as well. She hoped fervently that he would have long forgotten one acerbic comment in an argument that she faked her orgasms, but convinced herself that a good blowjob would certainly reassure him of his sexual prowess.

Tilina vamped into Restorante Berinato shortly after 7pm that Thursday; she had forgotten how dark the place was but rationalized that the soft candlelight would flatter her tannish complexion. Glen rose from his seat at the bar the moment he saw her, appearing unsure as to whether he should shake her hand or give her a hug. He settled for a warm smile instead.

The restaurant owner, Marco, fussed over them seemingly oblivious of their newly divorced status. Having ushered them to his best table, he reappeared, and with an exaggerated flourish, presented Tilina with a red rose. "*Una rosa rossa per la tua bella moglie* - a red rose for your beautiful wife." She gushed with thanks while a flustered Glen buried himself in the wine menu, "*Aah* Mister Avery, I do have your favorite *Pio Cesare Barbaresco* in the cellar."

"You've just made my day Marco," he said turning to Tilina. "Are you okay with that one?"

She nodded in agreement and Marco disappeared. Tilina was a little off center at that point, the restaurant was stirring long buried memories of happy days from the past. She assumed this was deliberate on Glen's part and after the first few sips of wine, she settled comfortably back into her chair to study the menu and choose a great meal.

They ate and drank like the king and queen they once were together, their conversation at first was a little strained but as the wine calmed their nerves, they chatted and laughed together. Tilina's heart soared with happiness; their divorce seemed like it had never happened. Sipping their liqueurs to top off the meal, she noticed a quietness come over him.

"We need to talk Tilina."

"Maybe we need to go someplace private?" Hoping that her tone would indicate an understanding of his nervousness, she suggested they have a nightcap at her place. Tilina had mentioned earlier in the evening that their son was staying with a friend, so they would be able to talk openly.

Oblivious to her intentions, Glen agreed and they shared a taxi to her home, a beautiful family house situated a few suburbs away from their former marital home. A freelance interior decorator, Tilina invested a sizeable amount of time and money in creating her dream home and flushed with pride as the cab rolled into the driveway, the headlights highlighting the stylish landscape of the front garden.

Tilina was now on home ground and immediately seized the advantage. The evening went exactly as she planned it; the stage was set…low lights burned in the living room and the music was mellow and soothing. The wine had relaxed Glen and his long lean body sprawled into the soft comfort of the couch.

"You've done a great job on the décor." He smiled surveying the contemporary-styled living room. The bright yellow walls harmonized perfectly with the mottled brown hardwood flooring, creating a warm ambiance. He had always been amazed at her ability to pair unusual colors and patterns, gray cushioned armchairs complemented the dark coffee table placed in the center of a beige colored area rug. A family collection of Chumash baskets her ancestors made was displayed in a glass stand, tastefully backlit to show off the weaving patterns.

Her divorcee living space bore no resemblance to their former marital home which had been very cowboy country, but dotted around the open area, he recognized pieces of indigenous painted rocks they had picked out purchased together to honor her Chumash heritage.

She poured two large cognacs and took a seat in the armchair next to the couch; estimating the proximity to be comfortably close enough for conversation and the odd physical touching gesture for punctuation purposes.

"Our divorce is one of the toughest things I've ever had to deal with," Glen looked straight into her eyes, "there were times I thought I would crack."

Tenderly she placed a hand on his arm. "Indeed, it *is* amazing how time can bring perspective." She watched carefully, gauging his reaction then continued, "I have ground away and finally dealt with my anger and truly agree with you now, a reconciliation is possible." Encouraged by his silence, she elaborated, "Of course family therapy would probably be beneficial but personally I believe that the best part of fighting with you has always been the make-up sex afterwards."

Glen shifted uncomfortably, then his initial look of discomfort was replaced by a genuine sadness. "Tilina, there were times I'd have given anything to hear those words."

"I'll say those words as often as you need me to." Clutching at his obvious surprise, she used the opportunity to dramatically sink to her knees at his feet. "We were married for twenty-two years, we have two beautiful children who need us. My darling Glen, our bond can never be broken." She looked up at him through tear-filled eyes—knowing Glen could never cope with a tearful woman.

"Yes, we said that, but it was a very long time ago." He sat upright and looked straight at her. "Somewhere in between then and now your anger and resentment chased away the love and joy we had. I hit Ground Zero, and as painful as it was, I had to move on." She laid her head on his knees and listened in silence as he continued. "I just couldn't cope with your anger."

"I'm not angry anymore," she said, as she reached for his crotch. "In fact, I'm very much in the mood for that make-up sex we spoke about earlier." She frowned as she saw Glen's face flush, unsure what he was thinking. "It's time for me to come home now and let's just pretend your little romp with Flossie the Floozy never happened."

She looked at him in confusion as he angrily brushed her hands aside, this was not going the way she thought it would. "Even if you were the only woman left on this planet, I can assure you that a reconciliation between us will never happen." He dropped his voice into a low and even tone, "I saw the true side of your character; your unquenchable need for money still disgusts and haunts me. The less I have to see of you, the better it is for me." His voice took on a warning tone, "And Stephanie's absolutely out of bounds, I've watched your dirty tactics with her and it's not working."

"Then why did you ask me out for dinner? What is it you wanted to talk to me about?" Tears were forming in her eyes as she looked at him.

"Stephanie felt I should be the one to tell you that we're getting married," he said quietly. "A wedding was always on the cards for next year but we just found out that we're expecting a baby and have decided to bring the wedding plans forward."

Tilina was stunned by the news. Her initial anger was quickly replaced by sadness; tears flowed freely and genuinely as she comprehended the terrible truth…her husband now belonged to someone else…her actions and opinions were of absolutely no importance to him now. Glen had built a new life for himself which included another wife and family.

Scene 3

The full impact of the divorce hit as menopause walked into her life and her youngest child left home to attend a college three states away. Tilina wallowed in the misery of her life as she watched everything crumble around her; she became as invisible as she felt. Settling into some semblance of single life, she kidded herself she was happy. She shared time with her new companions: loneliness, bitterness, and cyberspace. Saturday nights were spent searching for old friends and contacts on Facebook. She prided herself on her new found popularity by the number of Facebook friends she had racked up in a short space of time and spent hours writing witty comments and posting "likes" on every status that popped up on her home page. This was how she finally managed to link up with Ruby and then through her Charlotte, Alex, and Michelle.

The five of them used to hang around together in middle school and then on through high school. Michelle had been the core of the group, a friendly girl who befriended the waifs who didn't have a group of their own. Michelle gave them all a sense of belonging. Undoubtedly, Ruby was Michelle's closest friend but the others somehow fit in and the group became its own unique entity during their high school years. After high school their individual lives diverged onto different paths with careers and husbands establishing the direction for each. Michelle maintained contact with Ruby and over the years they managed to link up from time to time. The Facebook craze crested again during the home isolation orders given in nearly every state when the corona virus hit; this new online activity suddenly brought them into more regular and reliable contact and now, a year later, it was online that they had agreed to a reunion to celebrate their "Big Oh" year.

The plan was to spend uninterrupted weeks in some exotic location. Since money was not an object in their lives; they decided to rent a luxury villa. Each woman had provided five nonnegotiable requirements as their personal wish lists. Based on these, Ruby, who was tasked as the location scout, set out to identify the perfect spot in all of the whole wide world.

The reunion was planned as a retreat just for themselves.

One week would be devoted to settling into their new environment, getting to know each other as mature women, and catching up on the gaps.

The following week would be based on reflection and truth.

The beginning of the third week would cover judgment; this was the part where they would bravely throw their lives open to discussion and judgment by each other.

The final days would be devoted to acceptance of where they were at in their lives and their plans for the future.

This was how the plans had evolved; whether or not they followed it would be determined as they went along.

LET THE FUN BEGIN ...

Chapter 6
Departure for Greece
Scene 1 - Charlotte

Months had passed since her mother's death. After the funeral memorial service, Charlotte took refuge from the painful void of the main house in her art studio. It was in this sanctuary that she explored the unfamiliar territory of grief through new artistic creation, the only emotional outlet she felt comfortable with. She obsessed with a self-commissioned assignment; a receptacle, the interior of which would hold the mortal remains of her mother and the exterior of which would detail their lives and bond and provide a beautiful physical eulogy to the wonderful woman that she loved and mourned.

True to highly defined artistic concentration and discipline, she labored for weeks, foregoing sleep and food for days on end until finally she completed her quest. The release of her pain and deep sense of loss into creative energy resulted in an excruciatingly beautiful work of art. Resting, Charlotte recalled that ultimate artistic nod that announced finality, it was a moment etched in time; the dawn was breaking, delivering delicate shards of daylight which danced on the studio mirrors. She stood in a humble silence before the urn, finally content that the intricate detail and design truly symbolized their bond. *How ironic,* she thought at the time, *that only in the final act of death, did I truly understand and conceptualize the immense depth of love I felt for my mother.*

A peaceful contentment flowed through her weary body as she lay on the couch, coffee mug in hand, watching the unfolding of Mother Nature's palette. It dabbled, mixed, then imploded the gray canvas of dawn. As the salmon-colored ball of light quietly made its way above the eastern horizon, bright shades of pink-tinged edges of cotton candy clouds scattered across the sky. The words of the poet Kahlil Gibran came to mind as she succumbed to physical fatigue, *No matter how long the storms last, the sun always shines.*

Charlotte's cell phone blasted her awake. Lela's cheerful voice bounced around the room through the speaker function, "Just a reminder of the meeting with the lawyer at lunchtime."

"Thanks Lela, call me when he arrives." Glancing at the clock, Charlotte staggered from the couch to the bathroom.

Charlotte's casual boho attire provided a stark contrast to the suited and booted Gilbert Mylechrest, who greeted her warmly as she ushered him into the formal living room of the main house. The room was tastefully decorated; priceless works of art adorned the walls, the muted opulence of the drapery and furniture provided a discreet hint of the family wealth which was managed within the solid confines of Gilbert's well-respected legal practice. Charlotte had never involved herself in the day to day intricacies of managing the family's financial affairs; this had previously been the domain of her mother. While the nitty gritty of daily dollars and cents alluded her, regular discussions with both Gilbert and her mother had provided her with a broad knowledge of the overall financial structure of her estate. Gilbert advised her that shortly before her mother passed, they reviewed the financial portfolio in its entirety together. "In hindsight, it's obvious she sensed her death," he said then explained the importance Marjorie placed on the smooth transition of responsibility for the oversight of the family's investments to Charlotte. Using a series of diagrams, he sketched the complex ownership structure, detailing numerous company structures which were ultimately owned by a family trust.

Several meetings followed with accountants, lawyers, and tax specialists who pronounced that all was in order and in good standing with the relevant authorities. Charlotte's father always believed in dealing with the best financial service providers, she recalled him saying that this was money well spent and that the family should never scrimp or try to save on these necessities. His prudent and conservative investment philosophy had, in spite of numerous economic crises, enhanced the family wealth over the years which barely took a dip during the corona virus outbreak.

Charlotte was surprised she managed to make some sense of the investment jargon. It was comforting to have Gilbert's guidance so she agreed with him that on her return from this extended trip to Greece they would meet again to discuss a philanthropic strategy.

Gilbert summarized the financial arrangements he made for the trip and handed her an envelope with an assortment of bank cards which would insure she had access to funds while travelling. Linking arms with him as they moved to the dining room for lunch, he flushed at her obvious delight when she saw the table set with the take-out food he had thoughtfully brought along from a Greek Taverna. "I thought it would be a great opportunity to introduce you to some Greek food and drink before your departure."

The server had recommended mezethes, explaining that making a meal of appetizers was a very popular Greek custom. Several small dishes and a bottle of Ouzo were placed on the table before them; each plate looking more enticing than the other, the smell of eggplant and rosemary permeated the air and Charlotte felt a thrill of excitement as the reality of her trip really dawned on her.

"I believe the urn's finished and it's a magnificent eulogy to your mother." Gently he took her hand and continued, "On your return from Greece, we can discuss the interment of the ashes."

She nodded blinking back tears that threatened to fall whenever she thought of her mother.

"I've been in regular contact with Ruby Campbell to finalize the financial arrangements for your trip. She sounds like an absolute character," he said with a chuckle. "I'm sure this vacation will be good for you. Charlotte, the rest from studio work, change of scenery, and company of friends…trust me, you'll feel much stronger when you return."

Charlotte smiled in agreement as she thought back to their school days; many years had passed since those carefree days when they hung out together and she was indeed looking forward to meeting up with the girls. The opportunity to lose her identity in a new environment within the safe and loving embrace of these women she had known from childhood was a welcoming thought.

The studio had been cleared of all outstanding work so there was no time pressure whatsoever. At this particular juncture, with the warmth of the Metaxa in her belly, she undertook to put her life in fate's hands to see where it took her.

In that split second, she decided to take her mother along—urn and all!

Raising her glass of Ouzo, she burst out, "Opa! Gilbert you better notify the Greeks that they're about to be invaded!"

Michelle on the Isle of Man
Scene 2

Michelle paced the hotel lobby anxiously; it was 5:30am and there was still no sign of the colleague who offered to take her to the airport that morning. She managed to rouse him on his cell phone a half hour earlier and it was very clear from his blurred voice he had overslept. *Probably as a result of a heavy drinking session the night before,* she thought impatiently. The tired-looking clerk at the reception desk confirmed the futility of trying to arrange a cab at this time of the morning, leaving her with no option but to wait for his arrival, painfully conscious of the minutes as they ticked by.

A problem with the acquisition of an investment company based in the Isle of Man had resulted in this unexpected business trip and her standing in a quiet lobby in a small town waiting. Emily had juggled travel arrangements from the home office and, with some skillful maneuvering, managed to co-ordinate her arrival at London's Gatwick airport to a few hours before the scheduled departure of the private jet the women had booked for travelling on to Greece. Of course Ruby, in true volatile form, had nearly had a breakdown when Michelle contacted her to warn about the very tight arrangements. Michelle reassured her that it was a short flight and there was ample time to retrieve her luggage and meet the personal flight manager that had been assigned to them.

Michelle fumbled with her bags the moment she saw a car screech to a halt at the curb. The business trip backed up to the extended duration of this Greek vacation meant she was not traveling as light as normal. *Damn,* she thought as she eyed the clock in the car as they sped down the road, *the luggage check-in will take time, things are already looking pretty tight and we still have at least another ten minutes to drive before we reached the airport.*

A grim-faced clerk eyed her suspiciously as she rushed towards the check-in counter. *Be pleasant, be calm,* Michelle muttered to herself as she presented the stone-faced woman with travel documents. Peering over bifocal glasses, she looked sternly at Michelle and said, "I am sorry Madam; the flight to Gatwick has closed."

Michelle stared, barely keeping her mouth from gaping open. "Has the plane taken off yet?" She gasped as one hundred mental images of doom, disaster, and even more terrifying, a tongue lashing from the red-headed Ruby, passed through her mind in that split second of disbelief.

"The flight leaves in twenty minutes but the flight is closed. Unfortunately this flight will be leaving without you." The clerk smirked maliciously.

Michelle backed away from the counter in utter despair.

She was tired and emotional and it took all of her might not to stand in the middle of that airport and throw the mother of all histrionic shit fits. Years of experience with air travel warned her that this type of behavior would only exacerbate the situation so she left her bewildered, hung-over colleague standing at the counter next to her luggage to think up a way to negotiate a solution to this situation. She, herself, just sat in a self-sorry daze, staring out of the window at the wet, gray weather. *No wonder the British are so fucking miserable, they have to live with this shitty weather day in, day out.* "Miserable people living in a miserable place," she muttered as she dug deeply into the depths of her purse. Retrieving a Tiger's Eye stone that her Reiki Master had personally blessed for her, she rubbed the stone between two fingers repeating a calming mantra that she felt was appropriate for this moment: "Fuck, fuck, fuck." It was muttered quietly but with intense feeling.

Some time passed before her colleague appeared at her side announcing that they had found a workable solution to the problem. Taking her credit card from limp fingers, he returned to the counter where he arranged a new flight path which would involve a flight to Dublin, and thereafter, a fairly tight but do-able connection to London Gatwick. He calculated that all going well on what would be two short flights, she would arrive about thirty minutes before her Greek flight's scheduled departure.

Handing him her cell phone she said, "Sweetheart, you can have the privilege of explaining the details to Grant, our very gay and very personable flight manager and my darling friend Ruby who has a temper like a tiger and a mouth like a sewer. I have no energy to take them on right now." She smiled sweetly, a begging for forgiveness in that sad smile. "And then you are going to buy me a pack of cigarettes and a very, very strong coffee."

"Hey Mitch, I'm really sorry about the fuck up. I'll buy you two of everything," he said good naturedly, "and don't worry about Ruby, I'll charm her with my very best British accent, not too sure about the gay guy but I'll do my best!"

An hour later, Michelle was on board an Aer Lingus flight to Dublin, praying fervently to the Pope, Mother Mary, and any other saint she could think of for a smooth and uneventful connection. Her luggage had been booked through to Gatwick, so all she had to do was start running the moment her feet touched Irish ground. Well run she certainly did. *Why the hell do they always have to schedule my connecting flights on opposite sides of the airport?*

She cursed to herself as she hot-footed it down the seemingly endless corridors of moving escalators and jet lagged passengers moving at a zombie pace. She was a dripping, panting mess by the time she collapsed on the aircraft seat assigned to her, clutching a carryon on her lap. She gathered her wits and seat belt, absolutely amazed at making it just in time.

Once airborne, she ambled down the constricted galley way to the restroom. Shuffling around in the confined space, she surveyed herself in the fluorescent lit mirror, shocked at the tired, pale face that stared wild-eyed back at her.

Holy shit, time to do some repairs! She heaved her large travel tote onto the lowered, paper covered, toilet seat and proceeded to freshen up in anticipation of meeting up with old friends. Michelle was a seasoned traveler and, in spite of the restrictions on liquids and gels, often bragged that she could do a full spa/hair session and wardrobe change from her tote. Her carryon baggage always contained several strategically planned clothing changes and personal grooming essentials; enough to last for a few days.

Fifteen minutes later she emerged, looking and smelling absolutely gorgeous and feeling like she had been reunited with the calm and restful person she had been trying to reacquaint with during the months since the big bust up.

She sipped a coffee as she gazed pensively at the mass of fluffy clouds passing the cabin window.

Michelle was pinning her hopes of a full emotional recovery on this trip; the past months had been a rollercoaster of mental anguish. Terrified by the accidental overdose which put her in the mental hospital, she since had shunned the use of any medication, choosing instead to challenge whatever demons she had to face during this self-proclaimed period of introspection and healing as sober and as in control as possible.

Nigel was an absolute blessing. Michelle clung to the presence of her ponytailed Archangel like a child, allowing his gentle and undemanding demeanor to fill the empty space in her life. She hadn't mentioned a word of what happened to her employer; instead Michelle switched her work life to auto pilot, and anyone from the outside looking in saw a semblance of normality these few months after her discharge from the hospital.

Yet privately life was a struggle.

Her sleep patterns were severely disturbed; she tossed and turned at night waiting for sleep to release her from a deep raw pain of betrayal and anguish.

She knew the drill by heart now; sleep would only arrive after exhaustion, a new best friend, came to the rescue. Assuming the fetal position, she would fall gratefully into the arms of oblivious slumber. At precisely 3am she would be rudely roused by the little green monsters she referred to collectively as gremlins. She knew each nasty, venomous creature by name; six inches in height, running amok across the bed sheets and taunting her with their vicious abuse.

The gremlins arrived in squadrons and she would lie rigid with terror as they lined up in formation and prepared for battle. Wave after wave the brutal assaults would come, General Self Doubt was always in command of this war of negative emotions and he was skillfully assisted by his reporting officers Major General Fear, Colonel Failure, and Captain Despair.

Night after night, under the camouflage of darkness, this war of mental anguish erupted. Sometime, just before the break of dawn, the gremlins would take flight and Michelle would crumble into a semi-dazed slumber only to be roused by the blast of her alarm clock, demanding her presence in the work-a-day world. Diligently, she plodded through her morning rituals, expertly applying makeup in such a way so as to mask all evidence of the black lines under her eyes and painted lovely colored bright smiles on her face with Chanel lipstick.

Ruby & Tilina
Scene 3

Ruby was in her element; she loved being in charge. Managing, directing, arranging, scheduling were all tasks that came naturally to her. Fired up by the stress, she tackled endless lists and obstacles; both the foreseen and the unforeseen, the tantrums, the planning. Within the chaos, a final moment would emerge when she would take a step back and observe the visions in her head magically coming together into that beautiful moment created in her mind. In that instant, all the angst, frustration, and hard work evaporated as she stood still and watched her carefully choreographed performance come to life.

Of course, the most important aspect of planning such a grand trip was a budget. Preferably a big spending one; it was amazing what a person could achieve with money and, when appropriate, a hard-assed attitude. Ruby's mane of hair screamed a warning to strangers of the archetypical personality trait under that fiery redhead. Her temper was legendary yet her beguiling manner meant that she seldom had reason to use it.

Ruby had arrived in London the previous week. She was anxious to put the final touches onto the trip and wanted to be perfectly acclimatized and in control of her thoughts, processes, and service providers before her beloved friends arrived from the United States. She planned this reunion to be an event of a lifetime, something they would all fondly remember right up to their dying days.

None of them anticipated the emotional setbacks each would encounter when they started to discuss the trip. Ruby thought of Charlotte's dark tunnel of grief; similar to one she passed through when her own mother died. They were all special friends but Michelle had always been her "best friend."

Ruby's heart broke with Michelle's the day she heard that anguished voice crying out for help from a clinic. Beautiful, gentle, and unflappable; Michelle was her surrogate sister, the calming influence that kept her grounded in the chaos of growing up with five boisterous brothers. In spite of the physical distance between them, they had religiously kept in contact; arranging trips to be with each other at least once a year. Mitch always made the effort to go the distance to be with her, making Ruby's wedding thirty-two years ago, at her side when both sons were born, attended christenings, and even pitching in to clean the guinea pig cages when she visited from time to time. Ruby loved Michelle with every fiber of her being, while being different in every possible physical way. They realized at a young age that they wore the same shoes, literally and figuratively, and that was what made them inseparable.

Tilina arrived on a late flight the night before, then checked into a hotel very near the airport. Michelle was set to land and rush to the meeting point. Charlotte and Alex were landing separately, each with two hours to spare. They had arranged to meet at the VIP Lounge of the air charter company a few hours before takeoff time.

The personal flight manager assigned to them was worth his weight in gold. Grant was flamboyantly gay and embraced the excitement of the occasion with tremendous enthusiasm. The rapport between Grant and Ruby was instant. They had a lot of fun *oohing* and *aahing* over the special details of everything. Ruby tipped lavishly which ensured that nothing would be a problem. Traveling by chauffeur-driven limousine, Ruby made her way to the airport arriving at the lounge ahead of the others to make certain the champagne was chilled to the right temperature and the onboard catering and Greek music were ready to set the mood for a perfect reunion!

Grant was on top of his game; he minced around making comical hand gestures to amuse her while talking into his cell phone's headset. *This guy is good,* thought Ruby as she watched him in fascination; it wasn't often she came across a person who rivaled her in theatrical dramatics and she was picking up some great moves from this guy. He took right over when the call came in from the Isle of Man, assuring Ruby that everything would be fine and keeping her informed of Michelle's progress all the way from Dublin. He had flight trackers on Charlotte and Alex's flights and could tell her at any given moment the altitude, speed and estimated time of arrival of each aircraft. Helpers were dispatched to the meet and greet points, their meticulous planning culminated in the simultaneous arrival at the VIP lounge of Tilina, Charlotte, Alex, and a luggage-less Michelle.

Squeals of delight rang out as they hugged and kissed each other, tears flowed as freely as the Dom Perignon champagne was served.

Luggage was loaded into the aircraft while the girls sat chatting together waiting for the all clear to board their flight. Ruby presided like a mother hen surveying her brood, the years that had passed in between melted away and it felt like just yesterday when they all had been together.

"Let the fun begin!" Ruby called out to the world in general as they were escorted to the Cessna Citation jet that awaited them on the tarmac.

Airborne
Scene 4

The women clambered into the spacious cabin of a midsized executive jet. The stand-up cabin boasted a full galley kitchen, restroom facilities, and on-board entertainment. Excitedly the girls took their seats and barely listened to the pilot's safety instructions. Buckling up tightly they taxied onto the runway and before they knew it, they were airborne!

They gazed out their own windows deep in their own thoughts as the aircraft nudged its way up through the dreary gray banks of clouds that hung over London, each foot of ascension distancing them from their real lives until suddenly they broke through into space, sailing into that place where the sun always shines and every cloud reflects the warmth of joyous sunbeams. The speaker crackled to life announcing that the aircraft had reached its cruising altitude. The pilot provided them with details of the flight path ahead; his smooth British accent adding an extra flavor to his voice as it assured them that they were in very capable hands. Their destination was Volos Airport, a distance of 1,379 miles. They would maintain a cruising speed of 500 miles per hour and the estimated flying time would be approximately 3 hours. They smiled when the pilot mentioned that the weather en route was clear and the weather in Volos was hot and sunny.

The on-board hostess served champagne and finger snacks. When they were all comfortably settled, Ruby stood up and proposed a toast. Holding her glass up high she started, "Let's join hands as we reunite in friendship. Many years have passed since we were all together, let love guide and strengthen us as we rediscover the true joy of each other's company once again, Yassas!"

Ruby flicked the switch on the remote control, instantly, a large plasma screen came to life, accompanied by the piercing strains of Zorba the Greek, vivid images that were instantly recognizable as Greece appeared before them. They sat mesmerized by the Aegean blue pearl seas and stark white buildings, wizened Greek widows, cats of every color, size, and description. As the final notes of Zorba faded, the girls applauded Ruby's efforts quickly followed by Alex repeating their ritual toast from years gone by: "Here's to those who wish us well," she said with great gusto and importance and then joined the rest in chorus, "The rest of the fuckers can go to hell!" Champagne glasses clinked again as they settled back into their seats laughing.

Cats were Ruby's lifelong passion; images of feline perfection came to mind when she studied her friends. Ruby surveyed her stage and cast; the details were as perfect as she imagined they would be. She cast a motherly eye over these four friends.

Charlotte, or Charley as they called her, brought to mind a skinny, straggly stray cat. Accustomed to living on the periphery of life, she was a solitary, seemingly independent being who drew comfort when concealed in the shadows, easily frightened by people. One had to approach her gently, with patience and perseverance. If she warmed to your presence, she would reward you by sitting close for just as long as she felt comfortable. Petite as ever, she never seemed to change; disheveled blonde-streaked hair framed a sharp face. Dressed casually, a fitted black t-shirt clung to her boyish frame. Dark blue skinny jeans, heavy boots and a black leather jacket gave her a mysteriously chic, androgenic look. Closer scrutiny of her pale face revealed dark shadows and fatigue lines around piercing blue eyes. *Yes there has to be some Siamese mix in there from way back,* thought Ruby. She watched as Charley carefully relaxed into the new surroundings, the soft purr of the jet engines in the background seemed to soothe her. Slipping off her boots, Charley curled her tiny frame into the seat where she quietly observed the other women, mesmerized by their simple acceptance of her.

Ruby sipped some more and turned her attention to Alex. Definitely a Havana Brown she decided as she cast her eye over Alex's glossy hair, with its rich mink-like mahogany color. Alex looked absolutely amazing, her usual slender body looked toned and muscular and her obviously newly purchased cleavage seemed to be doing wonders for her self-esteem. Alex seemed more charming and playful than Ruby remembered, noting an attractive confidence which seemed to ooze like warmed chocolate from her. She sat chatting in a soft and affectionate manner with the others. Her brilliantly green eyes sparkled with happiness as she playfully interacted in the excited banter.

Michelle held center stage; multi-hued golden hair cascaded abundantly into gentle waves down her back as she stood before the group mimicking the stone-faced woman at the check-in counter. A born story teller, Michelle was blessed with the ability to transform the monotony of daily life into a riveting soap opera. Her keen eye and zany sense of humor could spot a comedic moment in the most peculiar places. At the most inopportune moments, one could rely on her to come up with some candid comment, the obscurity of which could often leave a person winded, laughing, or speechless. Ruby's gaze registered the long and lithe body that was now on the borderline of being too thin. Mitch had always bullied her body into shape with grueling training sessions which involved exercise in any manner or form. The years of unwavering discipline were obvious in her toned arms and muscular legs—there was no doubt about it, she was a beautiful and refined woman. The ravages of her recent stress and emotional trauma had seeped into her being and she looked gaunt and fragile and somewhat broken. Ruby suppressed an urge to gather her up and stroke the sadness away. *Plenty of time for that on this trip,* she thought, making a mental note to help Mitch slow down on the exercise and eat more over the next few weeks.

Ruby adjusted her hips slightly to study Tilina who sat primly on her seat engrossed in Mitch's animated performance. The quintessential dark gray Tom cat immediately came to mind as Ruby took in the chopped bangs and straight off cut at the shoulders. Ruby could never understand why some women went down the au-natural gray road when there were so many wonderful hair color options available. Lord knows, Tilina certainly had the money to splash out on a decent hairdresser; she had made no secret of the fact that her divorce settlement left her financially secure for the rest of her life. So why would anyone ever want to look old when they really didn't have to…but that was the Tilina they all knew. Her once straight black hair was now shot through with more than fifty percent gray. Tilina's tailored pantsuit looked expensive but her overall appearance spelled "gray Tom cat" in Ruby's flamboyant and colorful world. Tilina maintained a self-opinionated, condescending air about her, a trait that had often riled Ruby during their growing up years—Tilina was an expert at meddling in other people affairs and provided her opinion, whether asked for or not, in a very self-righteous and harsh manner. She was not an unattractive woman but certainly could have made more of her appearance. Tilina had good bone structure and a great skin tone reflecting her indigenous heritage. She was in reasonable shape but there was an air of bitterness emanating from her being and this hardened her features. Ruby had the feeling that Tilina could lash out and scratch at any time without any provocation. *Perhaps she's just one of those damaged women who never seem to recover from divorce,* thought Ruby as she signaled to the attendant to top up her champagne.

Ruby promised herself to be extra kind and understanding towards Tilina.

Chapter 7
Arrival in Greece – Road to Lefokastro
Scene 1

On arrival at Nea Anchialos National Airport in Volos, the women busied themselves in the VIP lounge restrooms: last minute "tinkles and lips" before they climbed into an SUV rental for the one-hour drive to Lefokastro. In anticipation of the mountainous baggage requirements of five women on an extended vacation, Ruby had arranged a Cadillac Escalade which she had been assured would comfortably accommodate their requirements; Ruby also wanted everyone to feel comfortable and reasoned that a good solid American car would be more appropriate for them. There was also the question of image and she drew comfort from the fact that if an American celebrity the likes of Kourtney Kardashian drove such a vehicle, then it would be deemed befitting if they did also.

A loud commotion drew their attention to the gleaming black vehicle right in the center of the furor. Much to their collective surprise, there stood the diminutive Charlotte, her hands gesticulating wildly as she tried to communicate with two Greek men. At first glance, one could see that the luggage had been loaded into the vehicle; the uproar appeared to involve a large and oddly shaped box that was standing somewhat forlornly on the parking lot. More frantic hand signals pointing towards the roof rack of the vehicle took place. Charlotte objected loudly to this suggestion, appearing close to tears or murder before Ruby and Tilina stepped in to try to remedy the situation, the latter hauling the now weeping woman aside, while Ruby attempted to find out what was going on. Tilina stood patiently with an arm around her friend, waiting for Charlotte to gather herself, looking strong now that she had the job of caring for a friend.

"They say the box won't fit in the car," Charley sobbed, "and I have to leave it here and another truck can bring it; they just don't understand I just can't leave it here, just imagine if something happens and they lose her!"

"Her?" questioned Tilina. "What do you mean *her* Charlotte?" Looking at the oddly shaped box, all sorts of images came to mind. "Okay, spit it out, what's in the box?" she asked cautiously, peering suspiciously at the object with an expectation that it might just move.

Charlotte gulped while contemplating sharing her secret with Tilina, realizing the slip of the tongue just made. She knew there was no option but to fess up to the contents and face the consequences. "My mother's in the box," she sniffed, averting her eyes, waiting for the reaction, which came, just as she thought it would.

The no nonsense Tilina blinked in astonishment, clearly expecting any other answer: a cat, a dog but certainly not a Mother. "Honey," she said gently, "your mom cannot possibly be in the box," lowering her voice to a whisper, "she passed away this spring."

"Tilina, my mom's in the box, trust me on this one." More tears flowed as Charley explained to her friend that the night after her mother died, she came to Charley in a dream and asked her to take her to Greece. "So I made an urn and put her ashes inside and brought her along."

Tilina was a little unsure about the Greek rules and regulations concerning the importation of human remains…her pre-travel research indicated that Greeks at all levels of society (including the Greek Orthodox church) were incredibly superstitious. Not wanting to unleash any of these tendencies or risk any violation of Greek law that could bog them down for weeks and totally ruin the birthdays, Tilina decided there and then that come what may, that box was going with them and the men who were helping them load up couldn't find out why.

After a round robin discussion with the rest of the women and much hasty corroboration with the Greeks, the suitcases were unloaded, a seat in the extreme rear of the vehicle was lowered and "Mother" was placed across it, the adjacent window was opened and the box maneuvered to lean on the window ledge and protrude. Pieces of luggage were then arranged into every possible gap they could find. It meant that they sat with suitcases under their feet and vanity cases on their laps, a little squashed but they reasoned that it was a relatively short ride to their final destination so the discomfort would soon pass.

Spirits were high as they took off, Alex at the wheel and Michelle acting as wingman/navigator fiddling with the GPS as they left the airport. "Okay Alex, you need to turn right in four and a half *ah, ah*...kilometers! Oh my goodness everything is in kilometers—and we are looking for *ah, ah*...EO Karditsas Volou. I guess an EO is Greek for an interstate," she said with a chuckle as the huge American SUV hit the road.

Ruby took on the role of tour guide; she spent many hours researching their destination and was now a self-proclaimed expert on the Pelion Region. She was captivated by the romantic Greek Mythology stories and now, experiencing the magnificence of these surroundings first hand, she could understand why back in the day, this particular area was fabled to be the playground of the Greek gods. Mount Pelion provided a majestic background for the city of Volos as it presided over the calm, vivid blue sea of the Pagasetic Gulf. She could just imagine mythological centaurs—half horse, half human creatures that inhabited this scenic mountainous area. With a dreamy look on her face, she explained the mythical background of the region to her fascinated audience, casually punctuating each story with the names of famous Greek heroes and gods like Achilles and Zeus.

"I wonder if we'll find any modern-day Greeks at play in the Pelion Region," she mused aloud with humor in her voice, "of course I'm a happily married Grande Dame these days but there's still plenty of goddess in this voluptuous body of mine."

"... and goddesses just love a little playful flirt from time to time," Alex chimed in from the front of the car.

"*Aaaw* come on girls, deep down inside all of us lies a roguish flirt," said Tilina sassily. "I could quite easily be tempted to indulge myself in some Greek sweet meat dripping with honey." She laughed. "Nothing like a hot steamy vacation romance to get the waning hormones vamped up again."

They chuckled good naturedly as the big car made its way through narrow, curved roads, the crystal-clear waters of the sea on one side of them and hills of olive groves rising on the other. Slowing down as they passed through a small village, their eyes simultaneously fell upon a vision of great beauty and desire…a blonde man, stripped to the waist, digging in a garden. Embracing their newly found flirtatious selves, they sounded the horn while Ruby wolf-whistled through the open window. The man stood up, his perfect physique glowing from exertions under the sun and rewarded them with a smile and a wave as they drove by.

"Well, that looked promising. Adonis is certainly alive and well and living in the Pelion Peninsula," chuckled Michelle. It felt good to be in the company of happy girlfriends. For the first time in months she felt a surge of warmth in her frozen, broken heart. In spite of the years that had passed since they used to hang out as carefree teenagers, she was struck by the easy comradeship that still existed between them. It felt safe and nurturing. *Perhaps this will be a journey of healing; maybe this is the gift of guidance from the universal power that my Reiki Master alluded to.* She knew from studies and endless hours of Reiki therapy that she needed to open her spiritual soul and chakras to allow this natural energy of friendship to flow through her being.

Michelle's laughter was heartwarming, the girls were all aware of the torrid time she endured over the past months. Ruby warned them that she was "delicate" and not quite herself at the moment. Ruby further explained that Michelle's choice to follow a holistic path of healing was inspired by her brother's Reiki teaching. It all sounded very esoteric and airy fairy, especially to Alex, but hey ho, each to their own, whatever made sense to the individual concerned was the general consensus. Although it sounded a little too new age for Tilina, who was she to judge? In Ruby's mind there was nothing that a cooking session, a bottle or two of an expensive Merlot, and a few anti-depressants couldn't fix.

The Villa
Scene 2

The digital drone of the GPS announced they had reached their destination. Large wrought iron gates of a private estate opened and the heavy vehicle inched its way down the precariously sloped and curved driveway. Ahead of them, their villa stood majestically situated at the head of a bay, providing a sweeping view of both the Pagasitic Gulf and Pelion Mountains. Constructed from locally sourced stone, the dwelling blended perfectly with the natural surroundings of the mountainous area. Olive trees grew in abundance as did forest flora. To the trained eye, it was a well cultivated and tended garden that looked like it had been placed by a god.

The housekeeping staff stood at the entrance, eager to welcome new guests they would be caring for during a long stay in Greece. They would cook, clean, and shop, leaving the women with nothing else to do but relax and have fun. Althea introduced herself as the head housekeeper, it was her job to make sure that the service provided satisfied each guest; she was very experienced in dealing with specifically American VIP elite guests (who behaved very differently from the Europeans that usually visited). Althea understood that while they valued high-end luxury and pampering, discretion and an almost invisible presence was required. It was important for her to understand and manage the guest's expectations as early as possible.

The booking agents advised that the women would need assistance with their unpacking and that a welcome dinner of traditional Greek food would be best on the first night; thereafter, she would meet with the group and plan with them regarding their personal preferences for breakfast, lunch, and dinner.

Eucalyptus infused, chilled facecloths and iced homemade lemonade awaited the travel weary group in the hall. They followed the natural flow of the U shaped villa, the center of which contained the main living areas which were dominated by a large open plan living room where they sank into comfortable oversized white couches, taking in the surrounding sea view offered by shimmering floor to ceiling windows. The heart of the villa was an enormous open plan kitchen which also provided a large informal dining area. Adjacent rooms accommodated any need for more formal dining requirements or if one was in search of a quiet place, a large library provided an impressive collection of books, a desk area with discreetly placed internet connections and computer equipment, wingback chairs in which to read or enjoy a quiet game of chess or simply window gaze, were placed in clusters. A large outdoor patio encircled the main living areas and provided an effortless flow between indoor and outdoor living. Every possible whim was provided for: an infinity pool, al fresco dining area, garden seat under a lemon tree, tennis court, Jacuzzi, grand Steinway piano—no expense or detail had been spared in creating this perfect retreat.

Althea appeared in the living room, a little confused because she'd been unable to find Michelle's luggage and there was also the matter of a large box that needed to be removed from the vehicle. The girls roused themselves from their seats ready to assist with the formal offloading and placement of Mother. Ruby explained the dilemma of Michelle's errant luggage to a somewhat perplexed Althea, confident that an airline van would magically appear in the next day or so with the bags.

It was all hands-on deck as Mother was slowly inched out of the vehicle; Charlotte hovered over the precious package like a mother hen, emphasizing how fragile the item inside was and issuing orders of guidance as the box was steered through the hallway into the living room. Michelle, who was very much focused on attaining a higher level of spiritual enlightenment, looked pensively at the box and asked a question that raised the eyebrows of both Alex and Tilina. "Charley, where exactly would you like Mother to be placed? Do you think she would enjoy the view and companionship in the living room or perhaps the peace and quiet of the library?"

"Actually, I thought she could share my room, but now that you mention it, I think she would enjoy being part of the mainstream action with all of us. She really liked it when you all came over."

Alex, who had gleaned from tidbits of conversation at the airport that Charlotte's mother was the sole occupant of the box, now eyed the box suspiciously. An image of an embalmed Mummy came to mind and she was not exactly comfortable about sharing her vacation home with a deceased (albeit embalmed or cremated) person. The ever-present placating nature of Ruby sensed Alex's discomfort and, in an effort to make everyone happy, suggested that Charlotte unveil her work of art to all of them after dinner as a treat with dessert.

Charlotte's dazzling blue eyes welled up with tears as her face crumbled in relief. "I'd be honored to share this tribute to my mom with all of you. I poured my soul and my grief into this work of art, the only people who might understand, would be all of you, thank you," she said with such humility, neither Alex nor Tilina had the heart to refuse.

Almost on cue, Althea appeared with a team of housekeepers to escort them to their respective suites where they could take a nap, shower up, and chill for the rest of the afternoon until dinner. The bedrooms were situated on both sides of the living room areas; individual suites each with a magnificent en suite bathroom and den ensured maximum privacy in their personal space. French doors opened out onto the pool area, once again capturing that wonderful feeling of space, openness, and that ever important connection to the main living areas.

Naptime
Scene 3

Michelle was roused from an afternoon nap by a sharp object digging into her side; she rolled over to retrieve a large rock crystal lodged under her ribs. Nigel told her that the energy of this particular crystal would help to heal her broken heart. Following an intricate programming process, she dedicated the crystal to this purpose and each night before falling asleep, she placed the shiny stone on her heart while meditating. Mustering all the power of her mind, she willed the invisible energy fields to flow through her blocked chakras but still the pain in her heart remained and the incessant weeping when alone or when an emotional topic came up continued to the point that she thought she was surely going mad. One of the women in her Reiki class consoled her during a particularly heavy downpour of tears one evening, reassuring her that it was good to release this grief so that her tears could cleanse her soul and the upside of all this wet and salty emotion was that she wouldn't get cancer.

Steadfast in her belief that the spiritual approach would help, Michelle frequented esoteric shops of all descriptions, spending hours in the council of spiritual advisors and Reiki instructors and purchasing every remedy suggested. In a few short months, she had amassed a large collection of unusual crystals. With the help of Ruby's brother, the house was gridded with crystals; she chose Selenite because this stone provided both protection and angelic guidance.

Michelle found herself in a space she could never have imagined merely a year ago; she was a strong, intelligent, and independent woman who had fearlessly embraced the challenges of modern life with passion. Yet she'd been brought crumbling to her knees with just one sentence, "I never loved you, not in the way that a man should love a woman, you have never been my special someone." Over and over again she heard his words and that was when the tears would start to flow.

Through hard work and determination, she had excelled in her career, enjoying the sweet rewards of success that came in great abundance.

The relationship with Bradley provided a semblance of balance—while it wasn't perfect, she at least had someone special who she believed cared about her. The stark realization that he had never loved her, that she had been for him a pleasant convenience at best and a safety net at worse, left her with a deep sense of betrayal and an internal anger that burned constantly. She grieved for the many lost opportunities, the men that had shown interest, the relationships that could have been, and the children that she could possibly have borne, had he just been honest with her.

The wasted years were what hurt the most. How could she have missed the signs that were so obvious now? How could she have given so much of herself and her being then settled for so little in return? She knew her truth was because there was a deep sense of unworthiness that had plagued her since childhood; an omnipresent feeling that screamed "not good enough" day in and day out was what fueled a need to work harder, be better, love more. All in order to be loved and valued. She lay on the bed clutching the rock crystal to her heart and sobbed until there were no more tears left. She fell back asleep from pure exhaustion: mental and physical.

The calm from the crying release came as she knew it would. Feeling energized from her nap, she changed into the running clothes smartly packed in her carryon luggage. She knew the physical challenge would elevate her mood even further and put her in the right frame of mind for the welcome dinner Ruby had planned. She smiled as she put her body through the stretch and warm up. Enjoying the warm afternoon sunshine, she hooked in earbuds and jogged up the driveway towards the road, running to her favorite playlist.

Jogging was one of Michelle's many pleasures in life; within the first few minutes of exertion she knew this was going to be a great run. The sunshine, the music, and the sheer beauty of these surroundings lifted her spirits as she settled into a steady rhythmic pace. *This sure beats running on a hotel treadmill. I could get used to this very easily.*

Thirty minutes into the run she turned around and headed back for the house, looking forward to an exhilarating shower and wondering what on earth she could scrounge from Ruby's wardrobe to wear for the evening.

She only had a pair of jeans and two t-shirts packed and it was a little too warm in Greece for those at the moment.

Apollo's Feast
Scene 4

The ladies gathered for sundowner drinks on the patio while Althea's team of helpers worked tirelessly in the kitchen putting the finishing touches onto the meal. The menu Ruby selected was entitled Apollo's Feast and judging by the smells emanating from the kitchen and the platters being carried to the patio table; this was most definitely food prepared with the gods in mind.

The Greek Meze Table, the true essence of Greek casual dining, was what caught Ruby's eye in the brochure. Understanding they would all be a little travel weary, Ruby picked this option for their first night's dinner. It was all unfolding before her eyes just as she pictured it; an evening of laughter, conversation sprinkled with drink, and a delectable assortment of food.

Althea prepared a variety of Greek appetizers—mezethes. It seemed that each meze dish was chosen to specifically awaken their senses to the unique smells and tastes of Greece. Small, brightly painted bowls held olives of various colors harvested from the villa's own groves, then cured by the staff using family traditions passed down by generations before them. Herbed pita bread wrapped in thick serviette parcels to retain their warmth, partnered glass jars of taramasalata mullet garnished with fiery orange-colored cod roe. Wedges of freshly fried Saganaki cheese, drenched in a warm honey and oregano sauce nestled snugly in a large cast iron pan beckoned invitingly to be tasted.

Providing a commentary while pouring tumblers of chilled Limnia Gi, a dry white wine originating from the island of Limnos, Althea revealed that the colors of the olives provided an indication of the time of year in which they were harvested. The green olives are picked at the start of the harvest season in October, the red or pink in November and the black in December. She proudly informed them that The Pelion was indeed an olive connoisseur's heaven and that all the ingredients in their meal were either grown on the property or locally sourced from this region which was famous for its agricultural products; specifically olives, cheese, honey, and nuts.

Famished from travel and settling in the gorgeous but new surroundings, they tucked in, enjoying the communal plates and animated conversation at a leisurely pace. The food appeared in staggered waves, allowing them ample opportunity to savor the taste of each perfectly prepared dish. Char-grilled butterflied sardines drizzled with a dressing of olive oil, finely diced red and green chilies, garlic and lemon accompanied freshly baked sourdough bread to soak up the delectable taste of the sauce. This all provided an interesting curtain raiser to the main performance of the evening: slow cooked shanks of lamb served with homemade Greek yogurt, herbed roasted potatoes, fried okra doused in mint vinegar washed down with gulps of chilled Ouzo. They reached across the table with their forks, laughing as they bumped against each other in their hasty effort to taste and savor every morsel so lovingly prepared for them.

The atmosphere was warm and inviting; the years of separation melted away until things felt as if no time had passed. Shrugging off their shrouds they revealed the young women they had always been, the faraway friends that they knew, long before the compass of life took them along individual paths. They once again merged at this point of reunion, all distance of mind, spirit and body disappeared. At this table of joy, they came together and celebrated, united in that inexplicable and extraordinary bond of female friendship; a little bumped, a little bruised, an extra pound here, a wrinkle there, yet safe in the warm embrace of this empowering human connection they shared.

They each held the expectation that this plateau of love and acceptance would provide a resting place where they could lay down their heavy load and armor and then reflect and recharge. It was from this protected vantage point that they could safely cast their eyes of truth across the terrain of life they had traveled thus far, knowing that their sisterhood would soothe tumultuous inner souls and plug the emotional cavities formed in their lives. In the bosom of their alliance, they would gather guidance, strength, and sustenance for the journey that remained ahead of them.

Expectations can be such dangerous things.

Tilina fiddled with her camera; her sons had grouped together to purchase the expensive photographic equipment for her birthday and she had watched the complimentary tutorial sessions included with the sale. Her curiosity piqued, Tilina then enrolled in a more intensive beginners' course where she made the acquaintance of a stern, retired German woman, Hildegard, who took an interest (whether financially driven or based on some essence of raw talent she might have observed) in developing Tilina's photographic capabilities. They agreed that Greece would provide a perfect opportunity for Tilina to practice landscape, still life, and portraiture photography. So Tilina was duly tasked with an assignment: she would be expected to display to her fellow students on her return a diverse portfolio.

The girls had grown accustomed to Tilina idly snapping away at various subjects since the start of the trip and now paid no mind to the camera. Tilina, on the other hand, stared in astonishment at the dynamics of the images she viewed through the lens this evening. Inspired by the emotions stirring within her, she warmed to the challenge of capturing these spontaneous, fleeting moments of female energy and love in pictures.

Michelle made for an interesting portrait study this evening; forced to raid Ruby's wardrobe for an outfit, her usual modern style was replaced by one of Ruby's diaphanously flowing outfits. In the absence of Ruby's voluptuous curves, the outfit hung loosely on Michelle's slender body. She had pinned her long, golden hair in a scruffy up do. The oversized top slipped off her shoulder and the overall effect was a waiflike, orphan look. The usual air of confidence that oozed from Michelle was replaced by an underlying vulnerability which enhanced her beauty in a very soft and appealing manner.

Althea set a tray with liqueurs and delicate Greek pastries in the living room and discreetly took her leave for the evening. The girls moved to the comfort of the large living room, nuzzling like feline creatures into the peaceful pleasure of the oversized couches. The end of the long dining process allowed for a change of pace as Ruby took on the duty of serving the liqueurs and sweets. With her hostess tasks out of the way, Ruby declared enthusiastically to Charlotte, "I think it's time for Mother to join us!"

Alex watched Charlotte's blue eyes widen nervously, and sensing her apprehension, hugged her affectionately. "Do you remember how I would play the piano for your mom when we were younger?" she asked eyeing the gleaming Steinway Grand Piano deep in the corner of the room. "Why don't I play one of her favorite songs? Ruby can sing just like we always used to." Charlotte's eyes shone with tears as she remembered those happy days so long ago, she nodded in agreement.

Ever the performer and sensing a theatrical moment, Ruby sprang to her feet, Ouzo glass in hand, and immediately assumed the role of creative director. Alex was assigned to the music arrangements, Tilina placed in charge of photography, Michelle agreed to be stage hand which included lighting, Charlotte would lead the performance and Ruby would sing as requested. Under the supervision of Ruby, they dragged the heavy box to the center of the room and then collapsed back on the couch, huffing and puffing from the exertion. The box was heavy and each one of them wondered what the hell Charlotte had inside. Alex voiced concerns to Tilina and Ruby that it was an Egyptian sarcophagus with a mummified Marjorie inside. Ruby scoffed at the idea and Tilina, well, she just shuddered at any theory, that box had spooked her mind since she discovered Marjorie was inside. They agreed to keep calm and be accommodating of Charlotte's eulogy; but if it turned out to be a little too over the top, they would signal each other to help Charlotte wrap it up. In the meantime, Ruby and Alex had a quiet discussion about the musical arrangements, Michelle scouted around the villa for some additional lighting for the centerpiece and Tilina sat quietly fiddling with the light settings on her camera so she could capture whatever Greek comedy/tragedy was about to take place.

Silence embraced the whole room as shafts of light fell softly upon the box. As the outer wrappings were removed, the contents eerily took on a very definite human shape. Alex settled herself on the piano seat and quietly tinkered with notes, rehearsing in her mind the pieces for the unveiling process and creating a few back up pieces just in case things went awry. Charlotte nodded at Alex who took the cue to start playing; the steady rhythm of Beethoven's hauntingly beautiful Moonlight Sonata flowed through the quiet of the room as they watched Charlotte pull away roll after roll of protective wrapping revealing an object wrapped in purple velvet. Charlotte moved around the velvet mass, loosening the ties until it draped the object beneath like a cloak. As the final strains of the sonata sounded, Charlotte pulled one end of the cloth with a sharp tug and stood back as the soft fabric melted away to the floor revealing the most exquisite bronze statue of a woman. The girls sat mesmerized, studying this magnificent work of art that stood before them. The face of the statue was instantly recognizable as Marjorie.

As if reading their minds, Charlotte explained the significance and symbolism of this piece of work. "My earliest observations of my mother were at her dressing table where she would apply makeup and do her hair. I remember watching these beauty rituals in awe, thinking she was the most beautiful woman in the world. She was a goddess to my young eyes." Charlotte paused to control her emotions then went on wistfully, "The night she died, I held her lifeless body in my arms and I *knew* that she was the most beautiful woman in the world." Looking up at the statue, she continued with a smile, "I wanted to immortalize her and the first image that came to mind was a goddess. In my research, I looked for the one that epitomized my mother. Hera—Queen of the Olympian gods and goddesses—the goddess of women and marriage—was the one I felt was befitting as the vessel for the eulogy to my mother."

Charlotte captured Marjorie in the prime of life in a swirl of poetic motion, her delicate face framed by long flowing hair, held back by a crown. Her graceful, lithe body was swathed in gossamer garments covering her breasts and lower body. A fabled peacock stood at her feet, the eye patterns in the giant fanned tail protectively spread around her. She explained that her mother's ashes were contained in a hidden pocket within the statue and that as bizarre as it might seem, this was the only option she felt comfortable with. She mentioned that there was a memorial service to facilitate the internment of the ashes scheduled for her return to the States but in the spur of an Ouzo moment she decided to bring her mother to Greece.

The girls cheered in unison as Ruby congratulated Charlotte on this glorious tribute and proposed a toast to Goddess Marjorie. Taking her place in the curved space of the grand piano, Ruby started to sing Bette Middler's *Wind Beneath My Wings*, the lyrics seemed to have been written specifically for this remarkable mother and daughter.

Alex was an accomplished pianist and Ruby had always loved singing. Even to this day she still sang in the church choir. A born entertainer, her clear, strong, and melodious voice filled the room as she sang to Marjorie and Charlotte. The truth and beauty of the words took her to the place of grief she instinctively knew was Charlotte's—with tears flowing down her face the song drew to its close.

"Thank you," whispered Charlotte as she hugged each one of them. "Thank God for all of you and how you hold me up."

They topped up their Ouzo glasses in celebration, Alex guiding them from one mood to another, soon leading them to songs they sang as young teenagers.

Lost in the moment of their now, which was ironically taken from their past, they laughed as they sang and danced in gay abandon to Abba, The Carpenters…the music just kept coming.

MIDPOINT

WHEN IN GREECE...

...GO GREEK

Chapter 8
Sun and Breakfast
Scene 1

Tilina was awakened by bright shafts of sunlight dancing on her face; she had left the curtains open when she went to bed the night before to ensure she would wake early. She didn't want to waste a minute of this experience. Stretching luxuriously in the king-size bed, she was chuckling while recalling the events of the previous night. After so many lonely nights, it was a rare treat to immerse herself in the company of people who loved her, witch warts and all.

She took a large number of photographs and was suddenly curious to see how they turned out. Climbing out of the oversized bed, she fetched her camera and laptop to download and assess the previous night's takings. Sitting cross-legged on the bed, she deftly connected the equipment and sat patiently waiting for the images to appear. She was transfixed by her endeavors; yes, there were a few out of focus, but by and large she captured some great shots. Critiquing the pictures though Hildegard's eyes, she deleted shots that didn't meet the strict portraiture criteria as decreed by her German teacher. Tilina could hear that heavily accented voice in her ears as she studied the images. Purring with satisfaction she noted with pleasure that the study of Michelle was as stunning as she thought it would be. In fact, even if she might say so herself, it was perfect in every way: lighting, composition, focus, color— Michelle's fragility climbed out of the image and straight into her heart. She created a new file and backed them up on her drop box. It was a good start to her assignment and Tilina resolved to have her camera with her at all times.

A cacophony of sound drew her attention to the patio where she saw Ruby dressed in a brightly colored and outrageously short gown, ringing an oversized goat's bell to summon everyone for breakfast. They sauntered in from their early morning activities;

Michelle and Alex had gone for a long run together, Charlotte just finished a weight training session in the villa's private gym and Ruby had been in deep consultation with Althea regarding their housekeeping requirements. A light breakfast, presented buffet style, awaited them and the group tucked in hungrily. Fresh fruit salad partnered well with the home-made yogurt and delicious golden-colored thyme honey. Alex groaned as she negotiated a stack of tiganites (Greek pancakes), smothering them in grape molasses, and bemoaned the fact that she would have to double up on her exercise régime if Althea continued to turn out such incredible food.

Ruby scoffed at that. "Alex my darling," she said with a sweet smile, "the Greek way of eating is a perfect example of the Mediterranean diet trending now in the States. Trust me, one month away from the standard American junk food offering and we will all be dancing like Zorba."

Tilina nodded in agreement. "She's right you know, look at the old folks here, they're slim, active, and seem to have all their marbles in the right place, must be something to do with all the olive oil they eat here."

Michelle sat listening quietly. Ruby had a valid point. From what she'd seen thus far, the food was simple, colorful, and wholesome, locally grown then cooked with an abundance of fresh herbs. Since arriving in Greece, she was reacquainted with a very long-lost friend: her appetite. "Let's make a pact," Michelle said with a wicked gleam in her eyes. "What a miserable shame to count calories and forego all these amazing new tastes when on vacation. I propose Alex and I take charge of the daily exercise ritual and Ruby, you tell Althea to go Greek all the way!"

"All the way?" said Charlotte with a coy look on her face as she pointed towards the swimming pool. "Does that mean Adonis the gardener's on the menu?"

Their heads swiveled towards the pool and they immediately recognized the gardener they wolf-whistled at the day before and screeched in unison, "Oh my God...yes, most definitely."

"And served with honey," growled Tilina.

They collapsed in girlish giggles while sipping strong coffee and debating what they would do with the beautiful sunny day that stretched before them. Their unanimous decision was to spend the day on their private beach, priming their snow-white bodies in the vain hope that they would become golden across the next few days.

"I don't want to be a party pooper...but," sighed Michelle, "my carryon luggage wardrobe is such that I can handle with the greatest ease a business meeting with Warren Buffet, a formal dinner with Joe Biden, a heavy running session with Usain Bolt, and a steamy romp in the sack with Brad Pitt. Unfortunately, my Greek god play date commitment wardrobe is currently in the hands of Aer Lingus, so the closest thing I have to a bikini right now is a sweaty exercise bra and a black, see-through G-string."

The girls stared at Michelle, groaning in joint sympathy as she flipped through the limited options. Michelle's tall, athletic build would surely drown in Ruby's wild and colorful garments. She already looked totally ridiculous in the outfit she borrowed the night before. Charlotte's tiny, boyish frame meant that any donation from her closet would, at a stretch, cover half a nipple. Even the new sports-model-shaped Alex was heavier in the butt and boob department than Michelle, so that wouldn't work either. The last option was Tilina's dowdy, school headmistress type vestments. Michelle would have preferred to wear a nun's habit than go scrounging through that closet.

En masse they lamented the hopelessness of their situation until Althea provided the vital and critically important fact they had overlooked during their deliberating moments of anguish. Looking at them quizzically, she stood before them like the prophet of life and stated pragmatically, "Swim suit? In Greece, we have nudist beaches. What's the fuss about?"

The *aha* moment appeared instantaneously. Filled with their newly found solution, they headed for their respective suites to shower and cream up ahead of the arduous task of sunning their buns for the day.

The Birth of Aphrodite
Scene 2

They followed a snaky path through the garden to the villa's private beach. Michelle wrapped her dignity in one of Ruby's excessively decorated oriental silk sarongs. Matching flip flops, featuring gold medusa heads at her toes, caused shuffling with each step she took in the oversized footwear screaming brazenly Versace!

On the pretext of photographing some flowers, Tilina hung back from the mainstream of the downward expedition; a bemused smile crossed her face as she took candid pictures of these renegade women who, at this moment in time, she loved more than life itself. *Oh my,* she thought as she shook her head at the picture they made, *what chaos and adventures are ahead of us across these next weeks?* There was nowhere else in the world she would rather be than in this particular moment, in this particular place, at this particular time. *Oh my goodness,* she chastened herself, *I'm starting to sound like Michelle's Reiki Master.*

Arranging themselves on luxuriously cushioned beach loungers they surveyed the vast blue gulf of water that swayed before them. The day showed promise of scorching heat, but the crystal sea winked at them invitingly. Wraps were stripped off; Michelle froze in hesitance. The ever emotional, yet compassionate, Ruby sensed her friend was having a problem with the naked moment that was rapidly approaching. Spontaneity propelled Ruby to her feet and, assuming her best rendition of a majestic goddess, Ruby theatrically ripped off her bikini top, releasing her salacious breasts from restraint. They tumbled in poetic unison across her chest.

Aghast silence clung momentarily to the fleeting breeze until the chivalry of female solidarity took over. Taking on the persona of their favorite goddess, they shed their swimwear. The first thrilling moments of sheer exposure were replaced by the ecstasy of a new found liberation in their nakedness. Taking to the water, they strutted and posed for their equally naked paparazzi photographer. Playfully snatching Tilina's camera, they took turns at taking photographs of her also, then each other. Super model sultry poses, duck face pouts, and slinky naked movements framed loud peals of laughter as they reveled in this symbolic moment of truth. Masks and shrouds used in daily life were stripped, they stood before each other shamelessly and revealed their true naked selves; stretch marks, caesarean scars, cellulite, and all.

Adonis appeared in the midst of the horseplay, armed with a silver tray laden with sliced apple pieces, nuts, olives, and a bottle of Ouzo. Seemingly nonplussed by the abundance of naked female flesh on display, he set the tray down in the gazebo, filled the tumblers with Ouzo and walked into the sea with a tumbler of his own. "Attended by beautiful nymphs, she is born; let us drink in celebration to Aphrodite," his sage colored eyes fixed on Charlotte, "the goddess of love, beauty, pleasure, and sexuality…"

"Opa!" Their glasses clinked enthusiastically, Adonis smiled, threw his head back, poured the contents down his throat, cast a smoldering look at Charlotte, waded back out of the water, and disappeared up the garden path.

"OH, MY GREEK GOD, he's definitely Greek for Gorgeous," breathed Tilina looking up from the lens finder. "Is he hot or what? I wouldn't mind practicing some nude photography on him." She smiled lecherously.

"Forget it Tilina," teased Alex, "looked to me like our Adonis had an Aphrodite moment toward—" Alex nodded at Charlotte.

Charlotte smiled self-consciously; she was not used to being at the center of any male attention. "He'd probably end up mounted and immortalized in bronze," she laughed and swiftly changed the subject. "Come on, let's swim out to that rock over there," she pointed in the distance to a phallic shaped bolder that rose majestically from the water.

"Naked goddesses lounging on a penis shaped rock sounds pretty cool to me. Who knows what other idols might be wakened and then we can have an orgy," laughed Alex as she led the way.

Tilina and Ruby reached the rock sometime after the others; yoga and the odd game of golf was the sum total of their usual exercise endeavors and it showed as they huffed and puffed their way onto the rock. Still a little conscious of their nudity, they arranged themselves as modestly as one could when lying *au natural* and spread eagled on a rock.

The warm sun bathed their bodies as they lay in idle chatter. Ruby sat up and stared pensively at her friends. "Why did I have to be in the front of the boob and bum distribution line?" she lamented surveying her body. She had always had a well-rounded figure but these days the emphasis seemed to dwell less on the well and more on the round. "I dunno, since menopause reared its ugly head, it doesn't matter what I eat or don't eat, my body has determined it wants to be apple shaped."

"Try me," commiserated Tilina. "Mine's going pear shaped. I'm the perfect example of Newton's gravity theory, everything on top has fallen to the bottom. You two skinny asses," she said nodding at Michelle and Charlotte, "don't have to worry. The smaller the mass, the less gravitational pull."

"You know what they say, you have to choose between your ass and your face. We have wrinkles and turkey skin to contend with," groaned Charlotte.

"Right," added Michelle, "for what I've spent on anti-wrinkle cream and facials, my face should look like a baby's bottom. Once you cross that menopause line, it all simply goes down the toilet. These days when they try to sell me face and body lifting creams, I laugh in their sweet twenty-something faces and tell them, it simply won't work darling!"

"How about the mood swings, the insomnia?" sniggered Alex, whose new sporty image sat snugly in the middle of the body shape debate. "Or those hot, steamy nights when your heart races and you ooze sweat from every pore and then you wake up and there's not a man in sight…Hello hot flashes."

"Still a male orientated world I'm afraid. How come they get Viagra and we get KY jelly for vaginal dryness?" huffed Ruby. "I was reading an article on research studies for the female version of Viagra and the bad news is…not any time soon girls, the experts are worried they'll produce a generation of nymphomaniacs…I wish!"

Michelle wiggled her body into the warmth of the rock, thinking how comforting it was to be with girlfriends. They could talk about anything under the sun, no subject was off limits. They understood and best of all, being the same age, they could relate firsthand to the peculiarity of female issues. Her profession was largely male dominated and as much as she loved her testosterone infused colleagues, she could hardly imagine discussing hot flashes and vaginal lubricants with any of them—not even the gay ones.

Why do we spend so much time obsessing about our bodies? At the end of the day, we're all beautiful and special in our own unique way. She felt a now familiar wave of despair engulf her and fought to hold back the tears that she knew would inevitably follow if she disappeared into her own private cesspool of turmoil; she didn't want to spoil this moment with her pitiful self-loathing and neediness.

Despite a Herculean effort, her thoughts turned to Bradley… *What is he doing now? Does he miss me? Perhaps I was too hasty by packing his things.* Maybe having a crappy man was better than having no man at all. He had, after all, accepted her with all of her faults and yet she hated the person she had become in that relationship. The more distanced he was, the more attention she craved, giving the impression of being needy. No man wants a needy woman; perhaps if she were less pathetically needy, he would love her the way she wanted him to love her.

On and on her thoughts ravaged at her until a loud sob escaped from her mouth.

Instantly the playful banter ceased as all attention turned to Michelle.

"Don't mind me; I'm just a glob of icky human DNA at the moment," she sobbed. "It's these infernal tears that refuse to stop."

Everyone except Ruby was gob smacked. Could it be true? The invincible, beautiful, strong willed, in control of everything, Michelle, was this naked forlorn mess before them? Ruby hinted that Michelle was taking the breakup badly, but they couldn't have imagined the true extent of the damage.

Rallying around her in support, they listened, consoling her with soothing words and providing eight collective shoulders for her to cry on. They followed the age-old womanly pact: don't fix each other, just lend a hand and provide guidance along the dark road until a new dawn breaks.

* * *

Althea appeared at various times during the day leaving light snacks and beverages in the gazebo. They spent the rest of the day on the beach; walking, swimming, snoozing, reading, and chatting.

It was a time to reminisce about their school days and begin the catch-up process, filling in the years and the details of each other's lives.

Michelle listened quietly, thankful that she could let down her pretense that everything was okay with her at this present point in time. She felt safe and loved—a state of mind that had evaded her for many years.

Yet despite this all, a hard rock of panic was forming and growing in her stomach, it was fueled by worry that she would never be able to kick this sadness and would eventually end up living out her days in a mental clinic if this vacation was unable to work its magic on her dying spirit.

The Greek Taverna
Scene 3

Refreshed from a late afternoon siesta, spirits charged by a glorious day outdoors, the women emerged from their suites eager to immerse themselves in their new surroundings. Casually dressed for a little drive-by sightseeing expedition and in no particular hurry, they followed the road enjoying the elevated vantage point the Cadillac provided. Visual senses were drenched with impressive sea vistas as they spied a number of well-hidden villas and stunning beaches along the way. Through the open windows of the vehicle, they were serenaded by the faint tinkle of bells attached to goats grazing in the surrounding hills. Admiring the olive groves, they waved to locals as they passed by, eventually ending up in Lefokastro, a small seaside village situated a short distance away from their villa.

Bright blue, painted wooden chairs and tables beckoned them to the beachside patio of a tavern. Crisp blue and white check tablecloths were held in place by small vases of dazzling colored geranium flowers; a necessity lest a frisky breeze should try and ruffle the perfect order of this fabulous Grecian postcard scene. Mesmerized by the shimmering seawater, they gravitated towards the outside chairs, drinking in the sights, the sounds, the smells of this delightful place. Wooden racks of squid drying in the warm air advertised the delicacy this tavern was well known for.

The tavern owner, Kyri, greeted them eagerly; it was early in the season so he was happy to welcome guests personally. Times had been tough the past few years, what with the Greek financial crisis followed by the global pandemic, tourists needed to be fiercely protected and pampered and where better to wine and dine them but at his taverna! At the click of Kyri's fingers his mekro Dominique sprang into action. From nowhere jugs of iced water, baskets of fresh dark crusty bread, beautifully painted cruet sets of olive oil and balsamic vinegar, and bowls of olives were thoughtfully placed in front of them.

Kyri surveyed the women as he deftly polished glasses, arranging them carefully on a tray, the centerpiece of which was a bottle of his best Ouzo, accompanied by an assortment of mezedhakia. *Americans,* he smiled to himself, *US dollars and judging by the fancy gas guzzling SUV and designer purses, lots of them.*

He looked up quizzically and methodically counted: one, two, three, four, five…five little doves and no sign of any men to supervise them! Further scrutiny revealed not doves, no not at all. In fact, to the contrary, these women were extraordinary; not young women, but not old either. The usual telltale trout lips and rabbit like Botox faces of many of the "not young" American women he had seen, were definitely not on show here. No, these women, he decided as he allowed his eyes to rest on Ruby's voluptuous cleavage, could only be described as goddesses. "Hallelujah!" he muttered looking skywards in search of the choir of heavenly angels who brought them to his door.

With a flourish, he presented the tray in mock humble servitude and then quickly regaining his Greek god composure, pouring each of them a drink and toasting their beauty and happiness, the sun, the moon, and all of the stars and planets in this galaxy, and all galaxies beyond. The scene had just been unknowingly set for the El Greco Party, as it would become known in years to come.

Kyri possessed what many former Greek gods of the world use on a daily basis, an item Ruby comically referred to as The Adonis Mirror. This miraculous object provided a "not young" stud mental visual enhancement of their godlike, totally male bodies. Bellies were miraculously replaced by six packs, love handles became zero fat muscles, and lo and behold, penises were portrayed as phallic symbols desired by women of all ages. Sadly, Ruby commiserated, women end up with a cheap imitation of the proverbial magic mirror, one that magnifies the gory detail of crow's-feet, lip lines, cellulite, and gray hair.

What Kyri lacked in actual physical attributes he made up for in charm, warmth, and bravado. He was a very generous individual who believed in sharing unexpected windfalls with a group of much-loved male friends (who were also members of the former Greek God Club). After running through the menu specials for the day, he left his birds of paradise with menus and hurried off to invite some thoughtfully selected friends to come and enjoy the magnificent scenery in his tavern. He donned an apron and chef hat and proceeded to cook with a passion he hadn't felt in quite some time; deep down inside of his being, a volcano of testosterone that had lain dormant was coming to life.

Oblivious of the smoldering volcano in the kitchen, the girls sipped at their Ouzo while enjoying the tasty snacks Kyri included with their aperitifs. Dolamathes, cooked grape leaves stuffed with a mix of rice, beef and Pignola nut; Loukanika, cocktail sized Greek sausages made of the finest ground beef, pork and veal and served drenched in lemon juice; caviar balls; and Tirotrigona, a delicate triangular shaped Phyllo pastry oozing with a mix of Feta and cottage cheese.

"It's no wonder the phrase 'food for the gods' originated in Greece," sighed Ruby. "Did you know that Greek mythology suggests the god Prometheus, who was, by the way, the creator of humans and giver of fire, taught people to cook?"

"Well I would imagine having fire would've brought a refreshing change to eating raw food," replied Charlotte as they chewed away thoughtfully, "but I must agree, there is something uniquely delicious about Greek food. It seems so wholesome and I've noticed my sinus issues have improved, must be something to do with the yogurt and cheese made from sheep and goat's milk."

Alex's face lit up. "It's like a movie scene, any minute now, a gorgeous young Greek will magically appear and whisk our table and chairs into the sea."

At that precise point four men ambled into the restaurant and settled themselves comfortably at a table nearby.

"Looks promising, keep talking Alex, you're doing a great job," chuckled Tilina observing the new arrivals. They nodded at the women who returned their greeting with warm, friendly smiles.

Deciding to collectively sample the chef's seafood specialties, they ordered three different main course options to share: Kalamarakia Yemesta, oven baked, fresh squid, stuffed with a tomato garlic base of spinach, nuts and rice; Psari Psito, fresh Halibut steak oven baked and topped with bread crumbs, cheese and butter; the unanimous favorite was the prawn dish. A tomato-based casserole type dish, the prawns sautéed and then fired in Ouzo and Metaxa before being baked with a topping of crumbled Feta cheese. They chose a large Greek salad as a side and a fabulous Greek white wine to partner the meal.

Following Greek tradition, they took their time over dinner; the restaurant was well patronized by locals with a few European tourists in attendance as well. Beautiful Greek music permeated the night air and they visibly relaxed as they enjoyed the warm, unpretentious ambiance of the establishment. The meal and wine sat comfortably on their spirits. Declining dessert they ordered coffee and were quite surprised when an unusual coffee pot with small espresso-type cups arrived. A rich aroma of coffee hung over the table as the young mekro poured dark foaming liquid into the cups. He explained the wide, flat bottomed receptacle was called a briki and the tapering at the neck of the pot which burgeoned outwards into a wide rim allowed the coffee to form a creamy froth (kaimaki) during the brewing process. As they sipped the deliciously sweet coffee, Chef Kyri emerged from the kitchen and appeared at their table with a big smile and a bottle of his home brewed Raki.

Gushing with gastronomical compliments, Ruby asked him to join them and in what seemed a blink of an eye, he beckoned his friends over to come and meet the Americans. The conversation level rose as the music volume increased and then the opening melody of Zorba the Greek started. Fueled by the turbo-powered Raki, Ruby dragged Kyri to his feet and in a re-take of the scene from the movie, ordered him, "Teach me to dance…"

"Did you say dance?" he responded on cue.

Coquettishly she looked at him, blinked, and continued, "I never loved a man more than you…"

As the tempo of the music increased, the rest of the group was brought into sequence by Kyri's obliging friends until they were cavorting around like wild things, ending up in a sweaty drenched heap on the floor at the end of the song, out of breath and laughing hysterically in the arms of their new found best friends.

The combination of jet lag, a day at the beach, and the heavy dance session depleted their energy banks. Much to the chagrin of their new found best Greek boyfriends, the girls decided to call it a night. Hugs and air kisses were exchanged before they disappeared into the night, homeward bound, in their Cadillac chariot.

Their moods were high; they were not quite ready for the night to end although they were worn out. They settled into the deep comfort of the living room sofas where Ruby took command of the bar and dispensed nightcaps from the deep cave that housed a vast assortment of alcoholic beverages. Rewarding her labors, she poured herself a more than adequate glass of Merlot. Glass in hand she positioned the wine bottle neatly in reach while she nested herself into one of the ample armchairs. "Oh, what fun we had tonight! Did anyone catch the name of our new best friends?"

They shook their heads in unison.

"Nope," said Tilina dolefully. "Our hunting skills are obviously out of practice, five Greek gods, one for each of us, and we didn't even let on where we stayed."

"Never mind Tilina, we can always stage another chance encounter with the studs," said Alex with a chuckle. "There certainly seems to be an abundant supply of Greek mojo going on here and if we lose these five—I'm sure we'll make the acquaintance of at least twenty-five more."

Tilina rolled her eyes good naturedly. "I'm sworn off men for the rest of my life, they're more hassle than they're worth, too much pain, too much sadness. Nope, I'm not volunteering for that nonsense again."

Michelle stared at her, silently wondering if she would ever reach the bitter cruel place Tilina had stumbled into since her divorce. Tilia had always been a tough cookie, self-opinionated, but her edges seemed to have become razor sharp now and there was a scary brittleness apparent in her being. Michelle thought of groups of divorcées, the ones who never seemed to heal from the disappointment of their failed marriages. They sat like poisonous trolls, spewing venom on any man who might be brave or stupid enough to venture too close to them. Fear gripped Michelle as she visualized her own near banishment to the Divorcée Troll Club. She might slip into this type of character if she couldn't overcome this. Once again, those infernal tears appeared from nowhere as a dark, damp blanket of despair settled around her.

In a flash, Ruby was by her side, soothing her as she sobbed. For the second time that day, the women stared frozen with shock at the fragile state of their friend, the one of their whole gang who claimed the role of being an emotionally stable advice-giver. Now shattered.

"Fuck!" spluttered Michelle. "Look at the fucking mess I'm in, I can't stop crying. I sleep with fucking rocks in my bed. I can't sleep. I see green fucking monsters at night—not red ones or orange ones or even nice pretty pink ones...my favorite color? Nope, nope, they are luminous green slimy bastards and I've never liked the color green...and, and..." she hitched in a breath then carried on, her mascara smudged face, wet with tears..."Those little green fuckers tell me I'll be alone forever, I don't want to be alone, I'm so scared of being alone, alone sucks—I want a man who'll love me till I die, a man who will drink tea with me and hold my hand when I'm frightened in the night, I don't want to be alone, I don't want to be one of those alone women, alone women turn into crazy cat ladies!" she shrieked and then stopped, silently looked at the horrified faces staring back at her and started to laugh.

"Oh my God." Michelle clasped her hand to her mouth. "I'm so sorry." Her blue eyes round with surprise, she searched the collective faces of her friends. "I think I'm losing my marbles here," she smiled sheepishly.

"No, you're not," said Alex with sober authority. "You, girl, just simply need to get laid! It's a well-known fact the easiest way to get over one man is under another."

Ruby drained her wineglass, replenishing it with alarming speed and dexterity. "She's right you know."

Alex nodded. "But right now, you look like shit Michelle."

They clucked sympathetically in unison as they surveyed the pitiful state of their friend, the oversized Medusa flip flops clashed horribly with the baggy psychedelic leggings and matching top scrounged once again from Ruby.

Michelle's disheveled hair and tear streaked face added to the chaos of her appearance.

"I declare a spa and shopping day!" decreed Alex with the sternness of a British Headmistress. Casting a disapproving look to the right of her, she stated firmly, "Charley and Tilina you will also be active recipients of a makeover as well, all three of you look like you need a good hard fuck!"

"Ruby and I are happily married women and in the enviable position of having sex on demand so we will supervise and *that*, quite simply put, is *that!*"

Bronzed Queen Hera watched silently as calm returned to the evening.

Ruby slugged her wine in one pop and poured another round of drinks to toast the upcoming Spa and Shopping day.

Chapter 9
Dressing of The Goddesses
Scene 1

T he girls chattered like excited birds as they piled into their SUV early that morning. Alex and Ruby spent hours on their tablets, researching spas in the area. They finally settled for an exclusive boutique hotel located on the glorious Mount Pelion, very close to the village of Portaria. The illuminated route on the vehicle's built in GPS screen indicated an hour's drive that would initially hug the coastline for most of the way and then gently meander its way towards the mountain.

Although Greeks drive on the same side of the road as Americans, the size of the Cadillac made the small winding roads tricky to negotiate, even more so when sporadic donkey carts appeared. Alex distanced herself from the hen-like banter of her companions, her temple knotted as she concentrated on the twists and turns that were punctuated by instructions from the satellite system. Michelle sat up front and appeared more relaxed since her crying episode the night before. The glorious sun-filled day on their beach had given her skin a golden glow and apart from yet another superfluous garment borrowed from Ruby, she was starting to look a little less pathetic than at the start of this adventure. *Yes,* thought Alex, *looks to me like that luggage is lost, never to be found, so Miss Michelle, it's time to get you a new wardrobe.*

After the first few miles, Alex felt her body relax inside itself. She always enjoyed the think time driving allowed her. Some women cleaned when they needed to think; nope, not Alex, she liked to drive and meditate and this route provided plenty of interesting snippets of Greek daily life. Greece was like another planet in comparison to her home surroundings in Seattle. Olive groves stood grandly to the side of the road, how interesting to note that something as natural and earthly as an olive tree would signify health, wealth, and belonging, so different from the

American symbols where an Ivy League degree would be considered the equivalent of having made it.

Alex and Kevin relocated to Seattle shortly after the birth of their eldest daughter. Prior to this lifetime milestone, they were living in a tiny, rented apartment in downtown San Francisco, a marvelous location for young couples with a passion for outdoor activities by day and city life socializing by night. Career opportunities were plentiful and they loved the ethnic diversity and broad-minded morals, which seemed to be a byproduct of the famous hippie culture of the 1960s.

Accepting parenthood as their new future, they looked for a less expensive and more child friendly option. Seattle seemed to be the place best suited to fill the requirements of all family members. An affordable, large suburban house within close proximity to schools became their new normal. They still lived in that house, however, it hardly resembled the original dwelling that they purchased. Across the years alterations and renovations were undertaken. Numerous rooms were added: a home office for Alex, a study for Kevin, a playroom for the girls. They also created a wonderful indoor/outdoor entertainment area at the center of which was a heated swimming pool. The rustic ranch style home served their growing family in a quietly efficient manner.

Alex loved the effortless access to nature. Mountains, volcanoes, ocean, and islands provided wonderful places to visit for a family camping trip or picnic. Over the years however, the booming economy of Seattle attracted a dramatic rise in population, house prices rocketed and traffic gridlock became the new order of the day. The constant noise of property development drove her mental, the same with the incessant rain and freezing winters. Despite the number of years spent living there, she never adapted to the climate. The glorious Greek sunshine warmed her heart as she floored the accelerator down the EO 34 highway, whizzing past what was now becoming a familiar sight: the village of Affisos. To the right, traditional white Greek houses scattered along the hillsides, their shutters painted vivid blues and adorned with balconies providing panoramic views of beaches and sea.

As they inched their way down the beach road, they peered curiously at various eateries, brightly colored signs proclaiming various daily specialties. Alex's attention was caught by the village square. Lavishly shaded by massive plane trees, outdoor restaurants beckoned all and sundry to congregate in this ancient communal gathering place. A small stream passing through the square center, replenished the historic drinking fountain with cool mountain spring water as it trickled its way seaward. Alex wondered idly if the Argo sailors truly did exist back in the day, and if they had, as Greek legend would have one believe, then they used this exact village stream before setting out in their Argonaut boats on their long journey to Colchis to capture the Golden Fleece. Greece had always been just the name of a place in Europe to Alex. She had seen the stereotyped postcard photographs and names like Athens and Mykonos sounded familiar. She'd never heard one mention of The Pelion Region and was delighted to discover it was very much off the beaten path and as a result, this region retained old-world charm. She loved experiencing the cuisine of the Mediterranean, everything seemed to be cooked from scratch with the freshest and purest ingredients. Not a sign of a McDonald's burger or Wendy's breakfast jarred the senses and she was surprised at her realization that this strange and foreign place was literally eating its way into her soul.

Alex promised herself not to think of life back home in Seattle; it was too complicated and she'd deliberately planned this period of quiet reflection in Greece before the eruption that was rapidly approaching. It would strike when she returned to normal life. Alex had always been like this; her greatest strength was patience, and it had never failed in her life plan. Apart from a brief text message to her daughters and husband when she arrived safely at the village, Alex had focused on immersing herself in the **now** of her Greek vacation. She pondered on the melodramas of Michelle and Charlotte, both of them so painfully grieving their recent losses.

As a child Alex learned to be quiet and self-sufficient and had painstakingly conditioned herself not to rely on anyone. That fateful day in the coffee shop came back as a strong memory; the mental training that came from that day and her subsequent physical changes were still being felt in her soul. Alex knew that whatever happened, she wouldn't lie down and cry like Michelle was doing right now.

Alex caught a picture of Ruby and Tilina in the rearview mirror. *Are they, like me, distanced from their own personal Broadway productions of life?* The wisdom that comes with a lifetime of experience re-affirmed her belief that nothing is ever as it seems and that everyone has a story—why would it be any different for Ruby, Tilina, or her, for that matter?

Her mind drifted to Magenta, wondering idly how Arnie was getting on with the would-be suitor of her business. She smiled inwardly. *Everything will come in its own time.* Alex was in no hurry, in fact, any potential sale of her business at this point in time would play havoc with her carefully crafted plan. So, with the knowledge that time was indeed on her side, she mentally returned to her Greek adventure with a smile.

The road wound inland gradually, taking them past the ancient city of Boufa now known as Koropi; a picturesque place, interspersed lavishly with olive and pear trees that seemed to grow in any spare place they could find. Roadside shops proudly displayed olives of every description, shiny red tomatoes and deep green and purple grapes stood as silent witness to the colorful bounty that was harvested by the local farmers.

Unusual plump jars of assorted fruits; miniature green and red apples, golden pears, cherries and apricots, all stood proudly on shelves. Fondly referred to as Spoon Sweets, this confectionary treat dated back to the Byzantine era. Sliced, grated, or whole fruit produce was preserved in a thick transparent sugary syrup infused with indulgent spices like cinnamon or vanilla and served as a Greek hospitality treat ritual.

"Are we there yet?" whined Ruby as she scrounged in an enormous tote bag and dragged out a bunch of papers she began to study. Taking on the air of a tour guide, she shared snippets of information with the rest of her entourage. "Ladies," she drawled in a similar nasal tone to that of their GPS, "Listen carefully while I explain the wonderful itinerary my fellow tour operator Alex and I have spent hours planning for you frumpy, sexually frustrated women in dire need of a make-over!"

"Frumpy," coughed Tilina, "I will have you know that mine is a classic wardrobe put together by my personal stylist who just happens to be a…"

"Nun?" quipped Ruby.

They all laughed and listened intently as Ruby rambled on, "So, spa morning kicks off with an exercise hour for the more energetic of you, and those who have over indulged on Greek pastries," she looked pointedly at Alex and Michelle, "get to spend quality time with the resort's professional fitness trainer, Stavros. I'm told he shows no mercy. The gentler souls," she smiled sweetly, "for example me, are assigned to the delightful Goddess Angelika for an hour of low intensity Pilates and Yoga. And now I will hand over the hostess duties to our Spa Guru, Alex, who will explain the spa menu."

Keeping one eye on the road and one eye on the rearview mirror, Alex good naturedly took Ruby's signal for giving playful instructions. "Well ladies, currently trending in the hot spot spas in Europe are the Hammam and Gommage Rituals."

The girls looked quizzically at each other. "And what the fuck is that?" asked Tilina, snorting in laughter at Alex's fake accent.

They listened intently as Alex briefly explained that these rituals originated from the Middle East with Hammam being a body cleaning process using low mist and steam, very much like a steam room but with more ceremony, while the Gommage part involved a full body exfoliation process. Not wanting to spoil the experience by divulging too many details of the luxurious treatments they had booked, Alex assured them, "By the time we emerge from our treatments we will look and feel like brand new women."

As they approached the village of Portaria, the annoying GPS voice announced they had reached their destination. The hotel complex was surprisingly small but had a tasteful lavish feel to it.

There was no doubt that this was an upscale and very discreet establishment, frequented by those with means who were habitually accustomed to this type of indulgence. It was a perfect choice for this grand birthdays celebration trip; going all out for this once in a lifetime splurge.

They were greeted by their Spa Mentor, a charming young woman called Konstantina, whose sole responsibility was to indulge the whims and requests of these VIP guests who had reserved the spa for their exclusive use that morning. She graciously ushered them to the individual private room suites assigned to them which contained everything they could possibly need.

Charlotte, Alex, and Michelle opted to spend quality time with Stavros. It was lust at first sight when they spotted this vision of godliness through the glass door of the gym. "Oh, My Greek God," sighed Michelle, "he looks like the guy from the Kouros *eau de toilette* ads."

"Yeah, just with a t-shirt on," Alex said mischievously. "A bottle of Dom Perignon for the gal who gets the t-shirt off that fabulous body."

They high fived each other and the bet was on.

Stavros ran an appreciative eye over the three women; these were Sex in the City type chicks with authentic American accents to boot. He had always had a fetish for older women and these three were catering to every variation his young heart could desire.

The little blonde rocker chick introduced herself as Charlotte, he stared into her china blue eyes and felt his knees go weak. Just as he was recovering some of his machismo back, that body with the incredible porno tits was in front of him. Her name was Alex. Alex with a phoenix tattoo on her wrist; he felt faint at the sudden blood rush to his head. Michelle was the one who dealt the fatal blow, piercing his heart. Errant rays of sunlight caught the highlights in her hair, framing her sad but beautiful face in a halo of gold. As she stepped towards him, poor Stavros was besotted.

These women were fit and up to any challenge Stavros had in mind; they matched him in speed, style, and stamina on the warm-up run, swung with the ease of monkeys on the overhead gym bars, pushed weights and exuded a sensuality that the poor young man was finding difficult to cope with. He had never seen squats performed in such provocative style, watching those asses move in perfect synchronicity brought tears to his eyes. Those porno tits wiggled and jiggled in front of his eyes and when Alex leaned into her sit ups, he nearly disappeared into her cleavage. The girls glowed with perspiration, their well-fitting training gear clung to their firm bodies and accentuated their feminine curves. It was all becoming too much for Stavros who was sweating profusely and not from over exertion either.

Seizing the moment, Charlotte eyed the pool and asked Stavros if they could do their cool down and stretches in the pool.

He almost kissed her in gratitude as he readily agreed.

Stripping down to training bras and underwear, they rinsed off under the shower before dive bombing into the pool. They stared in silent fascination as Stavros removed his t-shirt under the shower and followed them in hot pursuit.

The stretching exercises that took place in that heated pool will be etched into modern day Greek mythology forever. This was Stavros's golden opportunity to get a little up close and personal with his fetishes and he did not waste a single moment. He rubbed calve muscles, stretched arms, massaged necks, lifted them out of the pool high above his head like nubile ballerinas—they collectively applauded Stavros saying it was the best workout they had ever had.

With a boisterous blush Stavros returned the applause and compliments, blowing kisses when Konstantina came to fetch them from the pool.

Arabian Rituals in Greece
Scene 2

Konstantina delivered the ladies to their suites and instructed them to shower off and slip on the beautiful, spice-colored satin robes and slippers which were provided as take-home gifts and souvenirs.

Feeling relaxed and stretched from the Pilates and yoga session, Tilina stripped off and stood under the shower, rinsing her graying hair in the process. The saffron colored robe looked so inviting; closing her eyes she focused on the belly warming comfort of the smooth, soft fabric as it enveloped her body. It had been quite a few years since she'd allowed herself sensual license and she felt pleasurably feminine and sexy. She noticed her name had been tastefully embroidered on the gown and slippers; the Europeans definitely possessed a flair for discreet and personal attention. Certainly, most Americans provided top class, service-orientated experiences, but in comparison to this, it felt loud and sometimes way too much in your face.

Tilina savored every moment of this European experience and the close-knit solidarity of their girl tribe; it provided a jewel-like sparkle that was tinging each day with a shimmery glow. She stared at her reflection in the mirror, assessing the woman that stared back. Contemplating her image, she recognized a foreign but vaguely familiar feeling…puzzling for a moment to identify what it was…and then, she smiled as she recognized the elusively beautiful butterfly of happiness that had settled upon her. She stood motionless, afraid to move lest it take wing and fly away; she admired the fleeting beauty of the moment and realized that too many years had passed since she had experienced this lightness of being.

A gentle knock on the door provided the cue for her to take leave of this private chamber and join her kin. In silent obedience, she followed Konstantina down a passageway marveling at the Arabian themed décor. Moroccan style glass lanterns, strategically placed in arched wall crevices, cast pretty illuminations upon the dune colored and sand textured walls, discreetly guiding their way.

The swish of their robes and their muffled footsteps followed them through the arched entrance to the Hammam. The windows were decorated with delicately crafted wrought iron screens which graciously allowed intermittent shafts of sunlight to stream through the intricate patterns creating a delightful mixture of light and dark. A lone musician played a string instrument gently in the background providing a mystical, oriental atmosphere.

In a mosaic covered alcove, Konstantina exchanged the robes and slippers with a red checked pestemal, a garment which looked very much like a beach sarong, before directing them to the entrance of the hot room. The five of them were left alone and slipped with ease into ancient Hammam traditions catching up on all the gossip of the morning. Unusually, it was a much-animated Charlotte who, obviously enthused by her victorious scoop of the Dom Perignon prize, related the Stavros story to Tilina and Ruby. Michelle and Alex nodded in unanimous agreement as Charlotte described in artistic detail the physical attributes of God Stavros right down to the bulge in his Calvin Klein underwear adding that he would make a fine model for a bronze statue and that maybe she should ask Tilina to photograph him so she had a guide to follow.

As they became accustomed to the heat of the room, they began to relax and take in the opulent splendor of their surroundings. Lounging on gold-shot slabs of white marble, they examined the granite covered room, laced with hypnotic mosaic patterns. A large dome dominated the center of the room beneath which the göbektaşı—an elevated marble platform embellished with Byzantine styled copper and brass basins—had been constructed above the source of heat.

After twenty minutes of lying on the göbektaşı, the girls worked up a healthy sweat. Five estheticians entered the room. Their bodies were soaked with warm water, lathered with savon noir, a soap blend of crushed olives, olive and eucalyptus oil, and exfoliated with a kessa glove. Their feet were placed in a mint footbath, hair and faces were cleansed and bodies gloriously slavered with a sweet-smelling mix of clay and shea butter. The ritual ended with a traditional dousing of orange blossom and rose water, leaving them well prepared for the twenty-four carat gold facials and body massages that followed.

Their mani/pedis, hair and makeup were performed in the Harem Salon where they reclined on sumptuous crimson velvet beds propped up by vibrant orange silk cushions where one and all imbibed Middle Eastern tea while nibbling on sweet cakes.

After much persuasion by both Ruby and the hairstylist, Tilina parted with the drab *au natural* gray and ventured into the realms of a radical platinum blonde pixie cut; the transformation was amazing—Tilina stared at the foreign face peering back at her from the mirror, not quite sure how she would ever pull off the look.

Once again, the ties of female companionship rallied around her, assuring her that she looked incredible and making *oohs* and *aahs* in all the right places. The cut and color were far too new for Tilina to realize that she looked like a supernatural guardian of nature, straight out of lore from her First Peoples' Chumash tribe, the tribe that gave Malibu it's famous name. She virtually glowed with power from the mix of platinum hair over light brown skin.

The spa morning over, the girls set out on their next excursion: a shopping afternoon in the city of Volos.

Stavros proudly escorted them as they made the short journey down the mountain. He was easily persuaded to join them for a light lunch. He engineered a seat opposite Michelle and took every opportunity he could to study the radiating beauty of his new found goddess. Nicole, their personal aide and shopping guide, arrived at the rendezvous point laughing loudly at the dramatic lipstick covered farewells that Stavros received. Herding them up, she set off for the trendiest of trendy, funkiest of funky, boutiques of Volos.

Nicole wasted no time in suggesting a fun El Greco holiday wardrobe for each of them. Satin and lace snippets of lingerie, negligees designed for hot summer nights were eagerly tried on.

Pastel sun dresses, tantalizingly sexy bikinis, wide brimmed romantic hats.

Daring each other to step out of their normal American casual style and embrace some Greek Goddess Va Va Va Vroom style; the women went all in on the shopping spree. Fitted capri pants in wild vibrant colors, prints, polka dots, and checks were coupled with body fitting, cleavage boosting, tops. Skirts were shortened and coupled with killer heels, dramatic jewelry pieces changed ownership, all payments were settled with shiny credit cards.

Saying their goodbyes to Nicole, they left the shop dressed in their favorite new outfits giggling like school girls, with high hopes to return for another round of binge shopping before their vacation ended. Clutching a plethora of shopping bags with a few essential items for the baggage-less Michelle, they climbed into their car and journeyed back towards Lefokastro feeling very self-satisfied.

Greek Tavern Brawl
Scene 3

The sun was sliding towards the ocean as they neared Affisos. On the spur of the moment, they made the unanimous decision to take Stavros's earlier recommendation to stop for a sundowner at one of the taverns perched along the water's edge. In high spirits they entered the restaurant, embracing the ambiance of the Mediterranean, they ordered Ouzo aperitifs with octopus, fried cheese, and a variety of meatballs as mezedes.

A sweet smell of aniseed permeated the air, the transparent liquid turned opaque as it embraced floating ice cubes. Raising their glasses, they joyfully toasted the success of their day.

Tilina casually surveyed their surroundings and was startled to make eye contact with a rather distinguished looking Greek man. Maintaining eye contact with a warm smile, he lifted his glass in salute. Somewhat flustered, she blushed in a most becoming way and nodded a smile back in his direction. It had been a while since a person of the opposite sex had shown any inclination of actually seeing her, let alone acknowledging her presence in such an unmistakable manner. She looked puzzled as she tried to fathom this new phenomenon, perhaps it was the new jewelry she was wearing. Tilina lowered her eyes to check that she was not flashing a nipple or two in the rather daring top Ruby had bullied her into wearing.

Michelle looked at her quizzing, "You okay Tilina?"

Tilina stammered self-consciously, "Not sure what to make of the guy in the corner who just raised his glass to me, maybe I should swap seats with you, it's kinda freaking me out a bit."

As if all on one neck, they swung round curiously just at the precise moment the man was looking their way, making it pretty obvious that Tilina had drawn their attention to him. His eyes portrayed surprise but his male bravado came to the rescue as he once again raised his glass, this time to all of them. The girls smiled warmly at him before returning to their conversation.

Ruby drew in a deep breath which accentuated her ample chest. "Looks like the new pixie hairdo has received the positive endorsement of a very charming and not bad looking Greek." She smiled. "Honestly Tilina, you look fabulous, few people can carry such a short hairstyle, you're certainly one of them. Relax darling, it's okay to enjoy the attention."

The girls nodded in agreement as they studied her; it was hard to reconcile the sharp featured, dowdy gray woman with this surreal heroine who now sat before them. That caused them to contemplate the work of the spa professionals on each other and while they had all emerged looking amazing, Tilina's transformation was absolutely astonishing. She looked she was the lead star in a marital art's movie.

"Promise you'll never let another gray hair show again," said Alex sweetly. Tilina nodded and once again they raised their Ouzo glasses. Alex grinned as a waiter approached them carrying a silver ice bucket, the telltale bottle of Dom Perignon peeked out from beneath a white napkin. "Time for me to settle my gambling debt and Charlotte to share the spoils with her BFFs!" They cheered when the cork exploded from the bottle and giggled as they once again related the details of their workout with Stavros, Ruby's chest heaved with laughter as Michelle mimicked Alex wiggling and jiggling her porno boobs.

Tilina scanned the scene through the lens finder on her Nikon; this way, that way, fiddle, fiddle, scanning, scanning…in search of a moment she could selfishly capture with the touch of a button and hold for eternity. The wizened face of an elderly fisherman caught her attention. With a deft wrist movement, her long-range lens brought him within breathing distance. Oblivious of this scrutiny, he leaned against a small boat at the water's edge as she quietly observed him in this voyeuristic world she was becoming more and more comfortable in each day.

From her vantage point, Tilina studied her subject as the dinner chatter swirled on around her. A humble life at sea had etched deep lines of experience into his skin. His face captivated her; she held him close, not daring to move, lest he discover her. In a split second, his green eyes, glazed with age, looked in the direction of the camera, for a moment she looked into the windows of his soul, marveling at the peace and contentment within him. *Click,* she pressed the shutter. "Focus, focus," she whispered, "check the four corners..." *click* again and again. Realizing what was going on, he smiled acknowledging her intrusion, then rewarded her perseverance with a wide smile, posing majestically against the tranquil calmness of the sea, where the sinking sun cast giant pink and orange shadows in its wake.

Laying her camera to rest knowing she had captured something special, Tilina took a sip of champagne, watching the evening star silently take center stage as she enjoyed the moment. A black velvet curtain of night cleared a path for a million smaller stars as a warm salty breeze came off the sea. The gentle sounds of a bouzouki guitar laced the atmosphere as she reflected on a day spent in the warm bosom of female fellowship, tuning into the playful banter and chit chat of good friends.

From the corner of her eye Tilina kept a discreet watch on the corner table noticing that Mr. Friendly was joined by four male friends. Certainly, the presence of five beautiful women hadn't escaped the attention of the newcomers who made no secret of the fact that their curiosity was piqued.

She smiled as she surveyed her friends, certainly all male fetishes and preferences would be catered for in this one little group. If you were into boobs, tums, and bums—Ruby would be the obvious choice. If tomboy, low maintenance was your thing—Charlotte would suit you to a tee. If you preferred a steamy sultry type—Alex would hypnotize even the strongest constitution in a matter of seconds. Michelle was the woman that would be any man's perfection. Tilina sighed as she studied that beautiful face which she had always envied. Michelle still was the "it" girl in an inimitable way. The years had certainly been kind to her face, obviously she hadn't had children so her figure was awesome and her current heartache and anguish just added a vulnerable aura that could drive a man crazy...*and me?* Tilina pondered sadly, *I wonder if there's any type of male taste I would appeal to?*

Tilina's attention drifted back to the corner table where the five guys were in deep conversation, using this gifted unguarded moment to study the decidedly masculine features of Mr. Friendly. *Fifty Shades of Gray,* she thought while observing his short but obviously salon styled hair. Dark eyebrows framed crinkled eyes, a strong jaw line softened with some age was giving him an air of gentle maturity. *Definitely not a spring chicken,* she thought as her eyes travelled over his casual gray/blue shirt, the rolled cuffs revealing muscular lower arms. It was his hands that captivated her attention. *Hands tell it all,* Tilina thought to herself, *his are elegant yet decidedly masculine.* She found herself wondering what it would feel like to be touched by those strong hands. Startled, she paused to think. *How long has it been since I looked at a man this way?* Since her divorce, the angry walls that insulated the iceberg that was now her heart kept such thoughts away, but something was changing here. Within the nurturing cocoon of female friendship, she was beginning to reacquaint herself with the woman she thought she had lost along the path of life. Here in this foreign land, she felt a warm shaft of light pierce hairline cracks that were developing deep within the barricades of her fortress. Tonight Tilina felt beautiful, desirable, light, and comfortable in her being.

The waiter brought Tilina's attention back to the playful banter of her friends as they mused over which fine Greek delicacies to indulge in. The Ouzo aperitifs, champagne, and fine Greek wine left them deliciously mellow as they settled comfortably into their chairs, watching in fascination the raw emotion of the lone musician as he sang a poignant Greek song soothed by the haunting metallic sound of the bouzouki he played.

It was a perfect evening, a gentle ocean breeze moved the air ever so slightly, the candle flames flickered in unison, casting fingers of golden warmth across the table. The smell of coffee permeated the air as the waiter sat down individual copper bikris filled with dark foamy Greek coffee in front of them. Another waiter materialized next to him holding a tray of Greek liqueurs. With a flourishing smile he pointed towards the table where Mr. Friendly *aka* Fifty Shades of Gray and his companions smiled and nodded graciously.

"Oh boy…looks like things could get interesting tonight," said Ruby flashing a most majestic smile across the restaurant in thanks, then studying each bottle while listening intently to the waiter's half English, half Greek (which sounded all Greek to her) description of the contents of each bottle.

"Tell you what," she suggested to the waiter, "give us a shot of each and we'll share glasses and taste them all."

The waiter obediently lined up five glasses down the center of the table and with much aplomb, filled each glass with a different liqueur. Acting as if there was a huge dilemma over the tasting, Ruby flashed her most beguiling, beseeching, Bambi-like "help me" eyes along with hands raised in a poise of despair. This was always an attention winner pose for Ruby. She then projected this dramatic performance towards the occupants of Mr. Friendly's table. Of course, being gentlemen of the purest of pure chivalrous male battalion, within seconds of receiving the damsel in distress call, the five of them descended upon the table, neatly placing themselves behind the woman of their particular fancy.

In order to provide a hands-on guide to the fine art of tasting the splendors of Greek liqueurs, they beckoned to the somewhat bemused waiter who returned with the bottles and another set of five glasses and chairs.

The most extroverted of the five Greek gods that were now firmly ensconced at their table was a tall, overweight man. Seating himself majestically at the head of the table, with Ruby and Michelle on either side, he introduced himself as Alexander The Lawyer. With a loud chortle he pointed to a large painting on the wall of a man and a horse, proudly informing them his namesake was none other than the almighty Greek military commander Alexander The Great himself.

Ruby stared in fascination at his extravagant gestures and the silver plumes of hair that sat like a startled bird atop his head. Recognizing a fellow entertainer, she smiled; he was obviously a man accustomed to holding court, she could just imagine him bullying both judge and jury into legal submission as he gallantly saved one innocent client after another from the menacing jaws of the Greek justice system.

He gestured to the waiter to fill the first glass with a clear liquid. "*Chios Mastiha!*" he exclaimed loudly, then with exaggerated drama held the glass to his atypical Greek nose, delicately inhaling the sweet aroma that teased with a hint of lavender. He explained this liqueur was made from the Tears of Chios; Chios being a Greek island nestled between Lesvos and Samos near the Turkish coast. The tears were actually created by resin drippings lanced from ancient mastic trees, a unique landmark of Chios.

His large chubby face softened visibly. "*Mikró peristéri*," he cooed softly as he handed the shot glass to a startled Michelle to taste. *What an exquisite woman,* he thought as he looked into her blue eyes and then to his absolute astonishment, big fat tears started to roll down her beautiful face. He looked quizzically at Ruby who (along with the rest of the girls) had become quite accustomed to the frequent deluge of tears from Michelle. Ruby took the glass from Michelle who dropped her head to the table for some silent racking sobs, leaving Ruby to continue the conversation. At a loss for words for a second, Ruby mustered one of her most dazzling smiles, gestured the sign of a broken heart, shrugged her shoulders and passed the glass to Greek god number two.

Alexander The Lawyer stood proudly. True to his namesake, he was a gallant and chivalrous man and the sight of this distressed and obviously very fragile woman reached deep into his broad chest, somewhere in the vicinity of where he believed his heart to be. He shook his head in pity, muttered something in Greek and reached for the next bottle, a sour cherry liqueur cultivated from Vissino cherries on the island of Corfu. Immersed in a rainbow of color, tastes, and aromas they sampled the distilled orchards of Greece:, Kitron Lemon from Naxos, a sweet and sour experience; herbal blends distilled specifically to aid digestion; Tentura, a sweetly spiced cinnamon delight. All the while the candles glowed as they engaged in polite conversation and got drunker with each toast.

At the head of the table, Ruby was in deep conversation with Alexander. He was well traveled, clever, amusing, and enjoyed his alcohol. Ruby didn't need much coaxing when it came to a drink or two or three so she was packing them away, one for one, with him. Michelle was determined to remain on her path of pathetic that evening, she sat quietly opposite Ruby following the animated banter between her friend and The Great.

Already smitten by Michelle's delicate beauty, Alexander found this waif-like behavior inexplicably desirable; suddenly he was determined to woo and bed this fascinating woman languishing across the table from him. Even spectators in the cheap seats would have had the sense to know he would have more chance of bedding Aphrodite that night…but the lawyer was a Greek with a namesake of Alexander the Great, a man held in great esteem for his military strategic skills. This trait was something Alexander constantly reminded himself about on a daily basis and tonight he was scheming, fueled by this self-induced importance.

Seated at the opposite end of the table, Alex was firmly in control of her vantage point. In spite of being fairly close to the villa, she took her duties as designated driver seriously and somewhere between the champagne and wine, she consciously put a brake on alcohol consumption and switched to Souroti, a much revered sparkling water with enough calcium and magnesium to give anyone a fifteen hour hard on. She smiled wryly thinking this as she studied the bright blue bottle.

Dionysus and Nikolaos planted themselves on either side of her; they were fun guys, and both married with children. Her American tongue refused point blank to navigate these unfamiliar names, so in an instant they became Dion and Nico. As with Alexander at the head of the table, there was much pride and discussion when it came to their names, she was intrigued by the Greek custom of Name Days. Pushing back mentally into the role of spectator, Alex marveled at this impromptu gathering which, with the help of numerous Greek alcoholic beverages, was starting to resemble a comical, chaotic scene from some movie.

High on Dom Perignon, Charlotte was in great form. Nico and Dimitrios were the men on either side of her. She cracked jokes and chatted comfortably with Dion, the owner of a tourist trinket store who was trying valiantly to explain the history of the Greek evil eye and why he carried a talisman to protect him from the curse of the evil eye. It was a brightly colored blue and white circular charm. Charlotte threw her head back and laughed deeply from the throat uttering disbelief when Nico and Dimitrios sheepishly confessed that they too carried such charms with them.

Tilina was getting along well with a very attentive Mr. Friendly who had introduced himself earlier and whose name disappeared from Alex's mind in a nanosecond. It was definitely an Ofolus of some sort she thought. Tilina seemed to be quite taken with him; a perpetual smile had replaced the usual tight-lipped scowl on her face.

Amazing, thought Alex, *she actually looks younger and quite attractive, what a difference a good haircut, color, and good old-fashioned smile can do for a woman. Will tonight be the night Tilina finally releases the anger about her failed marriage? Dammit, it's painfully obvious, the woman needed a good mind and body fuck and Ofolus looks like the right man for the job. All in time,* she mused with an inward smile, *it took years for me to get to the point of letting go.* Casting her mind back to her epiphany in that wet coffee shop. One more major change and the plan from that fateful day would set her up as a woman in control of her mind, body, and life and fuck anyone who messed with that.

A shriek of laughter from Ruby's end of the table drew her attention to where Alexander stumbled to his feet, glass in hand and proposed a toast to Michelle, declaring publicly that a night of love and lust in his king-size bed would cure her broken heart. Michelle looked positively horrified and took refuge in Ruby's back, a wall of sobs barricading her from the onslaught of Alexander The Lawyer.

Sensing fear in his wounded pigeon, he magnanimously, and drunkenly, offered that the bed was big enough for Ruby to join them if she so desired. This ridiculous suggestion was met by peals of laughter. Alex was fascinated by this absolute belief in his sexual prowess and healing powers.

He strode majestically to the dance floor. Placing a glass of wine in the center, he clicked his fingers loudly as he took command—Alexander The Lawyer was a lone figure. The musician plucked a few encouraging musical notes, a few side steps commenced around the glass. Arms raised on either side, he stood proudly, choreographing moves as he went along. The music tempo quickened in order to challenge the warrior deep within Alexander.

Alex did a quick 360 degree eye swivel around the restaurant taking in the audience; all eyes were on Alexander who acknowledged the attention with a series of more intense footwork, swift side steps. Sweeping alternate legs behind him and tapping his shoes loudly, he increased the pace with the music as he moved around the glass.

Ofolous tore himself away from Tilina for a moment and sat back to watch the spectacle, raising his glass and shouting *Opa!* when another daring plunge was made towards the glass. He explained that this was the Zeibekiko Dance: a traditional dance which the Greeks believe cleanses the soul of sorrow.

Alex was impressed. In spite of his size, Alexander was both agile and graceful with a keen sense of balance. Standing on his right foot with his left leg extended hip height in front, he slowly reached for his left toe and with amazing dexterity, sinking to the floor on one foot then rising again. Deftly he brought the left foot to the floor for balance and with arms stretched to the side he sank to the floor grasping the glass between his teeth. Rising to his feet while continuing to sweep and swirl, he downed the contents, before sinking again to his knees. Nearly break-dancing, he gyrated and gesticulated on his back with a leg tucked behind him and deposited the glass back on the floor. Then he was back on his feet in a flash. Aligning himself once again with the glass, he placed one foot over the rim of the glass and swiveled in circles with his full body weight on the rim of the glass!

Rounded eyes took in this incredible feat, more applause and shouts of approval came from the audience until he gingerly stepped off the glass picked it up and gently tossed it into the hands of a person seated close by.

Bowing graciously, he gestured to their table, wanting them to come dance with him. Ruby was on her feet in a second; she was a gifted dancer with an inborn sense of rhythm. Ofolous escorted Tilina to the dance floor, and taking charge of Tilina's camera,

Charlotte gravitated towards the floor, determined to capture photographic evidence of the newly infatuated couple. *After all, this could be the future Mr. Tilina and these could become much treasured possessions,* Charlotte thought with a wry smile.

Fueled by an overabundance of strong alcohol, a fusion of Greek Zorba steps, American hip hop, old-fashioned boogie woogie, and honest to goodness, artistic dance move interpretation, the joy and merriment on that dance floor rivaled any rum soaked, socca dancing Caribbean carnival. *Tomorrow won't be quite so joyful,* rued Alex with a smile, *it's actually quite funny being the only sober one here.* She took careful note so she could remind them all at the upcoming hangover breakfast about what they actually got up to the previous night... *Damn, why did I have to be designated driver tonight?*

While the raucous dance floor scene was still going strong, Alex spotted trouble entering the restaurant in the form of Stavros with an entourage of cloned Greek gods in his midst. Young Stavros quickly scanned the room, to his apparent delight, he spotted the recently vacated chairs next to Michelle. Like majestic eagles, he and his friends descended upon the object of his desire ...Michelle...who, after the slobbering grandeur of Alexander, greeted him like a long-lost brother. Being young and a true gentleman, Stavros grabbed a bottle of wine on the table and topped up her glass, emptying the rest into a glass for himself. Sensing the approach of imminent disaster, Alex discreetly gestured for the check.

A very generous gratuity ensured a deep sense of camaraderie with the server, which unbeknownst to her, would come in very handy in exactly seven minutes and thirty-five seconds.

Dripping from their exertions, the dance troupe returned to their table. There was a hint of male awkwardness as both tribes sized one another up. Ever the pacifist, Ruby took control of a delicate situation and introduced everyone as best she could. Sensing tension, Stavros's friends retreated to the bar, but Stavros sat glued to his chair, delighting in the attention he was receiving from Michelle. The conversation continued with the exception of Alexander who grew quiet and menacing as he downed one drink after another far too quickly. Stavros whispered something into Michelle's ear and was rewarded with a gorgeous smile.

Suddenly, Alexander saw his night of passion taking flight and it all became too much for him. Rising to his feet, he uttered some expletive in Greek and took a wild swing at Stavros, barely missing Ruby in the process but successfully knocking his opponent off his chair. A moment of stunned silence quivered before pandemonium broke out. In a split second, Stavros's second line of defense moved in, not understanding who had thrown the fatal punch they collectively plowed into Nico and Dion forcing Demitrios and Ofolous to join in.

Alex sprang into action. "Time to go. Car. NOW!" the only sober person yelled while practically dragging a tottering Ruby towards the exit door as they picked their way through the brawl and beat a hasty retreat to the car. "Everybody accounted for?" Alex surveyed the heaving mass in the back of the car. "Doors locked, belt up! Let's go!"

"Alex, Alex, wait," whimpered Ruby, "I've left my purse inside."

"You're kidding me, right?"

"Nope, it's on the back of the chair," she cringed.

"Anything of value?"

Ruby sighed. "My passport, my wallet, my Versace makeup bag, not to mention, it is my absolute favorite, Christian Louboutin," she sniffed, "Paloma Large Triple-Gusset Tote Bag," more sniffing, "that my beloved husband gave to me for Christmas."

Alex stared at her in disbelief, suppressing an overwhelming desire to wring her neck. "God that was stupid! Fuck! We can't go back there; it's a fucking war zone Ruby." Tears welled in Ruby's eyes, Alex rolled her eyes. Drunk women were the absolute pits.

Casting her eye towards the restaurant, Alex could hear shouting and the crashing of tables, no damn way any of them were going back in there. Then she spied the server at the edge of the patio trying to stay out of the way. "Payback time buddy," she muttered leaning out her window. Flashing a 200 Euro note, beckoned him frantically towards the car, Alex called out, "Sir, my friend." Pointing to Ruby in the back of the car. "She has left her bag on the chair, please go fetch, bring…hurry."

The 200 Euro note aided a rapid translation of what was required and he took off, while Alex turned the car around, revving loudly, ready to floor the accelerator if any Greek god came anywhere near them. A speedy handover of Euro notes and bag took place and the black Escalade roared off into the night, the women erupting into laughter once they were convinced no one was following them.

Ruby had crawled into the back of the SUV and was lying flat on her back clutching her precious purse watching the stars singing drunkenly an old boppy song from their high school days.

The rest of them joined in, Alex was shaking her head at the wheel, the more things change, the more they stay the same…

Ruby always sang that fucking song when she was drunk, *and she seems to be singing that song too often these days,* she sighed with a worried frown.

EMOTIONAL
MUSINGS

Chapter 10
Raw Hearts
The Hangover Part 1
Scene 1

As was their ritual, Michelle and Alex were up at dawn, running shoes laced, Fitbit monitors on, ready to run the gauntlet and work off the excesses of the night before.

"How you doing Mitch?" Alex smiled as she scanned the pale face, not sure if the puffy eyes were due to the plethora of alcohol consumed or a long night of crying. She hoped it was the former; Alex was a firm believer that a wild night out was good for the soul and the spirit, not to mention bonding effects. *In Vino Veritas,* her father's words rang true; he distrusted people who didn't drink; always wondered what it was that they were scared of revealing. *Perhaps it's alcohol **and** tears, a good combination if you get the mix right,* she mused leaning into her runner's stretches.

"Little rusty in the springs this morning," Michelle grimaced, "nothing a brisk five-mile run, two gallons of water, and at least forty minutes of Jon Bon Jovi whispering sweet nothings into my ears won't cure."

They kicked up the tempo of their warm-up, a few minutes running in place, a series of jumping jacks, and then turning to each other to set their watches, adjust their headphones, then they started a slow jog up the driveway, picking up speed once they reached the road.

Michelle increased the volume on her iPhone, allowing her breathing to pick up with their faster pace as they settled into the first mile, heading in the general direction of Affisos, while following a narrow road alongside the beach. *First mile is always the hardest,* she told herself. Running was not her preferred form of exercise. She was a strong swimmer and loved nothing more than to immerse herself in silent waters as she swam lap after lap, after lap. Swimming was an out of body, spiritual experience for Michelle. She solved many complex problems in the depths of the lap pool at her local gym. Then business travel kicked in with a vengeance and she was forced to rely on the treadmills of the Hiltons, the Sheratons, and the Marriott's in order to get her cardio fix. *Running is convenient,* she nodded, *easy, no matter where I am in the world, so long as I have a pair of running shoes, I'm in the game.*

Alex was also enjoying her run, she felt great for having held back on the booze the night before. She certainly enjoyed a good party but as designated driver and sober eye, she had probably saved them all last night; heaven knows what would have happened if they hadn't made a dirty dash out of that Taverna— that Greek comedy was tottering on the verge of a tragedy and they still didn't know how it finally ended.

Alex breathed deeply, looking around, taking in her surroundings. *How cool is this? I get to run by the sea looking at olive trees and goats. This is awesomeness all by itself.* Physical activity was still something fairly new to her; she was amazed that it took so long to discover it.

The success of her boob job motivated her to take her body to a new place and with the help of a personal trainer, Alex managed to figure out the difference between a squat and a push up and what exactly a dumbbell was. She studied all aspects of diet and fed her new physique carefully, taking pride in the radical change.

Her physical strength gave rise to a newly found confidence. Alex felt powerful, invincible, but always paid homage to the frightened shadow of her former self as it stood by, cheering her on with words of love and encouragement. She learned that security and strength emanated from within, so swore that every day that she lived she would remind herself of that. Never again would she allow herself to live in that place called obscurity, never again would she give anyone the power to make her feel meaningless.

They continued at a fast but steady pace. It was an easy, comfortable partnership, neither one trying to outdo the other, just an unspoken acknowledgement that they were exercising together.

It was something they loved and more fun to have a buddy chugging away next to you, keeping an eye out for traffic, goats, and potholes.

They swung around at their halfway mark, a pile of stones they set down some days back after measuring the distance in the car, putting their all into the last mile to end up back at the driveway breathless, dripping with sweat, but on an endorphin high.

"Let's do our cool down stretches in the sea," Michelle suggested out of the blue, "we can grab a towel on the way down to the beach, we don't need a swimsuit, this is Greece after all… nudity is compulsory," she laughed.

They spent a happy twenty minutes in the water before wrapping themselves in fluffy towels and heading back to shower off and face the day.

"See you at breakfast," trilled Alex.

The Hangover Part 2
Scene 2

Charlotte and Tilina were on their second mug of coffee when Alex and Michelle reached the breakfast table. A yellow, telltale bottle of Advil sat on the table between them.

"*Mmmm* feeling a little delicate this morning?" smirked Alex, "not the life and soul of the party this morning are we then? Speaking of the life and soul, anyone seen the belle of the ball yet?"

As if on cue, Ruby announced her presence at the breakfast table walking into the room with a loud groan. They turned to look at the bedraggled mess that suddenly appeared. She looked an absolute sight with a red, white, and orange psychedelic headband and a pair of red circular sunglasses doing a good job of covering both eyes.

"Oh my God, what the hell did I drink last night?" She sighed as if in deep pain. "There's a fucking symphony of goat bells going off in my head." Ruby plonked herself down at the table and turned a light shade of green at the sight of the food. Covering her eyes dramatically she wailed, "I simply can't face food in my current state—the only thing that's going to deaden the sound in my head is a bloody, Bloody Mary."

She lowered her sunglasses to her nose and looked beseechingly at Althea. "Tomato juice, celery, and a double shot of vodka please Althea."

Althea didn't bat an eyelash. Obviously accustomed to similar scenes in her hospitality career, she vanished from the room and within a few minutes, re-appeared at the table with a Bloody Mary and all of the required ingredients to make many more. By the look on some of the faces at that breakfast table, it certainly seemed this would be in order.

A quiet cheer rose when Althea set the tray down on the table. Tilina and Charlotte each grabbed a glass and starting pouring and before they knew it Michelle and Alex were sipping away with them.

Tilina smiled good naturedly, the color rose up in her face when Alex did an impromptu impersonation of Mr. Ofolous fawning all over her.

"Yeah, great friend you turned out to be Alex; for the first time in God knows how long, it looked like I was going to get lucky and you order everybody out..."

"That was Michelle's fault. Mitch, how could you make it so painfully obvious that Alexander The Great was not doing it for you by throwing yourself at Stavros? Shame on you, the young stud is half your age," jibed Ruby.

"That guy just freaked me out Rubes. My imagination just can't go there. You, me, and him in his love nest? Oh my goodness, I just kept looking at him and wondering if this is how my future single life will be? Old lecherous men, groping and making indecent suggestions...and then Stavros arrived and saved me, saved us. Didn't you wonder how we were going to get out of that hole that we dug?"

"Thank goodness for Alex," piped up Charlotte. "These Greek guys are something else." A look of disbelief crossed her face. "There are definitely two types, the ones who think they're Greek gods and the ones who definitely are."

Michelle helped herself to a bowl of thick yogurt, lashing it with thick dollops of golden honey. "So did you get Ofolous's phone number at least Tilina?"

"Nope," she shook her head sadly.

Ruby lowered her sunglasses onto her nose again, stirring her Bloody Mary vigorously with the celery stick she said, "What were you doing woman? All that chit chat and gushing and no phone number?" She peered quizzically at Tilina.

Tilina laughed. "I guess I'm all out of practice, it's been a long, long, long time since anything remotely male looking, besides a four legged one with a tail and bad breath, has shown any interest in me." She looked a little wistful. "If truth be known, I've sort of gotten used to being invisible these days, maybe I should move to Greece, these guys are something else here. They have great hair ...all over their bodies, and I must confess, I'm rather partial to hairy men for some strange reason. Sort of makes them seem manlier." Tilina giggled and deftly changing the subject, asking what the plans were for the day.

Ruby announced they were heading for the hills as tourists. She had a few village destinations in mind and thought they would stop in a small mountain village called Milies.

"After last night's excitement, let's aim for a quiet day and take in some of the ancient culture."

Trip to Milies
Scene 3

Alex climbed behind the wheel, typed Milies into the GPS, and sat waiting for the first instructions of the day. *Funny*, she mused, *I didn't need help getting home last night.*

She surveyed the motley crew in her review mirror; they all looked a little worse for wear this morning except for Michelle who was dressed in a stunning pair of well-fitted olive-green Capri pants paired with a strapless orange top and the cutest straw hat that looked awesome on her. It was good to see her wearing something decent for a change. *Thank goodness we went shopping yesterday. Maybe she'll feel more like herself with new clothes that aren't just for business.* She was amazed Michelle had been so laid back about her luggage not arriving; for any of them on a normal trip it would have been a drama, but Mitch took it all in stride, *probably too focused on that idiot ex-boyfriend.*

Alex wondered why so many women couldn't see the forest for the trees when it came to men. Always easy to see how it should be when you're in the spectator seats.

The GPS broke the morning silence, "Turn around where possible."

Alex checked the display with a puzzled look. "That's not right. I'm just going to continue to the top of the driveway until it gets its bearings." Alex turned left out of the driveway and then nodded as the GPS instructed her to continue straight for the next 2 kilometers.

The backseat drivers stayed unusually quiet as the huge SUV hugged the winding road that clung determinedly to the coast. Veering right they slowly made their way up Mount Pelion to Milies, a historical little village which, according to their version of Trip Advisor, dated back to the early seventeenth century. Passing through lush forests of beech, oak, and horse chestnut trees they admired traditional stone houses and magnificent mansions from bygone times. The differing architecture bore witness to the history of this village which, according to Ruby, endured years of occupation by both the Turks in the late 1800s and more recently the Germans in the Second World War. They parked in the village square for Ruby who wanted to visit an old church she'd read about.

"There it is! The Church of the Archangels!" Ruby pointed excitedly as they strolled across the paved, shady square. "The paintings and icons are amazing. Let's grab a coffee and figure out who wants to do what and then wander around." Surveying the numerous Greek rabbis, priest, and nuns passing by, Ruby added with a cheeky wink, "I don't think we'll find much trouble to get into around here."

They picked one of the tables under a magnificent plane tree taking in the daily life of the village. Obligatory cats and widows punctuated what looked like a movie set; in fact, the five visitors were the only ones who appeared to be out of kilter with the ancient scene.

Tilina's fingers itched for her camera as they sipped the strong coffee, she could barely restrain the desire to take on the persona of a Japanese tourist and click everything she saw. Tilina decided to take off on her own and spend a few solitary hours studying the idyllic scenes through the lens of her camera.

Unsure of her choice, Alex remained, watching Tilina disappear down one of the cobblestone streets and Michelle, Charlotte, and Ruby slowly sauntered across the square towards the old church.

What diverse friends I have. All together as one, but lost in their own individual stories. Her thoughts were interrupted as the server brought the tsipouro she ordered, accompanied by an assortment of delicious looking mezes which included a basket of freshly baked bread, feta cheese, tomatoes, ham, and olives. *Just what the doctor ordered,* she smiled and settled into her own, self-appointed, happy hour with some people watching on the side.

Michelle and Charlotte trailed in Ruby's wake across the village square towards a rather ordinary looking building showing no outward trace of being a Christian house of worship. During the Turkish occupation, the Greeks built their churches in this manner in order to escape detection. They entered the dimly lit narthex of the church and waited a moment for their eyes to get accustomed to the darkened room.

Ruby, who was raised by a devout Catholic mother and was accordingly well-versed in church etiquette, approached a table holding dozens of flickering candles. Without a word, she pulled a Euro coin out of her wallet, pushed it into the collection box, and selected a candle she lit and placed on the table. Making the sign of the cross, she closed her eyes and bowed her head in prayer.

Michelle followed suit. Although the candle lighting practice was not something she recalled doing in the Presbyterian Church, Michelle found the process strangely comforting. For some strange reason, the candle she selected had two wicks—of course, in her current broken-hearted state Michelle immediately decided this candle symbolized the current status of her doomed relationship; the two of them going up in flames. Her hands shook as she lit both wicks and placed the candle on the table. She stared in fascination at the collective flickering light of the dozens of candles placed there, each one representing a silent appeal to God in heaven to do, say, help something or someone. Each little flame represented the hopes, dreams, thanks, tears, or fears of another human. Her emotions welled up at the profound, sad nature of this thought.

She stared at Ruby and Charlotte who were still in prayer and decided if she wasn't going to become a blathering, sobbing mess, she should say a prayer. Her outwardly stoic persona gave no indication of the emotional anguish raging inside. In the deep recesses of her mind, Michelle knew the relationship wasn't good for her, but a fear of impenetrable loneliness smothered her being like a dark, damp, heavy overcoat of shame and regret. *If only I wasn't so needy,* she caught herself wondering.

Up until this point and regardless of what appeared to be a self-inflicted death, she had never once even thought of speaking to God. God hadn't been a conscious part of her adult life. She attended church for weddings, christenings, funerals, and on the odd occasion she spent Christmas with her parents, she went to the Christmas Day church service with them.

She bowed her head in prayer, wondering if she looked foolish. She hadn't spoken to God since she was a young girl. Vivid memories came to mind of a moment at the height of desperation during a history test…she deliberately dropped her eraser on the floor so she could get under the desk offering a desperate prayer to the merciful Father for help with question ten. Hours later, when she confided details of her beseeching prayer, she listened intently as the all-knowing Ruby admonished her foolishness and informed her it was not polite to ask God directly for things. Thereafter a debate followed as they discussed the part in the bible about 'ask and ye shall receive.' *We never did reach a conclusion on that one,* Michelle thought ruefully, *and I failed the history test.*

Okay God, if I can't come right out and ask you to make him love me, can I ask you for the strength to overcome the pain I feel? I need the presence of mind to know how to negotiate the obstacles in our path so we can re-unite in love and then the past ten years of my life won't seem to be a complete waste of time.

Her prayer turned to thoughts as her mind raced over this desolation and sadness, somewhere in the maze of anguish and terror, her prayers settled her and she sat in quiet contemplation watching the flame of her candle grow larger and the two candle wicks became one. Michelle looked around and guessed Charlotte and Ruby had moved on and for that she felt immense gratitude. There was something she needed to think about alone and this church seemed destined to be the place.

Michelle skirted past a small tour group as she entered the church nave and took a seat on one of the pews. The stark, almost windowless exterior of the building contradicted the colorful beauty and style of the interior; she had never been in a church quite like this. Her curiosity piqued; Michelle eavesdropped as a tour guide enlightened his band of followers. He drew their attention to the three aisled basilica architectural style, pointing out beautifully crafted domes, skillfully constructed in such a way that the outside of the building was in total denial of their existence. He explained the scenes within the magnificent frescoes that adorned the walls, emphasizing the underlying theme of good versus evil.

Michelle was fascinated by the depiction of the human life cycle using the Zodiac, something she never quite expected to see in a church of any denomination. It made sense as the guide explained the human symbolism of the three concentric circles of the Zodiac cycle, the inner circle depicted human vanity in the form of a king figure, the second circle used the four seasons to symbolize the stages of life from youth to old age. There was a profound understanding of human nature and simple wisdom in the folly of life contained within the inscriptions of the unknown artist. In spite of the many hundreds of years since the illustration was created, it was surprising to note very little had changed in human life beyond new technical gadgets.

The tour group moved on to examine the underground acoustic system of the church leaving Michelle uncomfortably alone with silence. Sadness and pain engulfed her as the interminable tears once again made their presence visible.

Unsuccessful in willing the infernal flow to stop, she fixed her gaze on an icon and with relief, recognized the familiar face of Jesus staring back at her. From nowhere a voice resonated, she looked around the church trying to identify the source, saw no one and quickly realized this was a voice coming from inside of her. It was a voice which quietly assured her everything was going to be all right and instructed her to let go of this pain, right there and then.

Breathing deeply, she responded to the gentle command of the voice; with every exhalation she consciously willed the pain and sadness to leave.

Each inhalation brought what she could only describe as a deep feeling of inner peace into her body. She sat quietly in the church and embraced a powerful new ally called faith into her life.

She realized she had to let go of all perceived failures, celebrate her humanness, recognize her achievements, accept she was worthy of giving and receiving love, and have faith that at some stage in the future everything would make sense...she would laugh and be happy again.

Bowing her head and opening her heart to the unfamiliar arrival and presence of humility in this church that had stood and suffered many wars, she knew a first step was just conquered. She wasn't sure how long she stood there savoring the gentle embrace of ego-lessness and acknowledging a blissful feeling of peace.

Light footsteps announced the presence of another person. Looking across the church, she saw Charlotte quietly making her way towards her.

They sat side by side, united by an unspoken connection of grief; Michelle by the death of her relationship, Charley by the death of her mother. Both of them lost, frightened, not sure how or where to move forward with their lives.

Their silence was comfortable as they allowed the peaceful tranquility of this amazing church to soothe their troubled hearts.

Tilina – Realization
Scene 4

Tilina made her way down the cobbled street, enjoying warm shafts of sunlight dancing through the heavy foliage of the magnificent oak and beech trees along the way. *In order to be a great photographer I have to* **be** *one. That means I have to develop my eye and look for shots that capture the beauty and the essence of what I see here.* Tilina heard the heavily accented voice of her teacher in her head: *Tilina you must look for the unusual angles, photography is the art of painting with light; compose your image, it must speak.*

So far she had taken countless shots of stone buildings, doorways, geraniums in pots, motley looking Greek cats; but nothing had spoken, not even a whisper. Hot and thirsty, Tilina made her way towards one of the many ornate fountains and re-filled her water bottle with the gushing, clear spring water. She spotted a bench under a shady tree and, peeling off the heavy camera bag, she kicked back savoring the unique experience of drinking pure mountain water from an arbitrary fountain built who knows how long ago. *You'd never see that in the States. Some jerk would have bought it, bottled and sold it.*

Since arriving in Greece, Tilina had started to allow her mind the liberties of wandering every so often, indeed an unusual state of affairs for such a matter-of-fact, self-opinionated woman who spoke her mind with rarely a thought of consequence. Without any warning her mind strayed to the prohibited grounds of Glen, ex-husbands, and the sad, angry divorced women who would have commiserated with her as she lamented her woes and helped her to pour venom on any form of nostalgic memories she might have.

She meandered down memory lane, reminiscing about the fabulous holidays they took during their marriage and wondering how he would have enjoyed this trip to Greece. It had been many years since she'd last spoken to Glen, their children were young adults so there were no more joint decisions required. She speculated about his marriage to Stephanie, had the arrival of children flung the fiery passion of a new relationship into the realms of the ordinary as they both negotiated parenthood and all the other complications of married life?

Her malicious self reared up as she contemplated Glen's probable happiness and then she disintegrated into a septic tank of self-pity.

Her attention turned to an elderly Greek woman slowly making her way up the dusty street. Swathed in black from head to toe and clutching a walking stick, she hobbled forward painfully oblivious to the camera trained on her. The powerful zoom lens revealed a startling portrait, made all the more haunting by simple human contrasts contained within her old body.

The smooth black fabric of the headscarf wreathed a crinkled face deeply etched in pain and snarled with grief. The woman's eyes, clouded by cataracts, reflected dark opaque pools of regret and sadness.

Instinctively, with every click of the shutter, Tilina knew that this was a photograph of a lifetime. This was an image that she could not afford to ignore; it would scream at her every time she looked at it. The illustration provided insight of what she could become in the future if she didn't deal with the anger, jealousy, and self-pity harbored inside of her. She had spent many years in mourning yet life had gone on; it was all but overtaking her. It was her decision, and her decision alone, to cast aside the metaphorical widow persona and embrace the joy of living again.

It was all up to her, her choice and no one else's. It was an astounding revelation. Her part in the demise of her marriage became clear and was accepted; and, in that moment, Tilina knew Greece had changed her life forever.

Alex and Ruby
Scene 5

Ruby tottered out of the church with a splitting headache from the festivities of the night before. Her feet were killing her. *Whatever possessed me to wear six-inch stilettos this morning? I must have still been in some state of inebriation when I chose these instruments of torture.* She seated her derriere on the church steps and with much sighing, removed the heels. Massaging tender toes already showing signs of blistering, she spied Alex sitting quietly in exactly the same spot they had left her in. Shoes in hand, she limped over, tip toeing gingerly across the cobblestones.

Alex looked up and smiled as she spotted a riot of color approaching. Ruby's penchant for dramatic dressing was legendary. She shamelessly mixed her wardrobe with the deftness and skill of an artist. Flamboyant geometric patterns were perfectly positioned alongside equally loud patterns. Her curvaceous figure lent itself well to soft, flowing garments, the central point of which was always deeply slashed cleavage; it was all about cleavage in Ruby's opinion. She'd been well endowed with beautiful breasts and was not ashamed to put them on display. Alex watched her walk barefoot across the square, a red satin stiletto carelessly hung from each index finger. As Ruby walked, the sunlight played with her thick, untamed bush of iridescent auburn hair and the image was quite breathtaking. She looked like a movie star.

Arranging her things at the table, Ruby beckoned coquettishly at the waiter and gave him her most beguiling smile. "I need a drink; I'll have whatever she's having."

"Michelle, Charlotte?" Alex asked.

"Last seen deep in prayer with a Do Not Disturb sign round their necks. We could be here a while girlfriend. Any sign of Tilina?"

Alex shook her head. "Sore feet?"

"Un-fucking believable. I must have been shitfaced when I pulled these out this morning. I used to be able to dance on tables the whole fucking night with stilettos higher than this." She shook her head and smiled wistfully. "The good old days Alex, oh how I miss them."

Alex nodded in agreement as the waiter approached with a flourish, carefully balancing a heavy tray. He made a huge display of placing Ruby's order on the table. Alex wasn't sure if it was the movie star appeal or the promise of a big tip or both, but he certainly hadn't made as big a fuss over her earlier identical order. It was always fun being with Ruby, she had a special way with people. She could tease a tiger out of a kitten or reduce a grown man to tears with an off color joke; one thing you knew when you were with her was there would never be a dull moment.

An easy silence ensued as Ruby swirled her drink taking a few sips. She leaned back and surveyed the square. It struck Ruby that she hadn't had much of a chance to spend quiet time with Alex since their arrival. Michelle had been at the center of her attention for months now, it came as quite a relief that her tear sodden, broken-hearted friend was in the care of the Archangels at this particular point in time.

Turning her attention to Alex, she noticed, not for the first time, how beautiful and composed she was. Alex was in great shape, the hours of gym work and the boob job worked wonders on her outward appearance, not to mention the boost in self-confidence. Ruby had always envied the cool, quiet composure and air of independence Alex had even when they were young girls. She knew Alex had a tough time of it with that family of hers, how she dealt with that mother, Ruby never knew.

Aren't we women amazing? If our bodies are in shape and our boobs aren't drooping, nothing can get us down. In spite of Alex's outward appearance, there was something that had been gnawing at Ruby since they arrived. Alex was just a little too composed and way too in control. It was almost as if she was afraid to breathe or move or sneeze in case something would be exposed to the world. *Yes,* ruminated Ruby, *under that air of imperturbability, my Alex is not happy, something big's cooking and I hope it doesn't explode.* Lost in thought, Ruby chewed on a piece of baguette.

Alex watched Ruby affectionately, she had always admired Ruby's 'couldn't give a shit' attitude and the bubbly, noisy spontaneity. While she had never been as close to Ruby as Michelle was, they had known each other for years and there was something that Alex just could not put her finger on, some subtle change in Ruby that worried Alex. Rubes had always been a party girl, the belle of the ball, the one that danced on the tables clad in a mini skirt, ridiculously sparkling stilettos, and a thong. Ruby was the one to knock back shots and cocktails and whatever else was going, but Alex noticed there was a different feel to the way Ruby was drinking these days, almost like she was drinking to forget something. *Yup that's what it is, that's the thing I've been picking up on. Ruby's hiding something, underneath all the glitz and razzle dazzle party girl image, My Ruby is unhappy,* she thought sadly.

They sat in quiet companionship, enjoying the warm summer breeze.

"Who would've thought back in the days when we were pigtailed schoolgirls with bangs and braces, that we would be gorgeous, successful old bags, celebrating our fiftieth birthdays in Greece," Ruby mused aloud.

"It's quite something to come together seeing where each one of us ended up. Thank God for Facebook," Alex chuckled, "we sort of lost touch for a while."

"Strange, I figured we'd all get married and have children; yet Mitch and Charlotte ended up unmarried and childless." Ruby stretched her legs out onto one of the vacant chairs. "Funny how messed up it all gets. When I was up to my eyeballs with snotty noses and shitty diapers, I used to envy Mitch's lifestyle, she was always in some exotic place, staying in the best hotels and just doing her thing."

"Yeah," commiserated Alex, "isn't it weird how fifty seemed so old in those days and yet in a blink of an eye, you suddenly realize that you're closer to the grave than the cradle. How quickly children grow up. Little and demanding, you keep wishing for them to get older and less needy and the next thing you know, they're gone and you're left wishing they could just be a little bit needy again." Alex looked squarely into Ruby's eyes. "If you had the chance to do it all again Ruby, would you? I mean knowing what you know now, would you?"

"Would I what?"

"You know, would you get married and have kids again?"

Ruby thought long and hard. "That's a tough one to answer Alex." She fiddled with her hair uncomfortably. "You know, you spend so many years living a selfless life, giving, caring, nurturing, everyone needs something from you. One day you wake up and they're gone, *poof,* just like that. Everyone's out there living their life and you end up wondering what the fuck now? Where am I? Nobody has time for you and yet you sacrificed everything of yours to be there for them and then you look across to the stranger in the room, you know, your partner of nearly thirty years and realize you are exactly that, strangers…and you? Would you do it again?"

Alex sighed. "You know Ruby, I love my girls, I can't imagine what my life would have been without them, but boy oh boy, kids are hard work and very self-centered. I guess I've been fortunate in that I was in a career flexible enough to adapt to the challenges of raising children and an absent husband and now, that's exactly what keeps everything in perspective for me." Alex laughed good naturedly. "In hindsight, maybe I could have done with a husband with a bigger dick who was at home more often, but all in all, I wouldn't change my kids for anything."

Ruby looked wistful. "I often wonder if I hadn't gotten knocked up and airlifted into marriage, who'd I be today? I mean …I know who I am, but I'm not sure I'm everything I could've been."

"Yes, I know exactly what you mean Rubes. You were a talented and promising musician, who knows which star, or planet for that matter, you would be living on if you'd taken the scholarship opportunity at that music university in Vienna."

Lowering her eyes to hide the sadness in her soul, Ruby gazed wistfully at her manicure. "I thought being a wife and mother was enough for me but now that the boys are all grown up, I feel so lost and alone. Life seems so empty—to answer your first question in the current space that I find myself in, taking the love for our kids out of the equation; Alex, the answer would be no. If I knew what marriage and motherhood would turn out to be for me, I would have swum across the bloody sea to get to Austria."

Alex was a little taken aback at the hint of underlying anger in Ruby's voice. Ruby was always one of those happy, smiley people; life never seemed to get her down. This was a side of Ruby she'd never seen before.

There was more to this, so Alex was a little sorry to see Michelle, Charlotte, and Tilina sauntering across the square towards them. Ruby perked up at the sound of their voices and that unguarded truthful moment between them vanished as quickly as it came.

Mother of Mine
Scene 6

Ruby stretched luxuriously as the movie titles came up on the enormous television screen. "Oh my gosh, when was the last time we all camped out in our PJs watching chick flicks?"

"Must have been in high school," smiled Michelle. "Do you remember how we'd declare a weekend pajama and movie session after too many crazy party nights and all sleepover at your place Charley? And your mom would make us mugs of hot chocolate with marshmallows on top?"

"My mom loved it when you all came by, she always worried I was too much of a loner and I think secretly she enjoyed the plain nonsense of just hanging out with a bunch of giggly schoolgirls." Charlotte gazed wistfully at the bronze sculpture of her mother presiding over them. "I'm sure she's very happy to be hanging out with us once again." Her eyes widened as she looked at them and whispered, "I know it's kinda freaky but having her remains with me helps to fill this big black hole I feel inside. I don't expect anyone to understand or even agree, but right now, I know I'm just not ready to let her go...you know what I mean, you know to scatter or bury her ashes. That's all I have left of her. I need them near me until I can come to terms with my grief, my loss."

Tilina came from the kitchen bearing a tray of steaming mugs of hot chocolate and they all smiled at the generosity and sensitivity of thought which seemed out of place from her usual brusque manner. "I often tell my boys; you don't know you can't live without your mom till the day she dies. Sadly, you don't understand till she's gone. My mom died of cancer; I watched this lioness of a woman wither away in front of my eyes. Even though I knew it was terminal and I had time for goodbye, part of me died with her." Tilina's face softened as she looked into Charley's eyes. "One day you'll be able to talk about her without crying but you'll never stop longing for just one last time to talk with her, hold her hand or tell her just how much she meant to you."

For the second time that day, Alex was jolted by another unguarded truthful moment, this time with Tilina, a person Alex tended to cautiously observe from a quiet and safe distance.

Tilina's words smashed home the reality that her own relationship with her mother had never recovered from the "oh fuck" baby days. The last time Alex saw or spoke to her mother was at her father's funeral where it was obvious that time had done nothing to mellow the angry resentment of the woman who had birthed her out of wedlock.

A bolt of lightning penetrated Alex's thoughts as she realized there was unfinished business between mother and daughter that needed to be resolved before that inevitable moment when death would separate them and it would simply be too late.

As they sipped their mugs of chocolate, Alex contemplated the years that had passed since those high school sleepovers and marveled at how comforting it was to know their unity and friendship had survived sufficiently for this birthday grand vacation.

In spite of all the happenings in their lives in the interim, just knowing the links remained brought comfort that these women were part of where they came from and would be there to support who they were yet to become.

AZUL
AEGEAN
DAYS & NIGHTS

Chapter 11
Alex's Bomb-Well Hello Kevin!
Scene 1

Ruby opened her eyes cautiously; the blackout curtains provided no telltale strands of sunlight by which to gauge the time. The house seemed unusually quiet so she figured it was either very early or very late. Groping through the darkness searching for the bedside light she knocked over a wine bottle in the process. *Thank goodness it's empty.* Scrutinizing her cell phone, Ruby was startled to see it was 11am. She was a light sleeper, could it be that everybody else was still asleep? Her mind flicked to the previous night...*nope, I went to bed when everyone else did, then had a solitary night cap and watched the stars.* She fell asleep listening to music and thinking about all sorts of things. *Did I finish that whole bottle of wine?* Clothes strewn all over the floor indicated so. She staggered to the bathroom and stared at the face in the mirror; bloodshot eyes and telltale signs of makeup smudges indicated one of those alcohol induced blackout nights. *Can't let the girls see me looking like this,* she thought as she hit the shower and soaped and scrubbed away the evidence.

A half hour later Ruby sat on the patio enjoying a late breakfast in quiet solitude. The girls had left a Gone Shopping note and Althea left a tray of pastries, fresh fruit, and yogurt in the fridge. The metallic blue shimmer of the distant water held her gaze as she sipped coffee and rationalized her late night and private over indulgence in alcohol. The chimes of the doorbell penetrated her thoughts, she frowned at the intrusion. A second round of chimes brought the realization that she was the only one at the house so she rose to answer the door.

"Ruby, how are you?" a male voice boomed into her senses.

Uttering a small gasp, she nearly yelped out. "Kevin...Kevin Gibson?" Ruby breathed cautiously, it had been many years since she'd last seen Alex's husband and while this man looked very similar, the unshaven and unkempt appearance didn't quite tie up to the smooth man Alex had been married to for so many years.

Ruby's 'oh shit' antennas were immediately activated; she wasn't sure why Kevin was standing on the doorstep of their luxury villa in the middle of Greece, but she immediately sensed trouble, as in *low-flying shit drama* trouble.

Ever the gracious host and summoning her most charming of raspy voices, she beckoned him through the door. "Come on in, what a wonderful surprise Kevin. I was just enjoying a late breakfast on the patio; can I offer you an adrenalin shot? Otherwise known as a Greek coffee." She smiled.

"I'm a little stressed, long flight from New York to Athens, didn't get much sleep, then the five-hour drive. If you don't mind, I'd prefer something stronger, double whiskey on the rocks maybe?"

Ruby reached for the bottle of Glenfiddich whiskey that had presided grandly over the bar since their arrival. With a forced air of joviality, she remarked, "*Aah* a fellow whiskey connoisseur at last! I've had my eye on this little baby since we got here." Displaying the bottle like a hard-won trophy, she added with a flourish, "Twenty-one-year-old single malt, distilled in Caribbean rum casks. They say it creates marvelous undertones of tropical fruits like bananas, figs, and ginger. Let's give it a go. The girls are out shopping, so could be a while."

Expertly she assembled a tray with glasses, ice bucket, and snacks, motioned to him to grab the whiskey bottle and beckoned him to follow her to the living room. Her mind was racing furiously. Alex never mentioned a possible visit from Kevin, in fact, come to think of it, apart from her reference to his small dick yesterday, she had said absolutely nothing about him, nor their family. On further consideration, Alex had been pretty tight lipped and aloof about everything pertaining to her personal life. Something was cooking in this marital kitchen and quite frankly, Ruby didn't like the smell.

Keep it calm, keep it friendly, girl. Keep smiling, dig gently, stay neutral and make sure he's not too shit faced by the time the girls get back …Small talk, small talk, lots of small talk Ruby. "So, Kevin," flashing her most beguiling smile she chatted along, "how long's it been since last I saw you?" Tactfully, Ruby managed to establish from Kevin that everything was okay with the girls and the animals and the house and after a few silent breaths of relief, more pleasantries were exchanged and chit chat continued as they whiled away the time waiting, sipping Scottish whiskey in search of the promised exotic Caribbean flavors. As the chit chat threatened to become mindless blabber and the search for more distant island tastes become more difficult, Ruby heard the Escalade SUV pull up outside. Then slamming doors were punctuated by the animated banter of the women.

Gathering her whiskey inspired calm, she gracefully sauntered out to the car to greet them and give Alex an advanced head's up that her husband was in the living room quietly assuring everyone that there didn't appear to be any problems or drama at home or with the children.

As they walked towards the house carrying the load of newly purchased groceries, Ruby paid careful attention to Alex's demeanor. Outwardly she exuded a calm and cheerful attitude but the determined way in which she held her composure added to Ruby's suspicions that all was not well in the kingdom of marital heaven.

Leaving the packages on the kitchen counter, they flowed into the living room. Charlotte, Michelle, and Tilina hugged him warmly before settling themselves into the deep comfort of one of the many easy chairs in the room. Ruby calmed her nerves by busying herself behind the bar. For the non-whiskey drinkers, she trawled through the wine refrigerator and selected a dry white wine produced by Argyros from the Santorini region. The guest information leaflet promised it to be a refreshing, citrusy combination with a lingering but delightful taste of pears and salty sea spray that would appeal to even the most discerning palate. *Who writes this bullshit poetic wine nonsense?* Ruby presented Kevin with the bottle and corkscrew—*well he's the only male in the room and this will provide a welcome distraction from the drama that is about to happen.*

Taking center couch, Ruby surveyed the stage and backdrops in place for the opening scene of this Greek drama: to her left were Charlotte, Michelle, and Tilina who remained blissfully unaware of the depth of what was about to come, on the couch to her right sat Kevin in a self-induced alcohol/jet lag bubble and next to him his gorgeous smiling wife Alex. The pop of the wine bottle cork … *and* … **action** …

As if the scene had been rehearsed several times, each person took their cue; glasses were filled and a brief moment of amity ensued as they saluted and wished each other long and happy lives. Alex chugged the first shot of whiskey back in a flash, declaring she could only taste vanilla/toffee undertones, extravagantly recharging her glass; she exuded positive relaxation as she tucked both legs under her and snuggled into the corner of the couch, sipping the delicious whiskey in pursuit of the much promised banana and ginger experience, and most importantly some liquid courage.

Zoning out of the trivial banter and conversation, Alex once again remembered that fateful day two years ago when a torrential rainstorm with earth-shattering explosions of thunder and terrifying flashes of lightening drove her to seek refuge in a coffee shop. Somewhere between the deafening crashes and incandescent shafts of light, her known world vanished. The time between then and now had been devoted to reclaiming her inner self and creating a life devoted to her needs. With the full knowledge of her being, Alex knew it would happen in its own time, although she hadn't imagined that this particular piece of the transformation would play out in Greece in the company of lifelong friends.

With a steady but deliberate calm, Alex took aim as she launched a missile into Kevin's life, and settled back to observe the ricochet of lies and deceit that would soon fly. She turned to her husband and looking deep into his eyes; smiling lovingly.

"*Mon petit chou,* tell us about your business trip or was it actually a family vacation to Paris? I understand Lily and her lovely mother, Vivienne, were absolutely delighted to see you. Tell me my dearest one, did you share your life story with them or are you intending to keep your mystery all to yourself?"

The girls looked at each other quizzically as Alex stared evenly at her husband and in a very calm voice invited him to share the happy news with everybody. "I wouldn't want to steal your thunder," she said with a wry smile. Taking a long sip from her glass, she held her gaze on him and patiently waited for him to speak.

An uneasy silence filled the room as a red faced Kevin rose to his feet appealing to the others for some privacy so that his wife and he could discuss some very personal matters.

Taken aback by his request and not quite sure where this was all heading, after a brief moment of hesitation they rose in unison to their feet only to be halted abruptly by Alex's raised hand firmly motioning them to stay. "Step into the light you filthy, slime sucking slug. Your penchant for operating under lies and deceit is now finally being exposed, your shameful secret is revealed to all who will listen."

"Alex," he looked at her imploringly, "not here, not like this, let's talk honey—I can explain." Once again, he looked beseechingly at her friends. "Please, can my wife and I have some privacy? We have serious matters to discuss."

Alex rose to her feet, something he said triggered a wrath of deep-seated fury. Her face was red with rage and her entire body shook as adrenalin surged like acid through every vein in her body. "Now, after all these years of secrecy, you wish to speak privately with me?" she spluttered.

His eyes widened in disbelief, he looked around at her friend's faces and registered their realization as their seismic shocked looks gave way to absolute disgust as they processed Alex's almost unbelievable allegations.

The cobra inside of her reared its head. "Bigamist!" she hissed as she released the venomous anger and betrayal. "My husband has been married to another woman for the past ten years and now he wants a **private** moment with me in order to explain his actions."

Echoes of her hysterical laughter bounced like shattered glass from the walls culminating in a deafening silence.

Gathering the crystal shards of her dignity, she looked squarely at Kevin. "These are my friends; the bond we share is beyond the understanding of any man. The love I feel for these women is beyond anything I've ever felt for you. Right now, I choose to hold them close to me because I know their unconditional love and loyalty will see me through this catastrophe. I've no desire to hear your explanation, there's nothing to talk about. Our marriage is over and lawyers will take care of the formalities. Please leave now so I can move on with the rest of my life."

Spit it out Alex!
Scene 2

Kevin visibly aged before their eyes. He sank into the chair sobbing, his head and shoulders stooped. Tilina rose to her feet. Braving the silence, she took Kevin's arm gently. "It's time to leave," she said quietly. He followed her meekly out of the room without uttering a sound. Muffled conversation in the hallway followed by the sound of a car engine announced the departure of Kevin.

"What the fuck Alex?" Tilina blasted back into the room, "Ten years, ten fucking years and you only just found out now?"

"It's a long story, let's open another bottle of wine and I'll tell you everything." She settled back, crossed her legs, and sighed as she searched her mind for an appropriate starting point.

Sensing her pain, Michelle urged Alex to take her time and start at the beginning, Ruby nodded in agreement.

Alex recalled the first time their eyes met across the boardroom table at a Civil Engineering company; she was a junior software engineer working on an IT project, he was also a junior engineer. Their attraction was mutual and there was never any doubt in either one's mind that marriage would follow, albeit somewhat quicker than expected when Alex discovered she was pregnant with their daughter Melanie.

Their marriage was peaceful, there was seldom any drama, they plodded through the early years, raising two daughters. They were both well-educated and earned reasonably well so there was never any major financial issue especially once Kevin specialized as a Structural Engineer and turned his focus to both the onshore and offshore oil and gas industry. By all accounts, he was a highly respected engineer but the nature of his specialized work involved frequent absences away from home in far flung remote places in the world. Gradually, the absences became longer but Alex's absolute devotion to both children and husband meant she was happy to sacrifice many aspects of her persona, including career aspirations and ambitions, in order to tend and nurture her family.

Looking back at it now, her pride in their peaceful and amicable existence was misplaced and clearly not appreciated by Kevin. She learned the hard way that any oversight or shortcomings in a marriage would bite you firmly on the butt at a later stage if not fully dealt with at once.

Alex wasn't sure when or how or why, but those seemingly endless years of raising children, being at their beck and call, basing all her life decisions on them first and foremost, actually came to an end sooner than anticipated.

Perhaps if she hadn't been so busy tip toeing through bitchy daughter adolescence times two, she might have been more prepared for it.

She still remembered Melanie's prom night, sadly Kevin was absent, working in Nigeria (although these days, she was never sure what was fact and what was fiction when it came to Kevin's whereabouts during their married life). A melancholy descended on her as she came face to face with the young adult version of Melanie and not that cheeky ponytailed little girl. In a blink of an eye, her younger sister was also strutting out of the house in all her prom night glory, once again Kevin was absent for Abigail's big night too. Where was he then? The Gulf or the oilfields of Uzbekistan? His absences were so normal, so frequent, and so far from home that over the years she stopped paying attention to where he was and what he was doing. She grew so accustomed to weeks of not hearing from him, although in his defense, as internet technology developed, their communication did seem to become more regular.

When Kevin was at home he was quiet, caring, and very dependable. He generally made a point of being home for the girls' and her birthdays and never, unfathomably given the circumstances, missed a family Christmas...ever.

He did tend to seek refuge from the hustle and bustle of daily home life in his study. Alex always assumed the isolated places he frequented were the cause of his anti-social behavior—how wrong could a wife be? She smirked at the thought, looking at her friends who nodded in sad unison as they listened.

Melanie was the first to leave home when she was accepted into the School of Engineering at Stanford University. Both parents shared her delight and excitement and advised her to live on campus to enjoy the total experience of university life.

Abigail, on the other hand, was a constant source of surprise bordering on exasperation and frustration. They never quite came to terms with her artistic tendencies. Alex, in particular, was very uncomfortable with her airy fairy, head-in-the-clouds approach to life. Unlike her sister who had her feet on the ground, Abby was the butterfly of the family, constantly in motion, flitting from place to place in search of sweeter nectar. Numerous mother/daughter arguments took place as Alex tried to preach the importance of a girl having a solid education and career. It was something that she felt very strongly about given her childhood background. Alex's words lingered in the air, unheeded. Kevin would step in and try to mediate between the two. He gently but firmly insisted that Abby obtain at the very least, an undergraduate degree in performing arts and so it was that she left home in hot pursuit of artistic freedom at the University of San Francisco, leaving her mother with more time on her hands than she knew what to do with.

Uncrossing her legs, Alex reached for the wine bottle, looking deeply into the faces of her friends. She was moved by their compassionate willingness to do nothing but listen right now. This was the first time she had broached the subject of Kevin's infidelity with anyone.

She was surprised at how easy it was to lift the lid on the secret she harbored for the past two years. As she spoke, her words illuminated the hidden passages and corners of what had been her life for the past twenty-plus years.

Heartened by their openness, she continued, delving into her story, slowly peeling away the layers in order to reach that moment of realization.

It was the changed order and predictability of daily life that triggered the inevitable moment of discovery. The innocence of how it all happened still skewed her grasp of the reality of the situation. She relived the events of that fateful evening two years prior, that night had been on automatic replay in her mind, relentlessly; she relived it and all the minute details that went with it at the oddest times every day since. Driving to work, taking a bath, sleeping, shopping, board meetings…there was no respite from that moment. Her eyes widened with a deep sadness as she recollected that fateful minute.

Kevin had been home for a few weeks, his company was bidding for a large engineering and construction project and long nights at the office ensued as the partners carefully put together their pitch. She was positioned in her home office, grappling with an intricate code when the playful ringtone of her cell summoned her attention. It was Kevin calling from his office; he had mislaid some important documents pertaining to the bid and was wondering if he had left them in his study. With the phone pressed to her ear, she went into his study and, guided by his description of the file, she spotted a large file filled with papers. Sensing his frustration at his tardiness, she offered to run it down to his office which was a twenty-minute drive away at this time of the evening. She remembered with a smile his sigh of relief and was happy that she could be of assistance during this stressful time for him. She was still sporting yoga wear from her earlier class and, with the large bulky file under her arm, she reached for her purse and car keys and headed out the door.

A speeding vehicle racing through a four-way stop brought her to an abrupt stop as she hit the brakes to avoid a collision. The car whizzed by oblivious of the moment of danger, leaving her to continue on her way while trying to pick up her purse and the file which had slid off the backseat and emptied its contents on the floor behind her.

She called him from her cell when she arrived at his office and while waiting for him to appear, she rummaged around the floor of the vehicle in search of the papers, re-stacked them and handed the file to him through the window. A perfunctory peck on the cheek in thanks and she returned home.

Perched in the driver's seat, she scratched through her purse in search of the house keys but couldn't find them—they must have fallen out when she hit the brakes. This time, she got out of the car and, aided by the dim interior light, she groped rather than looked under the driver's seat and hauled out some papers and finally, the keys. She sighed at the thought of going back to Kevin's office once again to give him the missing papers, but decided to have a look at the document and phone him to find out if he needed these before making the decision to return.

Making some tea, she ambled to her desk and sifted through the handful of papers retrieved from under the car seat. Her attention was immediately drawn to what looked to be a certificate of some sort. Holding the light blue paper to the light, the emblazoned title screamed at her. In a moment of confusion, she pulled back and then gathering her wits, she read closely.

BIRTH CERTIFICATE BRITISH COLUMBIA

Surname	GIBSON
Given Name (s)	LILY ROSE
Date of Birth	OCT 22, 2011
Sex	FEMALE
Place of Birth	VICTORIA
Registration Number	2004-59-405046
Date of Registration	OCT 30, 2011
Date of Issue	June 20, 2013
Name of Parent	VIVIENNE GABRIELLE MARTEL
Birthplace of Parent	ALBERTA, CANADA
Name of Parent	KEVIN MARTIN GIBSON
Birthplace of Parent	UNITED STATES OF AMERICA

A collective gasp engulfed the room as they processed this information.

"Sweet Mother of Jesus." Lowering her head, Ruby's right-hand moved towards her forehead, as her hand moved in a cross like sequence to her stomach and then each shoulder, a Catholic blessing could be heard, *"In nomine Patris et Filii et Spiritus Sancti."*

Relief gushed though Alex's body, finally she had set down the heavy load of secrecy. Her eyes filled with tears as she felt their shock, compassion, and loyalty.

Their wholehearted acceptance of her truth was received without any hint of judgment.

Althea popped her head into the room and announced a light buffet lunch in the dining room.

So many questions came to mind but for the moment, they were content to each give Alex a big hug and move the story to the dining room.

Stripped Naked But Not Alone
Scene 3

The sight of food reminded them of their hunger. The events of the past few hours galvanized them and any thought of daily functions vanished as they digested the news. Sensitized by the recent demise of her own relationship, Michelle could relate to some of the emotional aspects of ending a long-term relationship. It puzzled her that outwardly Alex's calm demeanor didn't correspond with not only the dissolution of her twenty-two year marriage but the appalling betrayal and deceit that had taken place for at least ten years within that marriage. Now, without any discussion between the two parties concerned, the marriage had somehow abruptly ended and the guilty party had been dispatched without ceremony. How on earth had Alex managed to pull that off and still remain so calm and in control? To say she was intrigued, beguiled, or bewitched by it would indeed be an understatement.

Sensing the myriad questions that seemed to float through the atmosphere like stars on a clear summer night, Alex picked up the story as they ate. Her gaze shifted angularly as if she was searching a far reached corner of her memory closet. "Blindsided!" It was the only word that adequately described the shock of seeing her husband listed as a parent of Lily Rose. All those clichés one sees in the movies or reads of in novels went through her mind in a flash. She wasn't sure how long she sat staring at the humble piece of paper she so innocently stumbled upon; somewhere in that cataclysmic state she recalled coming to her senses—standing in the kitchen holding a lukewarm mug. There and then she made a pact to say nothing for at least twelve months.

Alex knew the dire implications of the piece of paper she held, but she wanted facts so she could understand the truth, the whole truth, and nothing but the unemotional, emphatic truth of what was going on. There was absolutely no way she was going to jump into any conclusions or launch into any type of behavior that would unleash a tirade of more lies and more betrayal.

She tossed the contents of the mug into the sink and headed for the medicine chest in search of a sleeping aid. She settled for a generous shot of Nyquil relying on that wonderful ingredient that induced a deep and heavy sleep for flu sufferers and headed off to bed.

During the weeks that followed, old childhood patterns came back to haunt Alex as she tried to process her husband's actions. Once again that feeling of being unwanted, a superfluous object not worthy of love or devotion gripped her soul, her tortured spirit descended into an eerie silence as she relived every moment of this farce of a marriage, questioning the authenticity of every moment spent; what was real, what was true. She had no option but to draw the conclusion that everything was a lie.

Miraculously, she found herself driven by that storm into the sanctuary of a coffee shop two years ago, where water streaming from the dark, furious face of the sky resonated with her own internal anguish and upheaval. By some quirk of nature, as the thunderstorm subsided, calmness returned to her being and Project Phoenix was conceived.

Counseling sessions, along with enrollment with a life coach, helped her to understand that time and knowledge were on her side and it was her decision alone to decide how and when this would all play out. She understood that if she were to come out of this situation in a positive state, she would need to own her power, her strength. She needed to look after herself in every imaginable way as she undertook the journey of truth and today, some two years later, she emerged at the end point, a strong and whole woman in every sense.

Apart from the atomic bomb that ripped her heart, mind, and soul to smithereens, absolutely nothing changed in daily life while at the same time everything changed.

Kevin continued to work away from home, spending weeks at the satellite office he established in Fort McMurray, Alberta. When he did venture home, he maintained his usual late hours, laboring tirelessly on one bid after another.

Alex became discreetly attentive as she conducted a wordless surveillance of her husband's movements; she listened to his phone calls, watched for unusual texting or internet activities but saw nothing that would provide more clues. On weekends spent together, they dined with friends, went to the movies, had sex and shopped—all normal everyday marital activities.

She engaged a private investigator to build the jigsaw puzzle one piece at a time until a picture of a man living two separate lives emerged. Kevin had met Vivienne in the small town of Fox Creek, Alberta, while working on one of his many oilfield projects. It was a pretty basic story really, an attractive young woman, fifteen years his junior, no formal education, working in a local bar and restaurant. She got pregnant with Lily Rose, they shacked up together, moved towns a few times and as far as Alex was concerned, the rest was pretty much history. She had no interest in finding out the why and when of the circumstance, choosing instead to focus on rebuilding her life without the attachment of or to Kevin.

Establishing her own business, she ensured financial independence. Her daughters were happily settled in their young adult lives, she built a strong support network via her business and the pursuit of her own interests and hobbies.

She engaged a divorce lawyer eighteen months ago, instructing her to prepare the divorce proceeding documents for issue when instructed. The wooing of a potential purchaser of Magenta Holdings had been the trigger point to start the divorce proceedings. Alex had no interest in a prolonged court battle should it ever be perceived that she had assets Kevin could lay claim to. The divorce summons was filed on the basis of adultery, unreasonable behavior, desertion, and cruelty.

Kevin's reaction to the receipt of the divorce summons had been witnessed by all of them that morning—they stared silently at Alex as they processed the story.

Alex quietly answered the unasked question in each of her friend's minds. "He wanted a private discussion with me? What's to discuss? For ten years he lied and cheated on me and our daughters. Nothing more to hear."

Silence permeated the room. Michelle and Tilina shifted uncomfortably as they reflected on their individual reactions to the demise of their own long-term relationships. Also intrigued by the absence of wrath and retaliation, Tilina stared long and hard at Alex then voiced what they were all thinking. "How on earth have you managed to carry this load Alex? Where and how did you find the strength to remain silent? How did you manage not to murder him?"

"Yes," chirped Ruby, "I would've chopped his balls and dick off …and that would have just been the start of the process."

Wistfully Alex explained how that violent thunderstorm was the turning point. She realized marriage and motherhood had merely been a continuation of her childhood. She never dealt with her feelings of guilt and inadequacy as a person and continued to believe her life was all about nurturing and tending to the needs of her husband and daughters. She realized that they were all out living their lives because that's what she allowed them the privilege of doing. And as hard as it was to acknowledge, they actually didn't give a real shit about her.

Her self-sacrifice in family relationships hit her square in the jaw, it was a life-changing revolution and it was time to re-paint her life canvas. The energy of the storm had somehow allowed her spirit energy to emerge.

With the help of a life coach counselor, she found an inner strength she never thought she possessed. There were times she felt broken, nights she cried herself to sleep, but with each change she made in life, no matter how small or how large, her confidence in who she was becoming felt more grounded, inspiring her to quit 'making do' and pursue her quest to find the true Alex.

Alex nodded to them with a smile. "I finally understood and saw firsthand that in order to move forward in my life story in a positive way, I had to let go of everything, you know, just drop the whole pile of shit I was carrying. Toss it all into the garbage can. The low self-esteem, the belief I was not good enough, the daily chore of scrambling to gain the recognition, acknowledgement, and acceptance of others in order to feel good about me—well that all ended up on Mount Trashmore."

She rose to her feet and made her way to the bar fridge. Extricating a bottle from the chilly cabinet, she stood up straight and smiled.

"I figured that ridding myself of the heartbreak, grief, and sorrow I was feeling was my job and my job alone. I had to just simply 'Let it Go.' Kevin's affair had nothing to do with me, it was his decision and with or without him, it was not going to change the fundamental of *Me*. For the first time in my life, I decided there and then, to be Me and to give my story a happy ending...and here I am, at my happy ending, surrounded by my beautiful, caring friends, ready to crack open this bottle of Dom Perignon and celebrate my personal victory of self and the start of a new chapter in my life story."

Chapter 12
A Drop at Sea
Scene 1 - The Boat Trip

The shimmering waters of the Pagasitic Gulf and tranquil blue sky provided a preview of the day that lay ahead of them. After the calamitous events the previous day, they embraced the peaceful atmosphere as they quietly enjoyed an early morning breakfast on the outdoor patio overlooking the sea.

Ruby booked what promised to be a lazy day at sea aboard a wooden gullet boat. She considered hiring a private yacht but decided it would be more fun to mix with both an assortment of local and foreign passengers. After all, who knows who one might meet and how the day would turn out? After the dramatic Alex versus Kevin episode yesterday, social interaction with unconnected strangers would most certainly provide a welcome distraction for them all, especially Alex.

Her gaze fell upon Alex who, in spite of looking a little worse for wear, seemed to be coping quite well with the turbulent winds of changes in her life.

Gosh, what would I do if that happened to me? What if, after all these years of marriage, I found out my beloved husband was cheating on me and had an illegitimate child to boot? I certainly wouldn't have had the wherewithal to handle it like Alex. I'd have probably been a ranting, raving lunatic needing a stay in some mental rehab center for the safety of all concerned, including myself.

It was time to hit the road to Affisos where they would be boarding the boat. Michelle took the role of designated driver with Alex in the navigator seat. It took a while for Michelle to become accustomed to the meandering roadway, but once she negotiated the infamous T-Junction, she relaxed and took in the beauty of her surroundings quietly reflecting on the previous day.

Michelle was having difficulty in justifying her emotions when she considered the stoic manner in which Alex handled the betrayal of her husband. *I guess we're all different, what seems to be the end of one person's world can mark the beginning of another person's.* Alex's choice was to move on. In Michelle's situation, she felt compelled to end the relationship and couldn't understand why she was engaging in the drama that followed. Maybe she was being too hard on herself; she was still in the early days of finding her way and sooner or later things would settle down and a new life would emerge. *But what if things didn't?*

Some of Alex's words and mindset rang true to Michelle, *I will delve deeper into this thought process, but not today. Today, I'm getting on a boat and going out to sea.*

Michelle vowed to open herself to new sights and new people that she had never even imagined before. Yes, today she decided to greet the world with an open heart, thanks to her dear friend Alex. She felt a rush of warmth and love for this brave friend seated across from her and reached out to give her hand a squeeze. Their eyes connected as their souls sensed a knowing that they were safe, they had each other's backs unconditionally. *Strange,* Mitch mused as she parked the truck, *I never had this feeling with him, or any man come to think of it.*

The women ambled across the road to the quayside where their boat was docked. They were welcomed aboard by the crew and gravitated to the bow of the boat in pursuit of the upfront view. At exactly 9am the captain blasted the horn signaling their departure.

"*Wow!*" chuckled Tilina, "these guys are bang on time."

"Take her out to sea captain!" ordered Ruby as the engine of the boat powered up and they slowly left the dock. Once they reached deeper water, the engine was shut down and the sails raised, fluttering in the gentle breeze as the expert hands of the crew guided them up the masts. This was a leisurely day cruise that would hug the coastline from Affisos and make its way south towards Trikeri, a village located at the southern point of the Pelion Peninsular. Along the way they would stop off at places of interest, take in the sights and activities, swim in the crystal-clear sea, and enjoy the warmth of Greek weather and hospitality.

The serenity of the sea was infectious and they succumbed to the euphoric sensation of floating in the breeze with no particular place to go and all day to get there. They spread out their towels, coated themselves in sun lotion, donned hats and sunglasses, and lay back enjoying the warm sunrays on their bodies, which were now turning delightful shades of gold.

Using the shoreline as it's guide, the boat sailed slowly through gentle waters, revealing hidden bays and grottos only visible from the sea. Against the majestic backdrop of the Pelion Mountains, they admired the quaint seaside villages of Kalamos and Chorto.

Tilina and, with what was rapidly becoming her soulmate, her Nikon camera, traversed the length and breadth of the boat, constantly on the lookout for that perfect seascape, landscape, friendscape, photograph. Imitating a paparazzi photographer, hidden from view, she captured subtle and meaningful moments of friendship. She felt a preference for taking photographs of people, where hidden from sight, she would delve within the depths of her long-distance lens, searching for an unguarded moment with her subject and then patiently wait for that person's inner spirit to reveal itself in the form of an emotional expression—be it a smile, a tear, or a wistful expression. *Perhaps I should apply the same principle to photographing objects and landscapes. Maybe, if I just wait a while, the spirit of a building or bird or tree will reveal its essence to me.*

Holding this thought in mind, Tilina watched carefully as they passed the small village of Milina and headed seaward towards the island of Alatas. She stared in fascination as the boat slowly circled the small island, silently revealing another smaller island. Surrounded by blue tinged mountains, Prasouda, a tiny oval shaped island, drifted into view, the vivid blueness of the surrounding sea was sprinkled with lighter colored ripples which appeared to draw the boat closer.

Prasouda, bathed in glorious sunlight, revealed its majestic soul. Surrounded by a sturdy rock waterline, the image was softened by generous green vegetation in the form of trees. From deep within a zoom lens, Tilina found the heart of this mystical island: a monastery dating back to the Byzantine period, long deserted but still standing solid in its remoteness. Quietly she captured the image and then took a step back to admire the glory of this moment. She stared in silence as the boat passed close to the shore and wondered how a person's faith could be so deep that they willingly spent their lives in this remoteness, dedicating their waking hours to the worship of God.

Tilina's contemplation was interrupted by Ruby, who had taken a stroll around the boat in search of some refreshments and, accidentally on purpose, stumbled into the captain's cabin. Never one to hold back, she introduced herself to Captain Costa who didn't seemed to be the least bit bothered by the invasion of his space by this American woman. As Tilina passed by the cabin, camera still in hand, she was hauled in for another round of introductions. Spotting the camera, Ruby insisted that Tilina take a photograph of Captain Costa and her. Ruby promptly removed his naval hat and, placing it in a most becoming lopsided manner on the side of her head, pouted and posed and draped herself around Captain Costa.

As Tilina focused the portrait shot in her viewfinder, she noted that Captain Costa was not short in the good looks department, there seemed to be no end to the supply of Greek idols in the Pelion Region. *I guess this is why it's famously referred to as the playing fields of the Gods.*

Charley happened to pass by as the photo shoot was taking place and, much to the delight of the newly found Greek divinity, she was promptly seated on his lap. Charley was a little stunned by the intimacy of the impromptu gathering but couldn't deny the sudden whoosh of chemical attraction that blasted through her body when it came into contact with Costa. The attraction appeared to be mutual and, in an attempt to savor the moment a smidgeon longer, Costa grabbed his cap off Ruby's head, placed it on Charley's and beckoned to Tilina to take another shot. This time, he leaned close, gently brushing her cheeks with his very sexy, one day, not shaven beard and mustered up the biggest smile he could for the camera. There followed an eruption of giggles as they disentangled themselves and gave Costa back his cap.

He pointed to the island of Paleo Trikeri which suddenly appeared in front of them, his Greek accented voice stated, "This is the highlight of the tour, there's so much to do, you must walk, you must eat, you must swim, and then you will enjoy it very much. When you return, we'll drink Ouzo and dance into the sunset."

They nodded in unison and headed back to the front of the boat to find Alex and Mitch.

Paleo Trikeri was indeed amazing, a tiny island situated off the southern point of the Pelion. Abundantly adorned with olive and citrus trees, amazingly, there were no cars or roads on the island, you either walked, took a mule, or a boat to get to where you wanted to go. The women took to the dirt tracks as they explored the glorious flowers and vegetation, taking in the magnificent views of the peninsula.

"Who'd have thought such a place could possibly exist now, let's not tell too many people about it. They'll want to come and see it and ruin everything," quipped Alex who was in hiker's heaven, loving every minute of the natural surroundings.

They passed through a massive olive grove which, judging by the size of the trees, had been there for hundreds of years. "Did you know olive trees can live for five hundred years? I wonder what stories these trees would tell if they could talk?" asked Ruby.

Michelle frowned. "According to the tourist guide, the history of this island is tragic, pirate invasions and revolutions in the early 1800s and not that long ago, this was a political prisoner camp during the Greek Civil War. I guess these poor trees along with past generations of Greeks experienced a lot of misery and suffering."

Ruby responding partly in jest, "I think they deserve a hug for all they've been through, don't you?"

"What a great idea," trilled Michelle, "your amazing brother Nigel told me I should hug lots of trees because tree hugging increases your levels of the hormone oxytocin which aids holistic healing."

With that, she stomped up to the biggest olive tree she could find and flung her arms around it. Standing there with tears rolling down her face, she challenged the rest of them to just let go and act a little crazy. "Who knows, it might just help."

Tilina shot a few photos and then she too embraced the absurdity of the moment and found her own tree to hug, laughing from the bottom of her heart.

They continued their hike, climbing to the highest point of the island to see the monastery, built by the islanders for protection from invading pirates in 1838. The monastery was dedicated to the Virgin Mary and was still used by locals. Ironically, no monk ever inhabited the monastery. A beautiful place of extreme peace and serenity, providing no inclination of the turbulent history it witnessed across the years.

Within an hour they had walked the length of the island and worked up an appetite so visited one of the few tavernas to enjoy local cuisine fresh from the sea, washed down, of course, with a glass or two of wine.

The harbor town was vibrantly colorful, a happy place which crept into souls assuring all of a lifetime memory of the moments spent there.

Rock the Boat
Scene 2

They re-boarded a few hours later and in the sanctuary of a secluded bay, the captain dropped anchor, affording them the opportunity to enjoy the crystal sea water. Mimicking their teenage years, these five were the first ones in the water and the last ones out. The water temperature was heavenly and they swam and floated until Captain Costa hit the horn again.

The sun took its downward track towards the sea and in honor of the sunset, the bar was open and beautiful Greek music played.

The rest of the passengers had lightened up from the morning, hanging out in the bar area on the stern side of the boat, chatting away with new acquaintances, marveling at the unique sights experienced on their trip.

Alex took a side seat, savoring a marvelous tasting red wine while surveying the world. It was a time to reflect. The unexpected arrival of Kevin marked an ending planned for the past two years.

She cross-examined herself about how she felt about everything. Her honest response was happy and relieved to have everything out in the open, but nervous, fearful, anxious, about where her future lay and hoping Kevin didn't fight the divorce and got it over with before the media ran with any stories about a Magenta buyout.

Outraged at the betrayal? I used to be, came back the answer, *but I let it go, I couldn't begin my journey holding onto all those negative emotions.*

She smiled when considering how far she had come already, here she was, having a blast in a country never on her list to visit, with friends made nearly a lifetime ago.

She spotted Tilina on the port bow side of the boat in deep discussion with another photographer. From the finger pointing and dial fiddling that was going on, Alex figured it had something to do with the approaching sunset.

Mitch was snuggled in the corner of starboard quarter, two Italian guys were making a connection with her while she just sipped away at her wine, smiling sweetly, unaware of their manly intent.

Dearest beautiful Mitch, so oblivious of her own incredible internal and external beauty and strength. Alex could empathize with where Mitch was at this point in time, it wasn't that long ago when she was languishing in the same muddy pool of self-despair. Somewhere down the line, Mitch would figure it out.

Alex caught a glimpse of Charley standing at the bridge in deep conversation with someone. That baffled Alex a bit, Charley was such a complicated, yet uncomplicated individual. Always a contradiction, femininely petite in a masculine type of way, beautiful, kind, academically challenged, but artistically brilliant, and Alex was seeing an unusually animated version of this generally quiet and subdued person. She raised her eyebrows wondering what was cooking on the bridge.

And then there was Ruby…the glittery social butterfly in full flight, sipping away at a glass of Ouzo, swaying in time with the music and surrounded by a mixed group of Spanish tourists who were as keen to party as she was.

The crew circulated amongst the guests offering heavily laden Greek mezze platters: an assortment of dips and snacks garnished with pine nuts and fresh parsley.

"Orgasmic bliss." Ruby's eyes rolled as she approached Alex, clutching a lamb skewer in one hand and a milky Ouzo on the rocks in the other.

Tilina moved towards them, a look of amazement on her face. "I just learned astrology signs are linked to Greek mythology; did you know that?"

Ruby and Alex shook their heads as Mitch fused into the group.

"Just been discussing centaurs and was told Sagittarius is a centaur named Chiron—fancy that…Greece is fascinating, can't imagine why I've never been here before, no wonder the chick in *Mama Mia* decided to stay here."

"Actually, parts of the movie were filmed right here in the Pelion area, on the Aegean side," Mitch informed them.

"Awesome movie," chuckled Tilina. "Just loved the dot, dot, dot parts—speaking of which, here comes Charley dot, dot, dot."

Charley blushed as she saw the questioning faces in front of her.

"The bridge dot, dot, dot?" jibed Ruby

"Just chatting with the captain, interesting fellow, an artist when he isn't sailing the seas."

The others chirped in unison, "Dot, dot, dot."

Don't Rock the Boat Ruby
Scene 3

The hum of light hearted chatter and chuckles flowed with the wooden vessel as it navigated classic blue seas; sunrays tumbled as the setting sun leaned towards the warm calm waters in search of its resting place, leaving streaks of apricot in its gentle wake.

Leaving the craft's wheel in the hands of his second in command, quietly Captain Costa materialized beside Charley. A bouzouki strummed the familiar opening chords of *Zorba the Greek.* With outstretched hands he beseeched, "Dance with me into this sunset."

Holding hands, they moved towards an open area with three crew members forming a dance line. "Follow me," he whispered, "don't worry, I will lead you."

Joining the center of the line, their eyes met, and taking their cue from him, the dancers joined arms at shoulder height. Gently steering her, he quietly instructed, "Left foot, step forward, tap right foot next to left heel, swing right leg forward, kick—"

"Whoops," she gasped as she faltered and strengthened her hold on his arm,

"*Yamas!*" Ruby raised her glass, her face a picture of joy as she watched them move in unison, left and right and in and out, to the tune of the famous music.

Spurred on by the enthusiastic cheering of the audience, they continued their dance with perfectly timed, in and out and left and right, movements.

The crew beckoned to other spectators to join them. Within minutes, Ruby was in the center of the action, the party had begun, the boat rocked in harmony on its homeward journey.

Leading Charley away, Captain Costa bowed as he left her in the company of Michelle and Alex and headed back to the bridge.

"Whoo hoo, Charley, I think someone's got their eye on yoo-hoo," teased Alex.

Charley brushed away the suggestion. "I bet he does that to all the girls," she chuckled.

The tempo of the dance picked up as they moved closer to port. Ruby was dancing with a Spanish woman she had been chatting with earlier in the evening, both of them looked well on their way to Shit Face City.

Simulating a Burlesque movement, a gasp of shock blew skyward when Ruby tossed aside her bikini top, tumultuously exposing impressive breasts.

Michelle was at her side in an instant. Draping a towel over Ruby, she dragged her from the limelight, forcing her to sit. "Enough is enough Ruby," her words lashed out in anger. Ruby quietly conceded defeat and by the time they docked in Affisos, Ruby was passed out.

The departing passengers filed past them quietly, leaving the friends to figure out how they were going to move this unconscious mass off the boat.

Captain Costa came to the rescue, carrying her unceremoniously off the boat and placing her into their car.

Chapter 13
My Boat is Sinking
Scene 1 –Ruby is Drowning

Rainy weather set the tone for the morning after the cruise. Predictably, Ruby didn't surface for breakfast. Concerned, the rest of the tribe topped up their coffee mugs and took up residence in the living room to discuss.

"Do you think she's an alcoholic?" Tilina threw out to all of them.

"Dunno," shrugged Alex. "I know nothing about alcoholism." She looked at Michelle questioningly, "I grew up in a house where alcohol only showed up for Christmas, we drank tea…by the bucket load."

Charlotte piped up, "Well she's not sneaking booze; my mom had a friend stay with us and the housekeeper alerted us to bottles of vodka hidden in the guest bathroom and under the bed. Turned out what we thought was water was pure vodka—haven't seen Ruby drinking much water, anyone else?"

Reaching for her cell Tilina pressed a button. "Siri, define alcoholism." She paused, reading the screen. "This definitely speaks Ruby…binge drinking, episodic excessive drinking; for women, four drinks consumed on one occasion at least once in a two-week period." Tilina rambled on, churning out statistics, her face registering shock when she saw a disheveled Ruby holding a coffee mug, scowling in the doorway.

"What gives any of you the right to discuss me behind my back?" Her voice trembled with controlled anger. "I'm here. Say it. Ask it. Fire away!"

Awkward silence prevailed as she wobbled across the room, plonking herself in an arm chair and glaring. It was obvious she wasn't fully sober, but now was as good as any to tackle the alcohol-infused beasty everyone saw but didn't want to talk about.

"Tilina? You had a lot to say when you didn't know I was here, speak up," Ruby demanded aggressively.

Tilina stiffened, never one to cower from confrontation, she lashed back. "Your behavior last night was shameful, embarrassing to say the least."

Ruby shrugged. "It was a party night, what's your problem?"

"You're the one with the problem Ruby."

"And what might that be Tilina?" a ruffled Ruby bit back.

"Booze, alcohol, every night you're shit faced."

"So…what's the problem?" Ruby smirked.

"It sucks to be us. When you're drunk, you lose ALL filters."

Ruby reeled under her harsh wave of criticism. "Filters? You, point fingers at me, about filters? You don't even know what the word means. Bottom line Tilina, you're a self-opinionated bitter bitch with a poisonous mouth."

Wounded by Ruby's bullet, Tilina exploded, "Really? Rich coming from you Ruby, Queen of all Bitches, that always has to be center of attention." Tilina yelled, pointing a finger aggressively, "You don't give a shit how the spotlight finds your fat face, even if it means flashing your tits and shocking the shit out of everyone, so long as you're at center, that's all you care about."

The warriors raised swords as they moved into battle.

"I'd rather be Queen Bitch than Super Witch, Tilina. There's no truth in you. I see you playing victim by day and scheming vengeance at night where no one can see your spite and envy." Ruby was referring to the drama of Tilina's divorce, a lengthy drawn out courtroom saga, driven by greed and desire to punish. "Me? Attention seeking? Really Tilina?" Ruby raised her eyebrows sarcastically. "Why didn't you settle privately out of court or were you enjoying the stage show too much?"

"He tried to rip me off, take what was rightfully mine," snorted Tilina.

"The judge didn't think so."

"Bullshit," Tilina's voice rose defiantly.

"Your memory's gone whoopsie, go read the court judgment again, it's all there, your whole story plastered on the internet, payout details, alimony, legal costs."

Tilina slumped, Ruby sneered. "Didn't you know a court judgment's a public document?"

Tilina shrank internally, Ruby struck a nerve; the pain triggered icy fury. Retaliating, Tilina calmly aimed for the heart. "Ruby…I'm your mirror, what you despise in me is the reflection of your own alcohol ridden shortcomings, deal with it…"

Alex called time out as Ruby hissed in breath getting ready to respond, attempting to conceal the truth just hurled at her.

"Slow down Ruby."

"We're worried about you."

"It's not criticism," chirped Charlotte nervously, "this isn't you, something's wrong Ruby."

Wide eyed, Ruby turned to Mitch for help but it was apparent Mitch was taking their side, four against one! Anger collided with desperation as the long-concealed alcohol laden bomb exploded, scattering a shower of smoldering shrapnel over all in close proximity.

"None of you are in a position to judge, you're no better than me. Divorce Troll Tilina, look at you, a wonderful loving husband and what did you do? Shove a rifle up his ass and fire the divorce bullet, now you're a bitter lonely bitch. Lucky you! Charley, when you gonna grow up? Live in the real world? How the fuck will YOU survive without your mother pandering to your whimsical behavior? Alex—" Ruby shook her head, sucking in air and rushed to continue before one of them could interrupt the flow. "The Great Pretender, cool and calm outside, all screwed up inside. What the fuck? How come you didn't figure something was up in your marriage? Too wrapped up in those spoilt brat daughters I guess." Ruby then glared at Mitch, who shrank back from the anticipated lashing. "Did you really try to commit suicide or was it just attention craving?"

"I can't believe you said that Ruby—"

"We're all thinking it Mitch." Ruby gazed at the shocked faces. "What the fuck? You've got it all, kick ass career, don't have to answer to no-one, the world's yours and you sleep with fucking rocks in your bed." Her chest swelled with contempt as she delivered the punch line, "The Michelle I knew is invisible, like a ghost, all I hear is the intermittent sniveling and howling of a lost soul with nowhere to go. Mitch, you've disappeared, so who the fuck are you to criticize *me?*"

Confrontation was not Mitch's style, tears welled in her eyes. Taking Ruby's hand, she dropped to her knees. "I look up to you Ruby," she said quietly, "you're everything I try to be. I envy your life. *Exotic career life?* Really…any idea how lonely a career can be? Those nights I called you from hotel rooms, alone in far flung places, your husband answered, I heard your kids squabbling in the background, I'd have traded places with you anytime."

"Bullshit," responded Ruby, "don't blow smoke up my ass. You wanna be like me? Ha bloody ha. I'm fat, I'm a drunk, only time I'm worthy is when you need something from me?"

Michelle began to sob, Ruby rolled her eyes skywards. "There you go, I'm so sick and tired of the constant wailing for sympathy and attention. Michelle, he's not coming back, he doesn't want you and I don't blame him. Deal with it. Move on, get a life."

Michelle screamed hysterically, "I can't handle anymore hurt, I'm outta here soon as I can get a flight, you're a drunk bitch."

Ruby promptly burst into tears as Michelle fled to her bedroom. Silence interlaced with loud sniffles rained upon the rest as they sat shell-shocked from the confrontation.

"Sorry," Ruby blubbered with a feigned smile, "peri-menopausal flare up."

"Not buying that." Alex shook her head. "Flat out, you're out of line, you're drinking's over the top."

Tilina and Charlotte nodded in agreement. Ruby conceded defeat. "You're right, I'm wrong."

"What's up?" Charlotte challenged not sure if she should be friendly or stay on the defensive.

"I'm pissed off, thanks for asking."

"C'mon Ruby spit it out. Why? What? Something we've done or haven't done, what's up?"

"Just hit a rough spot, pissed off, kids don't give a shit now they're in college, husband engulfed by his business, I feel abandoned, alone. I gave up my dreams, my life, for them and now I wonder why…"

Tilina commiserated, "Yup you were a talented, promising musician. I've often thought of how far you could have gone."

Alex sighed. "The lost scholarship must be a tough rock to chew, if only we knew where naïve decisions would lead us in later years." She smiled pensively.

Ruby wiped a stray tear, "My motherhood role's redundant."

"They'll be back when they need a babysitter Grandma," chirped Tilina.

"Ain't buying into that crap, done more than my share of shitty diapers," she squealed and they all chuckled.

Not letting up, Alex stated firmly, "Ruby, you said some awful shit to all of us. The booze issue is real, you need to sort it out before it gets worse."

Ruby flopped forward. "I'm sorry," she mumbled.

"What about Mitch?" Alex asked. "Ruby, you were rough on her." Charlotte and Tilina nodded looking harshly at Ruby.

"Somebody's gotta spit the truth. Tough Love," Ruby hissed. "She'll be okay, there's no scheduled flights into Volos, she's gonna have to hang around till we all leave."

The sound of a truck pulling into the driveway startled them. They listened as a car door slammed and moments later, the doorbell rang.

Alex, returning with a smile and look of relief plastered across her face announced, "We have a visitor."

Unaware of the drama that he'd escaped by a whisker and his presence just defused, Captain Costa, dressed to impress in a Greek captain's uniform, entered the room clutching a box of pastries in one hand and Ruby's bikini top in the other. His face lit up the moment he saw Charley. Taking a seat next to her, he graciously enquired after Ruby's health. Slightly embarrassed, Ruby re-assured him she was fine and politely thanked him for his kind assistance the night before.

He nodded in acknowledgement and proudly announced his intentions as a suitor for Charley's attention. The girls smiled sweetly at Charlotte wondering how on earth she was going to negotiate this declaration.

Chapter 14
Suspended in Mid-Air

I t had been a rough last week for all of them; wallowing in
Michelle's continuous misery, Kevin's unexpected arrival,
revelations about Alex's marriage—Ruby's harsh words hit
all of them and they found themselves facing inward as they tried
to digest facts from emotions and fiction.

Not paying much attention to the details, Ruby went along
with recommendations from her travel advisor and booked a
private day trip to some faraway place that she struggled to
remember the name of. Meta something. The only detail she
recalled was a long drive to historical sites which entailed an early
start and a late return trip. Hopefully it would provide distraction
from the drama of the past few days.

Just before 6am, an impressive black Mercedes SUV drew up
at the front door of the villa. A charming, energetic, and
effortlessly cool man in his early thirties introduced himself as
Dino their chauffer and guide for the trip. The five of them piled
into the luxury of the GLS 550.

The sun was rising as they hit the road. Settling into the lavish
comfort of the vehicle, they listened carefully as Dino briefed
them about the road trip that lay before them. "We're travelling
inland, heading northwest, approximately three hour's drive," he
said with an air of authority. "We'll pass by a few cities, Larissa,
Trikala—nice places to stop and visit but Meteora's our final
destination. There's a lot to see there, so no time to stop along the
way."

He glanced into the review mirror. "What do you know about
Meteora?" he asked and was somewhat taken aback by the blank
faces staring back at him.

Ruby fidgeted in the front passenger seat. "I booked the trip
but didn't elaborate on the details."

He chuckled, turning his eyes in Tilina's direction. "Glad to see you're camera ready, those photos will blow your mind for sure, you've been warned."

Curiosity getting the better of her, Tilina shifted forward and peered round the driver's seat. "So, what's Meteora, some kind of meteorite?"

"You're close, the word Meteora literally means 'hovering in the air' which brings to mind a meteor I guess."

Charley joined in. "So we're going on some kinda space odyssey?"

"Yup, thousands of tourists consider Meteora a pilgrimage."

Ruby smiled, dear Dino had caught their attention. *Thank heavens since we certainly aren't talking to each other yet.*

"Welcome to the voyage into the beginning of time…are you ready?" he asked.

"You bet," uttered Ruby, as the tribe nodded in agreement.

"Tell us more," Alex demanded, "it's my first time to Greece, I have to admit, it's been far from what I imagined."

"Indeed," said Dino. "Greece is more than white stone buildings, islands, and beaches…much, much more."

Slowly he drew them into the story of Meteora, going back millions of years, when the Meteora region was submerged deep, deep under the sea. He explained how tectonic earth movements forced the vertical fault lines of the ancient seabed upwards, forming a definitive plateau. The formation process under driving winds and lashing waters combined with extreme fluctuations in temperatures joined forces to fashion the combination of sandstone and conglomerate into boulders and enormous pillars of rocks.

The story telling timing was perfect because at that precise moment, a jutting, majestic column appeared to the right of the vehicle. "Meet Theopetra," he gestured. They stared in fascination at the massive limestone formation, craning their necks upwards to take it all in.

Dino used his announcer voice: "Within that looming rock, Theopetra conceals a massive rectangular shaped cave, covering an area in excess of 5,000 square feet, the entrance of which lies at the foot of Chasia Mountain over there." The girls stared at the rock shape, trying to visualize a massive cave within it.

His riveting story continued as he described the archeological evidence that provided proof of human life dating back to Neanderthal times, and plausible testimony of the abandonment of their hunter/gatherer lifestyle as they transitioned into the more modern-day human activities of farming.

"How on earth do they know that?" Tilina questioned in disbelief.

"Discovery of simple stone age tools dating back to the time of the caveman, as well as the detection of late Stone Age farming tools," he responded. "Archaeologists have been excavating in this area for more than twenty years now."

From a distance, dramatic pinnacle rock formations crashed upward, towering above Kalampaka, a town situated at the foot of the Meteora rocks. Just looking up their sheer cliff sides could give one vertigo.

As they drew closer to their destination, Dino continued with the enthralling story of Meteora, pointing to the massive pillars of rock, he said, "The first documented people to inhabit this area were ascetic hermit monks living in solitude in those hollows, crevices and fissures you see there. Renouncing all worldly possessions and human comfort, they dedicated their entire being to the worship of God and pursued salvation of the soul."

Approaching the outskirts of the city of Kalampaka, their travel path veered sharply to the right. Gaining altitude, they left the little town at the foot of the mountains, following the road as it weaved its way around the rock formations, into the heavenly sky.

Dino pulled into a viewing point; against this dramatic backdrop, with outstretched hands he declared, "Welcome to Meteora, the sacred Holy Land of Greece."

Surrounded by mountainous columns with skyscraper-like cliffs and maddeningly deep drops between them, the girls stared in amazement at the gigantic natural pillars which appeared to have been pushed from the bowels of the earth directly into the realms of heaven, epitomizing a force of strength and power that only God could have mustered.

The breath-taking silence and solitude of the sacred site of Meteora simply basks in the holy presence of the Divine.

In the distance, the calls of falcons, eagles, honey buzzards, and the haunting peel of monastery bells, summoned the faithful to worship in all ways. In the late 11th century, Skete of Stagoi, a monastic state, was formed and towards the end of the 12th century, large numbers of the ascetic community descended upon the region, occupying caves and coming together from time to time in unified worship. Towards the end of the 14th century, the Byzantine Empire was threatened by Turkish invasions. Hermit monks retreated from the invaders and during this period, twenty-four monasteries were built, each containing a church, monks' cells, and a refectory. Strategically positioned on the top of the cliffs, restricted access via rope ladders or windlass structures provided sanctuary and protection from conquerors. Only an eagle could drop in on them unexpectedly.

"Six of the original structures remain fully functional monasteries," explained Dino herding them back into the car. "Tourist flock from all over to visit. It gets pretty crazy here especially at the height of the summer season, but it's early, we're ahead of the bigger crowd. We'll make our first stop, the Great Meteoron Monastery, the highest, biggest, and oldest of all."

They approached Platis Lithos, an enormous rock pillar which rose 2,000 feet into the sky.

Dino explained more: The Great Meteoron Monastery, occupying the entire fifty acres of the topmost surface, cast its Godlike presence before them. Zig-zagging stone walls concealed multiple steps which facilitated modern day access to the monastery. Alongside the tower, cables bridged the chasm, providing rock-hard evidence of the legendary rope ladders, windlass, and nets which transported monks and goods to the safety of this bastion centuries ago. Today, a funicular car slowly chugged its way across the gorge, delivering supplies to the monks. In the 14th century, Saint Athanasios led the cloistral movement, the construction of the Meteoron Monastery, establishing the first monastic community which embedded monastery life in the Meteora.

Traversing the hundreds of steps fashioned into the rock in the early 1920s, the friends' physical efforts were rewarded by the elegance of this miraculous structure. Passing the central courtyard, they made their way to the main cathedral, where every inch of the walls was covered with beautifully painted frescos depicting the life of Christ. A history museum and library showed off irreplaceable treasures of ancient books and manuscripts, religious icons, and military uniforms.

A wooden door with a glass window revealed remnants of previous residents in the form of skulls and bones, neatly stacked on shelves in a corner. It was hard to believe that resident monks continued to follow the disciplined monastic way of life, in spite of the tourist invasion that occurred on a daily basis.

But the best was yet to come…

The view from the backyard of the monastery was indeed an astounding sight to behold. They stood spellbound, taking in the vista which featured the Rousanou Nunnery and Monasteries of Varlaam St. Nicholas and Anapausas against the spreading backdrop of the other pillars.

The women made their way on foot to the Holy Varlaam Monastery, situated on a neighboring rock pillar. They imagined welling power filling out goddess wings for them to soar across. Playground of the gods indeed. Enjoying the warm breeze, they crossed the bridge like mere mortals along the crafted steps. "That was easier than the last one," huffed Tilina as she reached the new summit.

The physical presence of monks was comforting as they observed their divine habitual abode and were rendered wordless by the simplistic, peaceful aura of these dark cloaked men going about their everyday life.

The ballistic episode of two days ago had impacted Michelle hugely. Not a person to be easily shaken by confrontation or arguments, her internal being's protection mechanism quietly measured the blatant transgressions levied upon her by the outside world. The peace of the monks helped to accelerate this mental work.

Silently it transformed them into gentle raindrops falling noiselessly into the river deep within her soul, creating a tranquil watercourse of human and life experiences. There, the water levels used to rise and fall in unison with day to day life until that massive blow-up gave her internal safety systems an overabundance of rain...one raindrop too many hit her yesterday, triggering a torrential flooding of her emotional pool with catastrophic results.

Michelle was aware that her river was full and recognized the risk facing her.

Ordinarily she would have brushed aside Ruby's self-centeredness, considering the drama as attention seeking, but at this particular junction in her life, she was still trying to cope with the turbulent emotional upheaval within her. Ruby was famous for engaging her mouth before her brain, never stopping to think of the impact of her words. Michelle knew deep down inside that Ruby loved her dearly, but for now, she had to step away from the external noise and find a safe place of sanctuary, high above the raging deluge of her emotions...or quite simply she would drown.

How bizarre is it I find myself in a soaring place like Meteora? I feel like I'm sitting on a throne looking down on the world, beyond its touch, beyond my own feelings.

Michelle believed that a universal power had guided all of them to this peaceful abode in order to re-group after that turmoil.

The absence of any stabilizing medication since the botched non/suicide debacle and the scrambled path of holistic healing had carried her into obscure, off the wall places and situations.

Her memory conjured a pitiful sight of her lying face-up and sobbing on a wooden board while Reiki Master Teisha, a waif like, elderly woman with waist length, straggly white hair, strummed a wooden violin over her body, disappearing at times under the board where she rattled away on a Shamanic beater rattle which produced wild and wonderful sounds, designed to open blocked chakras. One day I will laugh when I look back at this, she had thought while strapped to that board. *Dear Lord, please let that day come quickly.*

A sense of calm passed through her as she opened her heart to receive the refuge that these strongholds had provided to troubled souls for centuries.

Lighting candles as she passed through the churches, she cast aside her spiritual barrenness and experienced a strength of faith guiding her through the darkness of this point of her life journey.

The peaceful serenity of this evocative ancient land embraced all of them as they moved from one monastery to the next, each new plateau leaving a lifelong memory in their minds.

It was fascinating to observe the parallel co-existence of intense spiritual devotion to God, the artistic creativity used to exalt the life of the Divine Being, the natural beauty of the Meteora region, and the intrusion of modern-day life.

Chapter 15
Painting a Thousand Words ...
Scene 1 – Group Photo

A strange sounding bell clanged as silent monks congregated in the church, their heads bowed in prayer, unperturbed by the increasing noise as the bell rang louder. Tilina awoke from a vivid dream; darkness engulfed her eyes as her mind struggled to identify her location. Turning towards the sound, she realized it was the alarm clock on her cell phone, she had forgotten to turn it off from the day before.

Switching on the bedside lamp, she moved across the room and silenced the incessant noise of her phone. Realizing that sleep would not return, she reached for her camera and laptop, anxious to view the images captured at Meteora.

Slightly miffed that photographic activity was forbidden within the interior of the churches and museums, she had turned her focus to the formidable rock structures, panoramic views, and architecture of the monasteries and, of course, her usual portraiture.

She paused to examine a fluke shot of two monks caught in a visitor restricted enclave. In spite of the distance, the shot was exceptional. Seated on a crude wooden bench on the precipice of their monastery, the rock-strewn landscape of Meteora provided a dramatic backdrop to the image. With their backs to the camera, the two robed-clad monks were deep in conversation, prayer ropes draped gently over their hands, one of them pointing towards a neighboring monastery situated in the distance. Their black, flat topped, brimless hats and overgrown beards provided a regal ambiance while their calm demeanor emphasized their peaceable presence.

"Black and white," she murmured to herself, as she quickly edited the photograph, marveling at the serenity that exuded from the colorless shot she just edited. A sense of reverence overcame her as she stared at these unique human beings who dedicated their lives to a service beyond themselves. *Mmmm, Hildegard will be impressed with this image,* she silently applauded herself.

Haunting images of Michelle stopped Tilina in her tracks. Mitch was a photographer's dream; it was difficult to take a bad picture of her. "The camera never lies," she muttered as image after image revealed a constant aura of deep sadness that engulfed Mitch and tore at Tilina's heart.

Intrigued by this discovery, Tilina flipped through her files, hunting frantically for something. Finally, she found it, scanning photographs dating back to their school days. Studying the photographs, she was re-connected with the Michelle she had once known…there she was, beautiful, and holding her own, the epicenter of their group. She was the glue that bound them together; they were all misfits, but somehow, it had been Michelle's tranquil presence that scooped them up into "The" group of eccentric loners that collectively stood out as the "It" group because of their unified differences.

Michelle was their rock; she was gorgeous and glamorous, clever and humorous, someone always there for them offering a smile or a ridiculous joke that would reduce others to a pile of hysterical laughter. If that failed, she would scoop you up with a hug or gently kick your butt with a motivational word of reassurance. Within Mitch's physical allure resided a gentle being, the kindest, most compassionate human being you could ever wish to meet.

Eternally the silent leader of all the mischief they got up to during their school years, somehow Mitch's presence bamboozled everyone, her respectful approach to the hands of authority could soften even the roughest member of the firing squad of teachers when they got busted for doing something off the wall. Always top of the class, first to hand in homework, well prepared for exams and a wizard at mathematics, Michelle spent many patient hours guiding them through the intricacies of calculus and calming them down when their art projects got messed up or some jerk of a boy turned their lives upside down. She had a hand in helping them all get through those adolescent days.

Turning back to the Meteora images, Tilina stopped as she studied a few group pictures that Dino took of them. The forced smiles and poses smacked her in the face. Pain ripped her heart as she noted the space gapping between all of them and most specifically, Michelle. It widened so dramatically, Michelle was literally hanging from the edge by her fingernails on a stone wall, the dramatic landscape of Meteora behind them demonstrated the deathlike consequences if she were to fall away from them. *Holy shit!* she sighed, *this isn't a blow up, this is a classic fuck up.*

Suddenly, Tilina was a woman on a mission. Arming herself with laptop and photographic evidence, she left her room in pursuit of her fellow tribe members. Pausing in the kitchen to kick start the coffee machine, she busied herself with connecting her laptop into the massive television screen in the den and then quietly headed off to Alex, Ruby, Michelle, and Charley's rooms, urgently summoning them to an important discussion.

Clutching a coffee mug each and looking somewhat bedraggled with rumpled bed hair and pajamas, the girls gathered on the sofa with squinting eyes.

"What the fuck's going on Tilina?" demanded Ruby quietly, the rest of them waiting patiently for an explanation.

"My alarm went off by mistake and I couldn't sleep so I started looking at my photos from yesterday." She pulled up the image of the monks. "Nice pic I thought." They nodded in confused agreement.

"Then these came up." They stared at photo after photo of Michelle. "Look carefully," she implored, "this is not our Mitch."

Their gazes fell upon the shrunken and disheveled waif-like image of Michelle. Tilina continued flicking through the group pictures that Dino had taken.

"What do you mean?" Charlotte asked blankly, just seeing pictures from this vacation and nothing out of the ordinary.

"Let me show you," Tilina responded as she pulled up the old images and pointed to the screen. "***This*** is our Mitch, our Rock, the center of our worlds, the one who held us all together through thick and thin, solving our problems."

They stared in silence, slowly digesting the gist of what Tilina was saying.

"During the planning phase of our reunion, no one envisaged the individual dramas that would reveal themselves."

"How could we know? All we see is the Facebook version of our lives which is a pile of painted bullshit."

Tilina nodded and continued, "That awful blow up, that's real fucking life." It was said with tears in her eyes.

The women shifted uncomfortably as the nasty truth that Ruby uttered about each of them came to mind.

"I understand truth hurts but tough love can motivate ownership and responsibility for one's actions." Tilina bowed her head as tears rolled down her face. Tilina explained that Ruby had certainly triggered that for her when she exposed the existence of the court judgment. She acknowledged that she couldn't escape the written, hard, cold facts or the comments of a qualified professional judge with no bias or emotion to sway his opinion. She admitted she lost the case but never her anger. Tilina went on calmly to challenge Ruby on her assumptions; clarifying that it wasn't greed that drove her anger, it was actually vengeance and emotional hurt. She described how, following Ruby's attack, she contemplated her situation and finally, after all these years, admitted to her own failings. She acknowledged that blame had always formed a huge part of her ethos and in spite of being the one to leave and file for divorce, somehow, she blamed him for the demise of their marriage believing he would admit to his failings and come back to her, never for a moment did she think she was replaceable.

"But this is not about me," she emphasized, "Ruby's been unkind to all of us including herself, but that's Ruby, she's always been like that. Life always revolves around her. Ruby is drama in capital letters and always the center of attention."

Still remaining calm and not accusatory, Tilina went on and explained that Ruby's loss of self as she faced the reality of the much clichéd empty nest syndrome and the realization that Ruby turned to alcohol in order to disguise feelings of anger and resentment towards the perceived abandonment from both her children and her husband.

"But this is not about Ruby either," Tilina continued, "let's consider the tragic passing of Charley's mom just weeks before our departure."

She clicked a button and the projection moved from a picture of Ruby in the island sun to Charlotte looking lovely on the beach. Tilina then began highlighting Charley's determination not to let go of her mother's mortal remains, emphasized an umbilical cord that had never been cut and that the path forward for Charlotte would be difficult as she traversed the challenge of shedding the habit of parental dependency and standing on her own two feet in an adult world.

Tilina continued on with her explanation and a new current picture, turning to the demise of Alex's marriage, a cold-blooded performance, the horror of which seemed to embrace all but Alex. The fact that Alex lived with the knowledge of her husband's betrayal for two years and had no support systems around her to share this terrible disappointment implied some deep issues that needed to surface before she could begin to contemplate her next steps in life. So often, we see people who are afraid to show their true emotions for fear they will be judged for their weakness and inability to deal with life.

"But, you know what?" Tilina questioned, "these things we can sort out in due course. We can blame them on raw emotion and that we spoke without understanding the full story. So we can easily forgive each other." Eye to eye, she regarded each one of them before she firmly stated tearfully, "Right now, Mitch is the one who needs us most and **if we fail her, the consequences for all of us will be life shattering.**"

She looked at Mitch tenderly while putting up the last picture. Tilina had set the scene well, the entire tribe gasped as they saw Michelle leaning away from them, nearly toppling back into a deadly fall down the mountain cliffs.

"Your botched suicide attempt, as unintentional as you might plead, points to massive emotional trauma. Depression is potentially a terminal illness with fatal consequences if left untreated. And it can get worse if not addressed."

Alex rose to her feet. "Tilina's right, so many loved ones have failed to acknowledge the potential warning signs, only realizing the true depths of despair when it's too late and they are left with a lifelong guilt as they wonder if there was anything they could have done to change the course of a suicide tragedy."

Charlotte moved purposefully towards Michelle seated on the sofa. Scooping the shaking, quivering heap of sadness and tears into her arms. "Don't worry, we've got you girl, we won't let you fall."

Inconsolable sobbing permeated the gray silence of the end of that night; a pale pink line marked the first hint of dawn on the horizon. As time passed, the color intensified into a deep rose sunrise, a new day had come to light and with it the opportunity to start afresh.

Battered and weakened from negotiating the turbulent waves of constant emotional upheaval, Michelle no longer had the strength to fight. Like a drowning person who had lost the power to continue, she simply stopped battling the raging force within her and accepted fate, even if it meant death by drowning. At her lowest ebb of despair, the impenetrable bond of friendship wrenched her from the jaws of anguish and sheltered her with unconditional love. As she lay on the couch exhausted by the exorcism of her fear and acceptance of her fate, a sense of peace engulfed her.

In that heart rendering instant, self-truth prevailed upon all of them. They bore witness to how their own individual life expectations had also collided with real life circumstances, leaving them with no alternative but to crumble, hit bottom, and start all over again. Anchored by friendship in the darkness of their despair, they faced their hidden feelings of sadness, disappointment, failure, betrayal…and simply let it all go.

The time had come to review the heavily laden emotional luggage and discard the excess so they could continue with life's journey.

Chapter 16
Beach Day
Scene 1 – Potistika Beach

E ager to catch a glimpse of the Aegean Sea located on the eastern side of the Pelion peninsula, Alex declared a full-on beach day complete with picnic. Althea recommended Potistika and Melani, two remote beaches situated an hour's drive from the villa.

Following a sand-strewn beach road through the tiny scenic villages, they travelled in a southeasterly direction enjoying the panoramic views of the Pagasetic Gulf as the road ascended the hilly landscape in a zig zag swagger, towards the village of Argalasti. Surrounded by olive groves, the little town sat impressively atop a massive plateau overlooking ancient byzantine terracotta roofed houses. Fig trees, grape vines, and cultivated olive plantations punctuated the lush green vegetation strewn lavishly across the agricultural mountainous plains.

Slowly they wound their way along twisting roads towards Xinovrisi, a quaintly serene, rural village, situated on the slopes of northeast Pelion which provided the entry point to a number of magnificent beaches.

The artistic hand of Mother Nature was strikingly apparent within this particular region of the Aegean coastline. The dramatic amalgamation of rocky mountainous cliffs as they merged and tumbled onto the shoreline, were skillfully crafted into a series of cove like inlets, spectacularly edged with interestingly shaped stony crags. In some places the cliffs were steep enough to seal off a bay area and in others the rocky outcrops were of a walkable height, creating an endless expanse of wide-open sand and pebble mixed beach.

An assortment of vegetation comprising wild flowers and grassy patches softened the coarse appearance of the rock surfaces. The final exotic touch to this already perfect landscaped canvas were enormous pieces of rock jutting out of the sea and multicolored boulders strewn haphazardly around the beach upon which the sparkling sunlight reflected tinges and tones of red, green, and violet.

The now unified She Tribe set up their day camp towards the south end of the beach in a carefully chosen area secluded by large boulders reasonably close to the sea providing a private beach aura. The beach equipment loaded into the SUV by Althea ensured a perfect experience for their ocean day. The picnic basket was a treasure chest of Greek specialties that would delight even the most critically acclaimed foodie and the cooler box held an assortment of soft drinks, water, and alcoholic beverages. Claiming a wide expanse of beach territory, the tribe spread out their lounge chairs and sun umbrellas and settled into their new habitat, taking in the various nuances and delights of their new surroundings.

Leaving Charley and Ruby sprawled out on their loungers, the eternal exercise icons, Mitch and Alex, opted for a lengthy beach walk trailed by the photographic prowler, Tilina, who ambling from one side of the beach to the other, was on the lookout for what had become an insatiable quest for perfect images of everything and anything.

Tilina's direct approach to voicing her observations of their various personal dramas and issues punctuated by the haunting photos of then and now, had brought a new found awareness of the united strength their friendship provided. They recognized the unique and priceless value of a childhood friendship. It connected them with people who had experienced and loved them as their childish, most natural selves. In the absence of adult responsibilities, they lived those endless days of youth with open hearts and an unquenchable curiosity which rendered them open to taking on life's adventures.

As they matured and suffered the bumps, bruises, knocks, and falls of life, they built barriers and regrets which slowly diminished their willingness to take responsibility for the challenges, choices, and lessons of life.

Instead, they opted to languish in the pity pool of sorrow, caution, and blame. Their confrontation of their own life path the day before reminded them of who they once were, back in their youthful days, when they didn't give a shit about risk or pain. That self-evaluation forced them to get their asses out of the sewer they were currently wallowing in.

Certainly, life in the fog and mud can be quite formidable, one can revel in self-indulgent disappointment, creating a million excuses for your doleful presence in a dark and gloomy place… and it is okay for a short while, to take a break and chill out in the goo and gunk of life's calamities…but the reality is, that is where you will remain if you don't summon up the courage to put the bullshit behind you and step back into real life.

Supported by their invisible glue of unity, they understood it was time to exit their dark caverns of terror and disappointment, even if it meant leaning on, or carrying, each other as they climbed out of the slippery mud and slime of despair. Today, on the beach of Potistika, was the day of their personal enlightenment.

The sun-kissed breeze embraced their presence on this beautiful beach, the gentle sound of the waves flowing to and from the shore and the silent flutter of butterflies in pursuit of wild flower nectar encompassed their newly found nimbleness of being.

The harmony was emitting a tender aura of happiness and contentment. Ruby and Charlotte chatted away, Tilina was flicking through the pages of a photographic magazine, Mitch was deep in a self-help book Alex gave her, pausing every so often to scribble something important in a notebook. Alex busied herself quietly surveying the beach and some of the distant boulders. "Oh shit," she blurted, "we're on a nudist beach!"

"You're kidding me, right?" Tilina looked up from her magazine, not daring to turn her head to confirm.

"Nope," behind the anonymity of dark sunglasses, Alex swiveled her eyes, noting the naked bodies of each person in her range of sight. "Just letting you know, we're the only non-naked tribe on the beach. This nudity thing in Europe is weird, imagine us walking naked on beaches in California or Texas?" She sighed.

"Well, I guess we need to get with the program," said Ruby. "I've always wanted an all over tan."

Charlotte giggled. "Ruby, what would your husband say if you went home with an all over tan?"

Leaning forward, Ruby removed her bikini. "I'm about to find out…always wanted to walk naked and unabashed in a public place, so here goes."

"Me too!" Tilina followed suit, leaving the rest in shocked amazement. She glanced over at them. "What the hell? No one knows us here. Who knows? We might just enjoy it," she tweeted, watching as Charley joined in.

A few minutes later, they were all lying awkwardly naked on their loungers, trying to look like this was the most natural thing in the world and failing miserably.

"I think we need to sun lotion up."

"Good idea Mitch, you need some help?" Tilina pointed a spray can towards her boobs.

"Watch this space *chicas*." They cracked up laughing as Charley put on a spectacularly sensual performance of sun tan lotion application.

"Mimosa cocktail anyone?" Mitch enquired sweetly.

Their heads nodded vigorously; the girls were back in town and the party was on.

For some strange reason, the Mimosas brought a sense of assurance to their naked appearance and it was not long before they were comfortable enough to head backwards and forwards to the sea for a good old-fashioned skinny dip, cooling down session, repeat, then dipping into the cooler box to replenish their Mimosa cocktail glasses.

The tinkling of bouzouki music from Alex's blue tooth speakers reinforced the incredible atmosphere and the realization that their Greek Reunion was back on track with a heightened level of happiness now that all secrets and dark moods were spread out in the sun. With no specific agenda other than to chill, the girls settled into their very special beach date, doing whatever, whenever.

Mitch remained glued to her book, her note taking became more intense and at times, she was seen to be drawing intricate diagrams as more and more of the content appeared to resonate with her. The absence of her usual tearful outbursts was deemed a positive sign by the group, as was her enjoyment of the Mimosa cocktails accompanied by a healthy intake of the delicious lunchtime snacks.

Obliviously unaware of their examination, Mitch devoured each page as she quietly engaged with the self-help suggestions. Reviewing her current status on paper, seeing both the negatives and positives, she was quite taken aback when studying both lists and noting that the positive factors actually far outnumbered the negatives. She sat up and gazed out to sea as she digested the fact that she was now in a position to do whatever she wanted without having to consider the critical objections and scrutiny of her former partner.

That was a pretty awesome revelation and she reached for her notebook and wrote in large capital letters, "SOOOOOO HAPPY I TOLD HIM TO FUCK OFF" followed by a large smiley face. On her **To Do** list she wrote 'get a smiley face tattoo just like Alex's Phoenix tattoo,' followed by a series of smiley face drawings.

Resting the book at her side, she took a sip of her Mimosa, a huge smile of contentment spread across her face as a deep sense of gratitude for this very special moment came over her. How fortunate she was to be in such a beautiful place in the company of friends who loved and cared for her.

She spotted Alex swimming out to sea, heading towards a rock. Assuming she was with Charlotte, her head turned back sharply to re-focus when she saw Charlotte, Tilina, and Ruby, wearing nothing but wide brimmed hats, sitting on their butts, cocktails in hand, enjoying the wave tumbles on the shoreline.

"Whose Alex with?" glass in hand, she placed her own naked butt in the sand next to Tilina, struggling to keep her drink stable as she took a soft blow from one of the waves.

"Don't know," came the reply, "she went out alone, been there awhile and next thing we see, another person, looks like a guy, then they headed off towards the rock."

"Water's pretty deep," chirped Charlotte, "they're both strong swimmers, so guess they're okay."

Watching the two swimmers in silence, their eyes widened as the sound of the opening ting tinging of the famous *Zorba the Greek* song resonated from the speakers, their bodies moved in unison with the music and before they knew it they were up on their feet, Charley leading them as they danced their own version of this famous dance.

So involved in the counting and the in, out, left, and right instructions in their heads, they were unaware of both the sea and beach audience that watched them as they frolicked like children, caught up in this amazing moment of bliss, just doing and being whatever, and stark naked to boot.

As the music came to an end they were surprised by the waving and cheering coming from the sea and the presence of other people dancing naked along the beach. A little embarrassed, they collapsed together in a laughing heap in the shallow water.

"Isn't this just the best vacay ever!?" shouted Tilina.

And they all yelled: "Yes!"

Greek Gods Must Be Crazy!
Scene 2

Swimming was one of Alex's most favorite things, she'd had her eye on that rock since they arrived that morning, but her usual training buddy was so lost in the book she gifted her, Alex didn't have the heart to pull Mitch away from it. That book had been recommended by her life coach and she owed it a lot of credit for her recovery from the demise of her marriage. When Ruby mentioned the breakup of Mitch's relationship and the profound effect it was having on Mitch, she bought a copy waiting for the right moment to gift it. She was so happy to see Mitch was connecting with the guidance and knew this was the strongest weapon to give anyone going through a life war.

Surprised by the depth of the sea so close to the shore, Alex was a little reluctant to attempt the rock swim alone and for safety's sake chose to remain close to the shore. Keeping her group of friends in close view and enjoying the strange sensation of swimming naked, she let loose in the water and hammered out a few long lengths along the shoreline. Taking a break, she stopped to catch her breath and noticed that she was further in the sea and closer to the rock than she anticipated and there was another swimmer in close proximity. Both perplexed and relieved by the company…as they drew closer, she noticed it was a man. Treading water, they nodded heads and greeted each other.

"Strong Olympic swimmer," his Greek accented voice acknowledged her presence across the rippling water. She smiled at the compliment, just nodding at him. "Sea's calm today, sometimes waves get very big, then only strong swimmers come this far into the water."

"Will you swim with me to the rock?" she asked him, a little surprised at her forwardness with this complete stranger.

"Sure, let's go," he beckoned.

Side by side, they swam; she sensed he had deliberately slowed his pace to match her and was a little overcome by the strong, manly veil of protection she felt in his presence as they negotiated the deep water towards the jutting rock.

Drawing alongside the rock, they stopped to catch their breath, bobbing up and down, treading water and making small talk. "You from here?" she asked.

"Yes, from Argalasti."

"I know it, we drove through the village, very pretty."

Recognizing her accent, "*Ahh* American, where you staying?"

"Near Lefokastro."

"Why you come to this beach, not many tourists here?"

"We like quiet, don't like crowds." She smiled as she studied the thick mop of salt and pepper hair surrounding his rugged, tanned face. Checking his hairy, muscled arms she thought, *Tilina's right, these Greek guys are sexily hairy in all the right places.* "I'm here with my girlfriends," she turned to point towards the tribe, amazed at the wild dance rendition of *Zorba the Greek* that was taking place at that precise moment.

"They look like fun girls," he smiled as she nodded her head laughing.

They watched the dance fiasco in silence, it was certainly a wonderful sight to see the women letting go and having a ball, it was then that it dawned on Alex, they were all stark naked and so too, was she! *Fuck,* she thought quietly to herself, *here I am in the company of a handsome hunk and I'm stark raving nude! I wonder if he knows?* Another even stranger thought raced across her mind, *Holy shit…is he naked too?*

"You okay?" he questioned, detecting something amiss. She nodded back as he looked deeply into her eyes, pointing to himself. "I'm Aristotle, you are?"

"Alexandra," she whispered.

"You are a very beautiful woman Alexandra," he uttered looking deeply into her eyes. "I'm honored to meet and swim with a goddess." Pausing, he breathed deeply, "Did you know that the name Alexandra was also a name given to the Greek Goddess Hera?"

Alex burst out laughing.

Aristotle looked a little confused at her reaction, "I'm speaking truthfully, why are you laughing?"

"Because, the Goddess Hera lives in our villa and I have been staying under her watchful eyes." Clearly, she had lost him with that comment, so she took a few minutes to enlighten him about the statue Charlotte made in honor of her mother and how they brought it to Greece with them. He still looked understandably confused through most of the explanation but let the discussion go.

They opted for a breaststroke on the return journey so they could chat as they made their way through the water. Literally submerged in the most bizarre situation that Alex had ever found herself, swimming naked with a strange man who thought and treated her as if she was a goddess, she realized the truth of her natural beauty.

This person was seeing and accepting her for what she was: sopping wet, naked, no makeup, no fancy car, or business status. An even scarier thing was she was seeing him for what he was and definitely liking what she saw. At this point however, she had bigger things to think about, like what she was going to do when she reached the beach…cower under the cover of water or step right out as naked as the day she was born.

Nature had it all worked out for both of them.

As they approached the shore, a large wave engulfed Alex and Aristotle, roughly rolling them into a twosome and unceremoniously dumping them onto the beach a few feet away from where the tribe were sitting. Three waves followed in rapid succession, each one whacking them closer together leaving them lying naked and laughing in the surf.

As the water subsided, Aristotle was on his feet in a flash, scooping his newly found goddess into his arms, he emerged from the water with the grandeur of Poseidon blissfully unaware that the center piece of his crown jewel collection was standing large and tall in respectful salutation to the sensual beauty of the five women scattered around him as he carried their friend to them.

"You can't make this shit up," chuckled Charley as she watched Poseidon plonk Alex on the sand.

"Looks like something from a movie," muttered Ruby who was desperately trying to maintain eye contact as he approached.

"Aristotle." He smiled as he shook hands with each one of them and then promptly plopped his bare ass on the sand next to Alex. It was plain to see the two of them were clearly enamored with each other.

"Mimosa's anyone?" enquired Mitch sweetly as she leaned into the cooler box in search of a glass for their newly invited guest. They sat in quiet contemplation as their glasses were filled.

"*Yasou!*" they shouted as they plinked their glasses and settled back into party mode, Greek nudist style. Huge smiles plastered across their faces as they engaged in idle chit chat. Aristotle was a friendly laid-back type and after a few more sips of Mimosa, they were roaring with laughter at some of his jokes.

The sound of a boat horn alerted them to the presence of an incoming boat.

"Oh look, it's Captain Costa!" Overlooking the fact they were stark naked, Ruby and Charlotte were on their feet, shouting and waving frantically at the approaching vessel.

Toot, toot went the horn again making it obvious Captain Costa recognized them. The boat drew to a halt and dropped anchor close to the shore. They watched as Costa and three other men waved frantically back at them.

"Come and join us," beckoned a slightly Mimosa saturated Tilina, as she raised her glass into the air.

Within minutes, the four guys jumped off the side of the boat, laughing and waving as they splashed their way to shore. Costa was the first to hit the beach, smiling broadly as he threw his arms around an equally ecstatic Charlotte. His eyes fell onto Aristotle.

"Ari," he shouted, "good to see you brother." Turning to introduce his friends, he was amazed to see the wide-eyed stares of the girl tribe.

"Stavros!" shouted Mitch, "oh my goodness is it really you?"

The gorgeous young Stavros puffed up his chest and laughed as he gave each of them a big hug. "So we meet again."

"Oh My God! It's Ofolous, looks like him and Stavros are friends again," Alex whispered into Tilina's ear who stared in disbelief at the older gentleman standing to one side. Could it possibly be "The Guy" who often crept into her mind the past few weeks, The One that had wooed her that night until they fled from the fight, leaving them with no way to contact each other until now.

"Orfeus Vakalopoulos," he bowed his head graciously as he took Tilina's hand, "happy to meet you again."

Somewhat taken aback that three of his buddies had already made the acquaintance of this bizarre group of women, Costa pointed quizzically to the other chap from the boat. "You know him?" They shook their heads in unison. "Eli Manikas, a very popular musician in Pelion."

"My bouzouki's on the boat, I'll fetch it in time for sunset," Eli promised with a smile.

Captain Costa explained that they were fishing earlier that afternoon and had arranged to meet his brother Ari for a birthday barbeque at sundown on the beach, the invitation to which was enthusiastically accepted by the female clan.

Removing some freshly caught fish from the confines of a fishing net, the men joined forces as they scrubbed and prepared the fish in the sea water, crabs scurried towards them in search of a morsel before the waves swept away the off-cuts to tiny fish scuttling together in anticipation of a bite. Ari and Costa cracked open a bottle of Ouzo as they prepared to slowly grill the fish.

Waves frolicked gently on the beach as they settled back to enjoy the serenity of the setting sun, slowly savoring the sweet smell of aniseed as they sipped their Ouzo. The smell of the sea intermingled with the delicious aroma of seafood emanating from the soft heat of the burning wood.

Peaceful bliss surrounded the newly found friendships as cultures from opposite sides of the world embraced. There was no doubt that mutual sexual attraction was a key component in the success of this liaison.

As the sun prepared to bid its final farewell for the day, Eli started to strum gently on his bouzouki, casting a romantic spell on his spectators. This was certainly one of those special moments that no amount of planning could inspire, it had all just fallen into place as nature intended it and they were all enjoying the experience.

Music formed the key element of Eli and Ruby's link, in no time they joined forces and the evening resonated with their harmonious combination, Ruby's beautiful voice complimenting Eli's instrumental music ability serenaded the amorous activities of the unconscious coupling taking place amongst the rest of the group.

Obviously, their collective nudity was silently playing a leading role. Two by two, they discreetly broke away from the group, leaving Eli and Ruby to keep watch over the fire while the others headed off to more private and secluded locations.

Chapter 17
The Morning After

S ong for the day." Ruby activated YouTube on her cell phone and the sound of Frankie Valli and The Four Seasons spurted forth.

They all joined in the *do do do ing* as they wiggled and waggled their way to the breakfast table.

"Wow...back to our teens in a nanosecond," marveled Alex.

"Who would have thought we could still break out like that?" agreed Charley. "Is there consensus on if the theory 'forget one in the arms of another' works?"

Alex, Tilina, and Mitch nodded, their faces lighting up as they privately reminisced about the indulgences of the previous night.

"So, did everyone get laid except me?" inquired Ruby.

They all nodded looking very pleased with themselves.

"Important boundaries were shattered last night," Tilina announced, "we're not too old, it's never too late to start living, and sex is awesome."

"Forgive me, I feel left out and need you to share the details to make me feel better." Ruby mimicked a sad look. "Mitch, tell us about that gorgeous hunk Stavros."

"Even more awesome than he looks," she laughed.

Ruby slurped at her coffee. "Only two full vacay days left, we need to agree on plans for our birthday party *chicas*; anybody want to put something on the To Do list?"

"I want to have a memorial service for my mom and leave her statue here in Greece. I'll fill you in when I've got the plan all sussed out."

"Selfish Wish Ceremony for me!" piped up Mitch.

Ruby pulled a face as she tried to plan for these two weird requests. "Anymore?" The rest of them shook their heads.

"Tell me more about this selfish wish thing." Tilina stared at Mitch across the breakfast table.

Shifting a little uncomfortably in her chair, she answered, "Well you know, when the shit hit the fan, I kinda got pulled into this new age stuff, which is pretty weird and wonderful." She chuckled. "But when hope's minimal, you'll hang onto anything." Mitch smiled, remembering some of the insane things she'd done in the dark privacy of her despair; like fluttering from room to room clad in a white robe, waving feathers, and burning sage in an attempt to cleanse her home of negativity.

"It's a new moon the night of our party which symbolizes new beginnings. We need to let the universe know what we want from life by writing a wish list, you know like kids do at Christmas. But it can't be for others, not world peace or something like that; it has to be selfish—something just for you. Then we dig a deep hole and bury the wish and in time, the energy of our wish is released into the universe and **bam,** if it is right for us, the universe will grant it."

"Lots of detail?" Alex prodded.

"Exactly," Mitch responded, "detail, lots of detail on the wish list, if you want a man, state how tall, how wide, hair and eye color, profession etc., be specific, very specific about exactly what you want, so you'll recognize your wish when it knocks at your door."

"Sounds interesting." Charley nodded looking at the rest of them. "We're in!"

"Great, I'll give you a few pages to write up your wish and tomorrow night after dinner, we'll dig the hole on the beach."

"Moving on," Ruby commanded. "Birthday party, who, what, where?" she gazed across the table, waiting for the answers to flow and was instead hammered by a barrage of questions.

"So, is this a just "us" party or can we invite a guest?" a vision of Orfeus came to mind as Tilina posed the question.

"*Mmmm,* difficult one," murmured Alex as she tried to imagine a fully clothed image of Aristotle seated at the dining room table.

"Let's put it to a vote," suggested Charley, the thought of a lost opportunity to spend an evening with Captain Costa not at all appealing. "Hands up, anyone who wants to bring a partner?"

Five sets of hands rose instantly in the air...

"Well that was easy," Ruby chuckled. "I'll arrange dinner for ten with Althea, please invite your guest, let me know about any food allergies."

Mitch handed them each a notepad.

"Be sure to explain the selfish wish process and make sure they have theirs drafted and in their pocket when they arrive."

Chapter 18
Selfish Wishes
Scene 1 – Mother's at Sea

With Captain Costa at the helm, the boat headed out to sea. Surrounded by her tribe, Charley sat quietly center stern with a small wooden box in her hand and a basket full of brightly colored flowers at her feet.

Charlotte had taken him up on his offer to have a memorial ceremony at sea where she would scatter some of her mother's ashes, followed by an Ouzo wake, a party she knew her mother would have loved. Charley believed this event would signify her first step towards accepting the loss of her beloved mother. She understood the grief would last the rest of her lifetime and no matter what, she would always miss her mom, but a different life was forming. Deep within her soul, she sensed the emergence of an unfamiliar strength providing the guts needed to direct her own life in the absence of the person who was once the rudder of her life ship.

The silencing of the boat engines brought them to a gentle stop. The girls stood beside Charley as she opened the box containing fragments of Marjorie's remains. Her hands gently touched the ashes and she faltered realizing that once she cast these to the sea, only memories would remain. Charlotte stepped forward and sprinkled the smoke-colored dust into the deep blue sea, her friends highlighting the area by tossing flowers in the water. A tremendous feeling of freedom emanated as, aided by the gentle breeze and the gentle ripples of the water, her mother's spirit took flight.

She let tears flow and opened herself to the warm embrace of her friends and finally the protective hold of Costa. She looked into his eyes knowing that a lifetime attachment had been cemented, where it would take them, no one knew, but for now, she was happy to have his arms around her.

They stood for a while, watching as the flowers floated away and with Ouzo glasses raised to the skies, toasted the life, the love, and the memories of Marjorie Stein, beloved mother of Charlotte.

It was at this moment that Charley's selfish wish was triggered by Captain Costa. Unaware at the time that Charlotte was the creator of this amazing piece of art, he had marveled at the beauty of the sculpture when he visited the villa on the fateful day of the big fallout. The fact that unbeknown to her, she had created and carried to Greece an image of the much-revered Goddess Hera struck him as a striking symbol of destiny.

Drawing her attention to the shoreline with his outstretched arm he spoke, "Imagine your eulogy to Mother, erected in that spot there. You should seriously consider donating your statue of Hera to the people of Pelion," he uttered quickly yet in a quiet voice.

Charlotte nodded, the thought of her sculpture watching over the beautiful sea was appealing.

Later that day as she sat down to draft her selfish wish, considering his proposal.

It made perfect sense; she was, after all, a famous artist in her own right and if placed in the right spot, it could become a tourist landmark at best, even at worst it would be something local women may come to for inspiration. Scribbling this seemingly wild wish, her thoughts conjured up the possibility of expanding her artistic endeavors by researching mythical idols and deities in other countries and following a similar path.

She wished that Pelion would accept her donation and that if the statue was finally erected, a small bronze plaque would be placed dedicating this work of art to women and that she would be invited to the unveiling ceremony.

White Flag
Scene 2

Tilina set aside time to seriously consider her selfish wish, she giggled at the ludicrousness of the process but as she sat at her desk, she was overcome by the deep self-analysis this project triggered.

*What do I **really** wish for in my life?* She leaned back to think. *Well, in the first instance, I want to let go of the past and move forward. I love my photographic moments, perhaps, more focus there? Who knows? Maybe I could become a famous photographer. Selfish wish number one,* she smiled as she started to write and was quite taken aback at how the words filled the page.

My theme song's always been that song of Dido's... White Flag; *and as the song encourages I won't surrender. I never thought he would stop loving me but he did and moved on so damn quickly. This song is right, I caused too much mess and destruction for him to ever speak with me again—for so many years I've lived with the hope he would at the very least forgive me, so I guess that would be a selfish wish, forgiveness and acknowledgement of the good times that we did have together, appreciation for the two beautiful children we have.*

Turning the spotlight back to herself, Tilina once again affirmed the reality that she had embraced financial greed instead of facing her marital issues and the twisted bitterness that engulfed her being when she realized that, unlike her, her husband gave up trying to reconcile and started a new life. He had moved on with another woman, leaving her to flounder in a twisted form of bitterness that caused her to do everything in her power to wreak revenge on him.

In that precise moment, Tilina understood that the bitterness she clung to was the sole reason for her inability to negotiate herself out of the divorce quagmire she had worked herself into. *Well there you go, another selfish wish, let go of my bitterness.*

Her inner voice spoke quietly to her, *Be gentle on yourself Tilina —at the time you made your decision, there was something driving you. For you to walk away from your marriage after so long, something must not have been working, something pretty big. I don't believe it was the money that drove you to do that. I believe it was fear that made you go for the money—now it's up to you to discover the spiritual belief that will allow you to find your wings and fly. We all have our shitty sides, no one is perfect, and the shitty side comes out when we're frustrated and fearful and unhappy with where we stand at that moment. Take that big step. Follow your photography, let it be your symbol of guidance. Forgive yourself Tilina—we all make mistakes.*

She sat back once again as the answers to her selfish questions presented themselves and she refined her list to reflect her desire to become an accomplished photographer, to travel the world, and to find a partner, a companion, who would love her for who she was.

Sealed with a Kiss
Scene 3

Ruby stared out the window in her room, the beautiful blue sea overwhelming her senses as she drafted her wish list.

I want to let go of worrying about everybody else and focus on myself. The majority of my life has centered around my husband and children. Somewhere, I forgot about me. I want to pick up my musical dreams from where I left them when I was pregnant. I want to study classical music and sing and dance professionally; even direct some type of musical, perhaps buy a small theater to put on shows in our little town. Didn't we just agree this morning that we had shattered all the preset boundaries and it's never too late to be who we want to be? I want to achieve great things in the music and entertainment industry, that is my selfish wish.

She contemplated her drinking habits in great depth and realized it was caused by her habit of giving too much with the expectation of something in return.

Her next selfish wish was to stop living life through others; instead, dare to step out and live her own dream.

Adding one last item, Ruby noted that she wanted to lose the fear of growing old, of losing her beauty.

With a chuckle she listed her selfish wish to remain forever mentally young and grow bolder, not older. Gently, she kissed the page, leaving a ruby-red lipstick mark on the pink tinged paper.

Gazing out of the window as she carefully folded her wish, her gaze fell on Alex seated by the swimming pool, pen in hand staring blankly at her notebook.

I wonder what her wish will be?

Memo to The Tao
Scene 4

"**S**elfish wish," Alex muttered to herself, recalling the very precise instructions from Mitch. *Mmm, can't wish for anything on behalf of others, can't wish for world peace either.* Mitch's words permeated her eardrums, 'don't forget, lots of detail, be very, very specific.' She sat for a while, chin in hands, both elbows resting on the table as she contemplated the future that lay before her. Her marriage was over, her children were grown up, Magenta Integrated Tech was a successful flourishing business with a potential buyer hounding her to sell. If she were to agree, she would probably receive sufficient funds to ensure she never had to work again..*and then what will I do with myself...curl up and die?*

Her brows puckered as Alex delved into her heart, then a voice within flared up: *Why is this so difficult for you? It's a simple, straightforward question...what do you want from life, what's your life purpose, what do you need to help you to determine your future path? An angry mother, a cheating husband? Sorry girl, they're not relevant in your life anymore, you're on your own, which means you call the shots from now on.* That reality dealt a direct hit to the heart. *Wow, this selfish wish exercise couldn't have come at a more appropriate time.*

Embarking on the unfamiliar feel of this new age approach to life and not accustomed to asking for favors, she hilariously chose to draft a formal memo to the most senior authority of the universe and respectfully make her selfish wish known.

To: The Tao, The Higher Spirit, The Universal Power, The Creator, God the Holy Father, The Unexplained Power of Life
From: Alex
Re: Selfish Wish

So there I was, cruising along the interstate highway of life, firm in the belief I was heading in the right direction, following basic life rules for happiness and stability, keeping to the speed limit, maintaining 360 degree visual through the rear & side view mirrors, all while keeping my eyes firmly on the road and hands on the steering wheel. And still, I didn't see it coming until illuminated road signs loomed in front of me, signaling the imminent closure of the highway up ahead and pushing me onto a diversionary route.

Instantly darkness descended. Speed reduced and clinging to the tight roadway, my vehicle's headlights struggled to keep up with the dramatic twists and turns as I passed through forests and over mountains and across valleys, towards this turning point in my life journey.

A riotously ridiculous moment in time indeed, an American science-based engineer, writing a selfish wish to the Managing Director of The Universe! A practical woman who spent the whole of yesterday being absolutely impractical, partying stark naked on a Greek beach, with an equally nude male Greek stranger who I met while swimming in the sea and spent the rest of the day having bare assed fun with.

As tough as it is to travel the unknown, if this is the outcome of a diversionary route...Wow no more interstate highways for me!

My life as I knew it has ended BUT I'm not dead yet, in fact I've never felt more alive.

My selfish wish is for the courage to embrace the fear of the unknown and look to it as my mentor, not my enemy, as I pass through this turning point on my journey.

I wish for a place where ego is not the order of the day—where my uniqueness and talents are accepted, appreciated, and nurtured so I can realize and further develop my true-life purpose, whatever it turns out to be.

I wish for warmth and love and passion but will not accept being treated as an object or an ornament that can be used at the whim of another's desire or wrath. So, if it is to be that I'm blessed with another lover, let it be a person of similar beliefs to mine.

Help me let go of expectations and open my mind to the silent instinct and intuition of life itself. I know, if it's good for me, my wishes will happen.

Respectfully: Alex

Coming Out
Scene 5

From nowhere, a message was quietly delivered to her subconscious mind and read silently the day before the nude beach escapade. Looking back now, Mitch could imagine the quiet contemplation that took place amidst the resonance of her anguish and the vibration of her uncontrollable sobs and tears. Her subconscious self, understanding the urgency of the demand for immediate action conveyed by the message, reached out for assistance from her inner voice and a decisive plan of action was formed.

Oblivious of the plot, Mitch, wallowing in what had become an affluent sanctuary of self-despair, was shaken by a strong voice shattering the dark silence of self-pity, commanding her to abandon the cave immediately. Shaken to the core by the suddenness of this intrusion, Mitch strongly resisted the authoritative order just issued.

An argument ensued, backwards and forwards they wrestled, each need that Mitch identified to justify a reason to remain in her dark confines were blown apart by her ruthless inner voice.

Finally, acknowledging defeat, Mitch requested permission to wallow for just a few more days. A compromise was agreed and true to her word, today was the day she slowly removed her body, mind, and soul from the grotto of depression.

Unaccustomed to the warmth and brightness of this new light, she blinked cautiously as she settled down to bring to fruition her selfish wish task. She had given her future a great deal of thought over this vacation and was quietly embracing a new found liberation. She understood it would be an arduous task to completely climb out of the deep hole she had fallen into, but the journey had begun the moment she had extricated herself from the dictatorship of self-pity and doubt.

Acknowledging that her grieving time had come to a rapid end, ruling out all possibilities of a reconciliation, meant the severing of all ties with her ex. No more midnight telephone calls, Facebook stalking…"Done and over with," she uttered.

Where to from here—what do I want?

While Michelle knew that within a few days she would be catapulted into the daily grind and stress of work, she understood that the most positive and stable aspect of her life at this particular moment was her career.

She loved her work; she had great colleagues; her talent was widely acknowledged.

She recalled numerous times she reluctantly turned down growth opportunities due to her relationship. She acknowledged she was ready for a massive change in life and that formed the basis of her selfish wish.

She was open to a transfer to the moon if that was what was offered and she was ready to take on the challenge of adapting to whatever change the universe decided to present.

She wrote a long list of preferences, wants, and desires…and three pages later, folded up the note which would be delivered to the earth later that evening.

Chapter 19
The Big Birthday Celebration

A black limousine drew up at the villa, five tuxedo-clad Greek gods alighted from the vehicle and made their way to the front door. Greeted graciously by Althea, they were ushered through to the living room where they stood collectively, admiring the beautiful view and splendor of the luxurious villa the women had been renting.

The click of stiletto heels alerted them to the arrival of their hosts, each one a goddess of her own type, dressed to impress in a stunning variety of evening cocktail dresses. The pop of a champagne cork signified the start to the extravagant birthday celebration. Ruby had commissioned Tassos, a professional photographer, to create phenomenal memories of this momentous occasion and within minutes, he had them relaxed and in fits of laughter as he expertly positioned them in various formal and some ultra-hilarious poses.

The setting sun bid its own golden farewell as they sat making small talk on the patio.

"What was the highlight of your holiday?" Ari asked politely.

"Wow, I wouldn't know where to start." Tilina looked at the tribe. "A thousand different memories immediately come to mind."

"Potistika Beach." Alex smiled as she cast an eye at Aristotle.

"Is this actually the same group? I hardly recognize any of you with your clothes on," Ruby joked as she surveyed the formally dressed men.

"Nudity is not common in America," Charley explained to a surprised looking Costa.

"What a shame, no sneak peeks at all those beautiful American women," Stavros commented with a cheeky grin. They all laughed out loud.

"It's been an amazing vacation; Greece is one of the most beautiful countries I've ever been to." Michelle added, "The food, the people, the culture, it's just so different to anything I've ever experienced."

The women nodded in agreement knowing that the memories would magnify around the fun they had once they returned to their everyday lives.

Althea prepared a magnificent meal in honor of their birthdays and at dessert time, presented them with a beautiful birthday cake, ablaze with fifty burning candles.

They grouped together and extinguished the fiery flames with a collective blow.

Tears formed in their eyes as Eli strummed the opening notes on his bouzouki and Ofolos led his fellow compatriots in the Greek rendition of Happy Birthday. It sounded so different from the usual English version and took on the sound of a happy love song especially as the guys formed a small rock and roll group as they joined in.

Group hugs and kisses and tears followed the celebratory song as Captain Costa, taking the lead, took them outside to where Althea had placed the pile of birthday gifts that the fellows had brought with them. After-dinner liquors were passed around, the centerpiece of the outside table was a stainless-steel garden spade adorned with a massive, multi-colored, happy birthday ribbon, awaiting the selfish wish ritual on the beach.

The birthday girls unwrapped their gifts, beautiful Greek authentic mementos, carefully selected by their purchasers to remind them of their vacation in Greece.

Each guest had chosen to include a very special piece of jewelry for their extra, extra special goddess that they had formed a bond with. More tears formed as their thoughtful generosity penetrated female hearts.

Chapter 20
A New Era

As the new phase of the moon shone down upon this happy group, prompted by Mitch, Stavros reached for the bow wrapped spade. The time had come for Selfish Wish Ceremony! Hands joined, happily they made their way towards the beach, the guys somewhat intrigued by this strange ritual that they assumed to be a part of American mythology, Alex had absolutely no intention of informing them anything to the contrary.

Stavros rolled up his sleeves and, assisted by Ari, started to dig and clear a fair-sized, very deep hole as instructed by Michelle, who had in the meantime, put on some beautifully calm Greek music and lit candles around them.

Under the pale light of the moon, holding hands, they gathered in a circle surrounding the hole. Mitch asked them to place their wish papers in their palms, hold them up to the moon, silently express gratitude to the universe, then place them in the hole. Silence overcame them as they stared at the small papers lying in a collective bundle in the deep sand, symbolizing the unity of their faith.

Emulating Mitch's movement, they fluttered their hands to the skies, bowed to their knees, and scooped the sand back into the hole, erasing all evidence of where the wishes were buried.

Returning to the patio, they chattered away the rest of the evening until the limousine arrived to take the dear men home. Tearful hugs and goodbyes were exchanged as they wished their new friends a safe trip back to the United States.

The women sat in the silence of the aftermath of their birthday celebration.

"What a fucking amazing trip this has been!" shouted Tilina as they clinked their glasses in unison and contemplated the past weeks.

Each of them had literally and figuratively stripped themselves naked in the presence of their trusted companions. They let appendix scars and stretch marks show in the harsh noon light and each of them embraced each other, warts and all. They soaked their battle-weary bodies in the warm Aegean Sea and then revitalized them with body polishes, facials, massages, manicures, pedicures. They adorned themselves in clothes suitable for goddesses, this time with an awareness of their imperfections but still with a love for their being. They laughed and cried as they stood in front of each other for judgment and guidance. Self-realization and the feeling of safety allowed them to review their lives as they were at that moment.

They were able to relish in the now, accept the past, both the fun side and the dark side. They survived the brutal honesty with which they had chastised each other and offered advice based on nothing other than a true love for each other, accepting no one was perfect. They would emerge from Greece with renewed purpose and hope for their lives knowing that they had a safety net to protect them with love if they should falter.

Each one of them would have eternal gratitude for this intense period of life reflection, judgment, realization, and acceptance. They had scrutinized their individual insecurities within the tight knit bond of friendship, each of them gained an understanding of who they were and acknowledged their own need and right to live a life that provided them with an overall sense of worth and purpose.

None of them knew where the future would lead, but they knew that what they experienced here had better prepared them for what life had in store...

The End

Love Books?

SUPPORT AUTHORS – buy directly from their publishers. This puts more royalty dollars into the pockets of your favorite author – and gives them time to write their next book.

Visit us for links to many vibrant publishing companies to find the book for you.

Americana with a Twist

These ARE The Books You've Been Looking For.

Go to: **vanvelzerpress.com**

to order directly / or for special Book Club pricing

About the Author

Sue Holmes was born, raised and educated in Harare, Zimbabwe.

Sue is an international career banker, specializing in Wealth Management – a profession that has allowed her to travel the world as career opportunities beckoned. She currently resides in the Cayman Islands.

Sue has firsthand knowledge of the many challenges that face women in their day to day lives, whether it is professional and/or personal.

Set in the exotic and unusual Pelion Region of Greece, *She Tribe*– Sue's debut novel—is a reflective character-based story, the emphasis of which is on seemingly normal day to day life choices made by the main female characters and the long term impact that these have in their later lives. These characters are believable because they deal with issues that all women of every race, culture and nationality deal with on a daily basis.